the
singer's
gun

8/14

Also by Emily St. John Mandel

Last Night in Montreal

the
singer's
gun

Emily St. John Mandel

UNBRIDLED
BOOKS

Unbridled Books

Copyright © 2010 by Emily St. John Mandel

First paperback edition, 2011
Unbridled Books trade paperback ISBN 978-1-609530-42-6

The Library of Congress has cataloged the hardcover edition as follows:
St. John Mandel, Emily.
The singer's gun / Emily St. John Mandel.
p. cm.
ISBN 978-1-936071-64-7
1. Families—Fiction.   2. Crime—Fiction.
3. Psychological fiction.   I. Title.
PR9199.4.S727S57 2010
813'.6—dc22
2009053826

1   3   5   7   9   10   8   6   4   2

Book Design by SH • CV

First Printing

To Kevin

Something about the tanks at London's Heathrow Airport changed my mind. Before they rolled into place, in the innocent days when security just meant men with submachine guns, a travel book could be fluffy, silly, familiar or carefully manufactured, and it hardly mattered. Afterward, every destination acquired a sudden glow of hellfire, every trip an element of thoroughly unwanted suspense. Escape has become a problem in itself. A travel book without danger—to the body, the soul or the future—is entirely out of time.

...We stand in need of something stronger now: the travel book you can read while making your way through this new, alarming world.

MICHAEL PYE

The New York Times, June 1, 2003

the
singer's
gun

In an office on the bright sharp edge of New York, glass tower, Alexandra Broden was listening to a telephone conversation. The recording lasted no longer than ten seconds, but she listened to it five or six times before she took off her headphones. It was five thirty in the afternoon, and she had been working since seven A.M. She closed her eyes for a moment, pressed her fingertips to her forehead, and realized that she could still hear the conversation in her head.

The recording began with a click: the sound of a woman picking up her telephone, which had been tapped the day before the call came in. A man's voice: *It's done.* There is a sound on the tape here—the woman's sharp intake of breath—but all she says in reply is *Thank you. We'll speak again soon.* He disconnects and she hangs up three seconds later.

The woman's name was Aria Waker, and the call had taken place fifteen days earlier. The incoming call came from an Italian cell phone but proved otherwise untraceable. Police were at Aria's apartment forty minutes after the call went through, but she was already gone and she never came back again.

Broden went down the hall for a coffee, talked about the baseball season with a colleague for a few minutes, went back to her office and put the headphones back on. She listened to the recording one last time before she made the call.

"Is that it?" she asked when the detective answered.

"That's it, Al."

"Please don't call me that. And you think they're talking about Anton Waker?"

"If you'd seen what his parents were like the morning after that call came through, you wouldn't ask me that question," the detective said.

"How's the investigation going?"

"Horribly. No one knows anything. No one even knows the dead girl's name." The detective sighed. "At least it's not as bad as the last shipping container we dealt with," he said.

"I suppose I should be grateful that only one girl died this time. Listen, I'm going to talk to the parents."

"I tried that two weeks ago. They're useless," said the detective, "but be my guest."

On the drive over the Williamsburg Bridge Broden kept the radio off. She called her six-year-old daughter from the car. Tova was home from school, baking cookies with her nanny, and she wanted to know what time her mother would be home.

"Before bedtime," Broden said.

On the far side of the river she drove down into Brooklyn, grafitti-tagged warehouses rising up around her as the off-ramp lowered her into the streets, and she circled for a while before she found the store: an old brick warehouse on a corner near the river, almost under the bridge, with *Waker Architectural Salvage* in rusted-out letters above the doors. She parked at the side of the building and went around to the front, where a woman was sitting on the edge of the loading dock. The woman was looking out at the river, at Manhattan on the other side. She turned her head slowly when Broden said her name.

"Miriam Waker?"

"Yes," the woman said.

"Mrs. Waker, I'm Alexandra Broden. I work with the State Department, Diplomatic Security Service division." Broden walked up the steel steps to the loading dock. She flashed her badge at the woman, but the woman didn't look at it. Her gaze had drifted back to the river, moving slow and gray on the other side of a weedy vacant lot across the street. There were dark circles under her eyes and her face was colorless. "I'm sorry to bother you," Broden said, "but I need to speak with your son."

"He used to sit here with me," Miriam said.

"Is he home?"

"He's traveling."

"Traveling where?"

She said, "In a far-off country."

Broden stood looking at her for a moment. "Is your husband here, Mrs. Waker?"

"Yes," she said.

Broden entered the warehouse.

"This one was saved from the sea near Gibraltar." Samuel Waker had been interrupted in the middle of repainting a figurehead. He had stared flatly at Broden when she came in, but seemed unable to resist giving her a tour of his collection. The Gibraltar figurehead depicted a strong-faced woman rising out of foam, her arms disappearing into the folds of her dress. Her gown ended squarely in an odd cut-out shape where she'd been attached to a ship. Another figurehead had been recovered from the waters off France, her entire left side splintered by the coastline. One had been pulled from the rocks off the Cape of Good Hope, and this was the one Samuel Waker was restoring. The Cape of Good Hope figurehead had hair the color of fire, and her eyes were a terrible and final blue. In her arms she cradled an enormous fish: a block away from the nearest river, it opened its gasping mouth to the sky.

"Is this figurehead fairly new?" Broden was looking at the iridescent scales of the fish. "It looks perfect."

"Restored," Samuel Waker said. "Had it before, bought it back from someone." He picked up a palette, and as he spoke he resumed retouching the figurehead's hair. His voice was reverent. "Can't believe my luck, getting it back again. I think I might keep it myself this time."

"Mr. Waker, I was hoping to speak with your son."

"Don't know where he is, exactly. Traveling, far as I know." Samuel Waker's voice was steady, but the hand that painted the figurehead's hair was trembling.

"Traveling where, Mr. Waker?"

"Europe, last I heard. He hasn't been in contact."

"What about your niece? You spoken with her recently?"

"Not recently. No."

"Mr. Waker," Broden said, "a shipping container came into the dock at Red Hook last week. It held fifteen girls who were being smuggled into the country from Eastern Europe, and one of them died in transit. I think your son and your niece may have been involved in the shipping operation."

"I wouldn't know anything about that."

"Mr. Waker, is your son dead?"

Anton's father was silent for a moment. "I'm offended by the question," he finally said. "Here I just told you that he's traveling, and now you're calling me a liar."

"Mr. Waker—"

"I think I'd like you to leave," he said quietly. He didn't look at her; he was filling in a worn-away section of the figurehead's hair with tiny, meticulous brush strokes. "I don't think I have anything to say to you."

Broden stepped out into the end-of-day light. The sun was setting over the island of Manhattan and Miriam Waker was a shadow on the edge of the loading dock, slumped over her coffee cup. It was November and the air was cool but no steam rose from her coffee;

the coffee hadn't been hot in a long time and she hadn't sipped at it for longer. Broden sat down beside her, but Miriam Waker didn't look up.

"Mrs. Waker," Broden said, "I know you were questioned about your niece by a detective two weeks ago. Has she been in contact since then?"

"No."

"What about your son? Have you spoken with Anton recently?"

"No."

"Mrs. Waker, I'm afraid that something may have happened to him."

"I don't know where Anton is." Her eyes had dropped to her coffee cup, and she was almost whispering. "I don't know where he is anymore."

"Well, where was he last?"

"The island of Ischia," Anton's mother said.

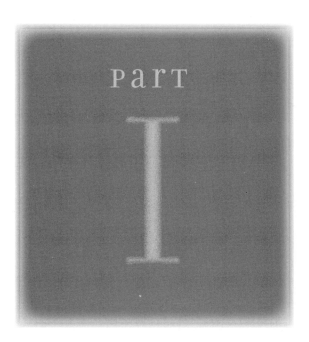

part

I

1.

For reasons that were difficult to think about in any great detail, let alone explain to his wife in New York, Anton had rented a room on the island of Ischia for the off-season. In exchange for a hundred euros a month and the understanding that he'd wash his own towels, he was given a small blue-painted room overlooking the Tyrrhenian Sea with the outline of Capri visible in clear weather against the edge of the sky. For the first few days the silence was miraculous, and he thought he might finally have found what he was looking for.

His wedding had taken place six days prior to his arrival on the island, after a long and frankly disastrous engagement: Sophie found a dress, bought it, had a panic attack when she tried it on at home, and canceled the wedding. This was a fantastically costly maneuver involving several dozen hours of therapy at three hundred dollars an hour and a mailing of two hundred uninvitations: "The wedding of Sophie Berenhardt and Anton Waker has been post-poned for personal reasons. Thank you for your understanding." She informed him that there was no hyphen in "postponed," took up meditation in addition to the therapy, and came to him a month later with the news that she'd had an epiphany: the wedding was meant to be. Two hundred and fifty all-new wedding invitations were mailed out, in shades of spring violet; the flowers blossoming in the corners of the invite, she told him, represented rebirth. Anton had just been reading about how violets pinned to a girl's lapel in a certain era had represented lesbianism, but chose not to mention this. Two hundred and one RSVPs arrived without incident. She showed up at work during his lunch break in tears, clutching the two hundred and second. All it said was "We're so glad for you! We'll be there!" and it was only from someone's obligatory aunt, but he knew before she spoke that the wedding was off again. She was scared, she said. It wasn't him. She just needed more time.

"Because I really love her," he told his friend Gary, in response to a question.

He canceled the hall and the caterer and sent out two hundred and fifty uninvitations in shades of blue. The wording on these was much the same, except that she removed the hyphen between "post" and "poned," and then he added the word "in-definitely" right before he sent it to the printers, and then he had to sleep on the couch for two nights. They spent a polite six weeks avoiding the topic. He wasn't sure what to do, but he told himself he'd always known she was flighty and should have seen this whole mess coming. Marrying her was the only course of action that seemed honorable. He was living in a strange limbo wherein he couldn't remember if he loved her or not and he sometimes felt he was losing his mind. He took endless walks through the streets of Manhattan and didn't sleep well. In the evenings while Sophie was working he spent a lot of time with his cat; Jim lay across his lap and purred while Anton read.

Their friends went to absurd lengths to avoid bringing up the wedding. Everyone was terrifically sympathetic. The therapy bills were stupendous. Topics of conversation seemed to change abruptly when they entered rooms where their friends were sitting. He tried to protect her from all this as best he could and to make things generally as pleasant as possible—coffee in bed in the morn-ings whenever feasible, flowers every Saturday—and he could tell she was trying to keep the mournful cello music to a minimum and tried to appreciate the effort. He sat on the sofa outside the closed door of her study with the cat on his lap and lost himself in the unspeakable beauty of her music.

"I don't mean to state the obvious, but being in awe of some-one's talent isn't really the same thing as being in love with them," Gary said, when Anton told him at the end of spring that Sophie was finally ready to get married again. "But what the hell, maybe third time's the charm?"

"Third time's more or less my outer limit," said Anton, and tried to convey this to Sophie in much gentler terms later on ("I don't want to pressure you, sweetie, but . . .") and she took it fairly well initially, but then played what sounded like funeral music in her study for days. When he cracked open the study door to see if she wanted to talk about it she just murmured, "I'm working," without looking up from the score, which forced him to close the door again because they'd agreed that when Sophie was working no one could talk to her. He took long walks, read in cafés, went out for drinks with Gary and made very little progress on anything that week.

The manager of the hall he'd booked for the two previous wedding attempts laughed and hung up on him, so he booked a new hall that was slightly more expensive and had been his first choice from the beginning, mailed out three hundred new invitations with a completely different color scheme, agreed with Sophie that it would probably be best if she let him handle the RSVPs this time, and set about relaunching the catering, floral decoration, and wedding-music operations. Some of her old friends from Juilliard had a rock band on the side, so he booked them against his better judgment and tried not to think about what the music might sound like.

All three hundred guests RSVP'd in the affirmative almost immediately—most, he suspected, out of sheer curiosity—and Sophie seemed happy and uncharacteristically calm, although she was playing a lot of frenetic atonal modern music in the evenings. On the day itself she was a vision, dark curls and white silk and the plunge of her neckline, blue necklace on pale skin. It was an evening wedding in a church lit with nearly a thousand candles, and time skipped and moved strangely in the half-light. He was watching her float down the aisle, there were candles everywhere and so many roses that the scent and the candle smoke made him dizzy, she was beside him, they were listening to the priest and he couldn't retain a single word that was being said. She was a mirage in the candlelight and he stood beside her in a kind of suspended animation, he was kissing her, Gary hadn't forgotten the rings, *I now pronounce you husband and wife.* The band wasn't nearly as bad as it could have been, his new wedding suit was less uncomfortable to dance in than he would have expected, they stayed at the reception til three in the morning, at intervals he heard himself laughing and he felt that he was observing the scene from some distance away.

Time seemed to be moving very rapidly now. He drank champagne and danced with his bride. His friend Ilieva put a flower behind his ear and he left it there for an hour. He felt strangely still inside through the whole thing, calmer than he thought a man getting married really should be—but it wasn't until he was thirty thousand feet over the Atlantic Ocean the next day, Sophie asleep in the seat beside him, that he realized he'd been confusing calm with indifference. He wasn't, now that he thought about it, calm at all. Nor had he fallen out of love, exactly—*indifference* was the wrong word, it was something softer and more precise—but he also wasn't at all sure that he should have married her. His exhausted bride slept on unaware.

He made his move on the island of Ischia. They arrived in the harbor village of Sant'Angelo in the late morning; a taxi let them off outside an archway beyond which no cars were allowed, and they dragged their suitcases down a cobblestone street to a pink hotel that stood by the water. It was a small two-story building with a half-dozen rooms on the second floor, the first floor taken up by a restaurant. There was no reception desk; the owner, a perpetually smiling man in his fifties named Gennaro, took reservations from a phone set up in a corridor by the door. The corridor led to the restaurant, and a flight of stairs led up to the rooms.

They checked in and spent the day wandering the streets of Sant'Angelo, and Anton thought it was the most beautiful place he'd ever seen. The village allowed no cars and couldn't have accomodated them; the streets rising up from the harbor were open-air corridors between the pale walls of villas, rough cobblestones turning every now and again into stairs. There were walled gardens glimpsed through iron gates, vines spilling over the tops of plaster walls. They turned a corner and the sea was brilliant far below them, bright-painted boats bobbing in the harbor waters. Three cafés competed on a large open piazza, and from the hillside above the harbor their umbrellas were sharp white circles and squares in the sunlight. Sophie and Anton ate dinner in the hotel restaurant and went to bed early, and in the morning they went down to the piazza and sat for a while reading the paper and drinking coffee together.

"You know," Anton said, as casually as possible, "I was thinking about maybe staying on a while."

She looked up from her café latte.

"Our plane tickets are for Thursday," she said. "We have to go back to Rome tomorrow."

"I was thinking if I stayed here for a little bit," trying not to emphasize the *I* too cruelly, failing, "I could get some traction on my book. You know, really write for a while."

"You're writing a book?"

"It's a new kind of travel book. I've been meaning to tell you about it. I just can't get going with it at home," he said, "but the atmosphere here . . ."

"A new kind of travel book," she repeated.

" 'We stand in need of something stronger now,' " he said. He was quoting a book review he'd read in the *New York Times* a while back, but he surmised from her baffled stare that she hadn't read it. He pressed on regardless: " 'A travel book that you can read while making your way through this new, alarming world.' "

"That's what you're writing?"

"Well, I haven't started yet. But here, you know, with no distractions . . ."

"Well, if you can't write it in New York City, Anton, you won't be able to write it here either."

"Bukowski," he said. "I like that."

"What?"

"Isn't that what he said? Something about writing in the apocalypse with a cat clawing up your back? Anyway, I just think—"

"No, he said if you're going to create, you're going to create with a cat crawling up your back while the whole city trembles in earthquake, bombardment, flood, and fire."

"Oh," he said.

She regarded him silently.

"As I was saying. I just thought . . . I just think it might be nice," he said, "after all we've been through, you know, it's been so intense with the wedding and everything, all the cancellations, I thought maybe we should be apart for a while. I mean, when I say a while, not a long while, just maybe a couple weeks. Sophie, please don't cry."

"I'm not crying."

"You probably hate me," he said. "Suggesting this on our honeymoon of all times."

"No," she said. She was digging in her purse.

"It's okay, I'll pay for your latte. Are you all right? Tell me honestly."

"Fine," she said absently, without looking up. Her handbag yielded a ferry schedule. She examined it for a moment, glanced at the antique gold wristwatch his parents had given her as an engagement gift, stood up from the table and started out of the piazza without looking at him. By the time he found a ten-euro bill in his wallet she was out of sight. He left the money on the table and ran after her, lunged through the door of the hotel and then realized at the bottom of the staircase that she hadn't gone in. When he came back out into the sunlight, blinking, she was already halfway up the road that led out of the village. He caught up with her as she was getting into a taxi.

"Sophie, what are you doing?" He thought he'd never seen her so calm before and wondered if she somehow thrived on catastrophe.

She said something in Italian to the taxi driver, who nodded and started his engine. Somewhat at a loss, Anton climbed in beside her and closed the door.

"Sophie, come on, this is unnecessary. Your luggage. Your passport."

"I carry my passport in my handbag," she said, "and you can dispose of my luggage as you see fit."

Sophie had nothing to say the rest of the way to the ferry terminal. He was on the shoreline side of the minivan; he stared out the window at the jumbled chaos of hotels and villas and the sea beyond, thinking of how beautiful the sea was and how much crassness and vulgarity lay between him and it. She had nothing to say at the ferry terminal either. She ducked away from his kiss and got on the ferry without speaking to him while he hung back uncertainly on the shore.

The way she departed: standing on the ferry moving away from him over the water toward the city of Naples, looking at him where he stood. She was half-smiling in a way that he felt was meant to convey something—sorrow, hope, reproach?—but he couldn't bear it and so he turned away almost immediately, while her features and her half-smile were still clearly visible and the boat still loud in the water, and he realized later that this had been the moment when the cord had finally snapped between them.

He found himself repeating the motion at intervals in the weeks that followed, trying to recapture the clarity of that moment at the ferry terminal. Standing on the road near Sant'Angelo and looking out at the sea, for example, he would turn very slowly and deliberately away from the sunset, and he was invariably disappointed by the lack of finality in the movement.

For the first two weeks on Ischia he did very little. Once he had explained to the hotel owner that he planned on staying a few weeks or possibly longer and worked out an arrangement for the off-season—"You will help me watch the place, yes?" the hotel owner said—the question of what to do next hung overhead like a cartoon thundercloud. He was waiting for an event, and thoughts of it crowded out everything else. He had ideas about his travel book but was too distracted to write anything. The room was so small that he felt claustrophobic unless the doors to the balcony were open, but then the sea was too blue, the air was too bright, and before long he found himself down in one of the cafés on the piazza with a glass of coffee and the *International Herald Tribune*, reading and absorbing sunlight and doing the crossword puzzle and watching the boats. Anton had no books with him that he hadn't already read, which was a problem, and there was an enormous amount of time to kill. He was startled by how much he missed his cat. He'd rescued Jim as a kitten two years earlier, and the cat had been an adoring orange one-eyed presence in Anton's life ever since. He went for long walks up the stairs of the town, past houses and gardens terraced up the side of the hill, and spent hours sitting by the harbor at night. On clear nights Capri was a distant scattering of lights. He could see it from his room but preferred to be down by the harbor, where you could walk to a certain point at the edge of the piazza, turn away from Capri, and imagine that nothing stood between you and the north coast of Africa. He harbored vague notions of escaping to Tunisia.

"Are you having a nervous breakdown?" Gary asked, over a phone line crackly with enormous distance.

"No," Anton said. He was leaning against a wall beside the pay phone in the Sant'Angelo piazza, looking out at the boats moving silently up and down in the harbor waves. Imagining the phone lines running under the Tyrrhenian Sea. The piazza was deserted. There were people inside a nearby café that was frequented mostly by fishermen, but the restaurants and shops were shuttered and dark. The wind off the water was cold.

"You'd tell me, right? Your best man and everything."

"Of course," Anton said. "The question's not unreasonable."

"What did you tell the office?"

"What did I tell the . . . ? Oh," he said. "The office. They've probably figured it out by now."

"You didn't tell them you were abandoning your job?"

"Well, the job abandoned me first. And I didn't know before I left that I wasn't coming back again."

"So you're not coming back."

"I don't know."

"You can see how a concerned friend might conclude there was something amiss," said Gary. "Even if he hadn't been your best man two weeks ago."

"I could. Yes."

"What's your means of support over there?"

"I'm expecting some money soon. It isn't expensive. I could last quite a while here."

"How long?"

"I don't know. Listen, I don't want to talk about this anymore. I'll call you later." Anton hung up and walked to the edge of the piazza to look at the boats.

Anton's job had faded out at the beginning of summer, slowly at first and then with increasing momentum, until he found himself alone in a dead-file storage room on the mezzanine level of the tower where he worked. The process began on the day his secretary disappeared, although it was far from clear at the time that things would snowball so quickly; this was near the beginning of June, and the third and final wedding attempt had just been scheduled for the end of August.

Anton was the head of a small research division at an international water systems consulting firm. Most of its projects to date had been in the desert cities, places like Las Vegas and Dubai, where some impractical visionary had once touched a point on a map and said, *Here*. Never mind that the place touched on the map was uninhabited for a reason: "But there's no *water* there," some inevitable naysayer would protest, and this was where Water Incorporated eventually came in. There was also work done in other, less glamorous municipalities around the world, towns from Sweden to Montana with leaking aqueducts and purification issues. But the New York City contract was something unusual, and the details made Anton shiver when he read them: most of the 1.3 billion gallons of water that flow each day into the city of New York are supplied by two pipes, completed respectively in 1917 and 1935. The conduits have become so fragile over time that the supply can't be interrupted in order to perform routine maintenance; the pipes are held intact only by the pressure of the water rushing through them, and the system leaks thirty-six million gallons of water per day. A third pipe has been under construction since 1970, but whether it will be completed before the older pipes fail is anyone's guess. If the first two pipes were to fail before the third pipe is ready, then New York City would be rendered uninhabitable overnight, the supply of drinking water cut off. Water Incorporated's contract called for studying the situation and coming up with recommendations on how to provide the residents of New York with a temporary supply of drinking water within twenty-four hours of a catastrophic pipe failure.

"All of you should be proud," Anton's director told the staff. "It's your good work that brought us to this moment." He was standing on a chair to address the troops. The New York City contract had been announced the day before and they were having an office party to celebrate. Anton was drinking wine with two of his staff: Dahlia, who he would have liked to drink with more often if he weren't already engaged, and Elena, his secretary, who he'd been secretly in love with since he'd met her under criminal circumstances two and a half years earlier. "Now, as you can no doubt imagine," the director said, "the systems we'll be studying hold significant interest for terrorists." He said *terrorists* in a slightly hushed tone, as if al-Qaeda might be holding a competing office party in an adjoining room. "We're talking about the New York City water supply here. So in the coming weeks before the project commences," he said, "we'll be performing background checks on all staff who will be involved in the project. It's a new regulatory compliance thing."

Anton excused himself and went to the bathroom to splash cold water on his face and stare at his own reflection in the mirror. A background check. He felt as pale as he looked. In the days after the office party life continued as normal, but three weeks later he arrived at work on a Monday to find that his secretary had vanished. An unfamiliar blond specimen was sitting in her cubicle.

"Where's Elena?" he asked.

The impostor, who was chewing gum, looked at him distastefully. "Who are you?"

"I'm Anton Waker. This is my office. You're sitting at my secretary's desk."

"They didn't tell me anything about an Anton," she said. "They said I was supporting Louise and Jasper."

"It's Gaspar, not Jasper. I'm afraid you were misinformed. Where's Ellie?"

"Who's Ellie?"

"Elena James? My secretary?"

"I'm your secretary."

"You just told me you weren't."

"But then you said I was misinformed," she said. He went into his office and closed the door behind him. He sat for a while at his desk going through yesterday's research reports, spent a half-hour on the phone with Sophie who was crying because someone had cut in front of her in line at the bakery and she hated people and why was everyone always so horrible and mean, and when he ventured back out a few hours later the new secretary was gone. He heard her voice from somewhere down the hall and walked in the opposite direction to avoid her. Later in the afternoon he asked Dahlia if she'd made progress on the report she was supposed to be writing, and she told him that actually she'd been told to report to Gaspar in the Compliance and Regulatory Affairs department from now on.

"But you don't do that kind of work," he said.

She was embarrassed but had no explanation. It was just what she'd been told. His other seven direct reports told him the same thing, awkwardly, with their eyes downcast. No one really knew anything. It was embarrassing. The sympathy in their eyes made him want to punch someone. He couldn't very well go across the hall and speak to Gaspar about it ("So, what's this I hear about my entire staff reporting to you now?"), and repeated calls to his supervisor were not returned ("I'm sorry, Anton, he's still unavailable. Would you like me to take another message?"), so he spent the day in his office with the door closed, waiting for an explanatory memo that never arrived. When he left at five his staff was in a meeting that he hadn't been invited to. He heard Dahlia's laugh and the strange new secretary's voice through the conference-room door. Anton felt very formal all the way home.

Sophie was working; he heard the cello through her study door. He turned on the television and turned it off again, ordered Malaysian takeout and ate alone in silence, read the morning's newspaper for a while and spent time with the cat, ate a few spoonfuls of ice cream, sat for two hours in the living room spellbound by Sophie's music. He talked with Sophie about the day's news headlines when she emerged from the study around ten o'clock, brushed his teeth, kissed her, slept fitfully, came back to the office at a quarter to nine. He was met at the doorway of his office by a man from HR. Jackson was about Anton's age and of similar build, but always slightly better dressed. He had a way of smiling a beat too quickly, and Anton had always found him somehow suspect.

"Anton," he said. His voice was hesitant. "It's good to see you."

"Jackson. Good morning. Do you know where my staff went?"

Jackson smiled. "I believe they're all in a meeting. May I talk to you a moment?"

"If they're my staff," Anton said, "and they're in a meeting, why wasn't I invited to the meeting too? I'm supposed to be supervising them?" He hadn't meant the last part to sound like a question.

Jackson continued to smile instead of answering, but his smile was strained; he had the look of a man who'd have preferred to be doing almost anything else. Anton closed the door of his office behind them. He wondered if this was the last time he'd ever sit behind his desk, and he glanced up at the diploma on the wall to steady himself. Jackson sat down on one of the chairs across from him.

"Anton," he said, "I realize the timing of this is a little unfortunate, but . . ."

"The timing of what?"

"As you know," Jackson said, "we've been conducting some background checks recently."

"Right, to prevent terrorist cells from infiltrating the office," Anton said, but Jackson seemed not to find this as amusing as he did. "Well. Is there anything I can clarify for you?"

"There is, Anton. Listen, this might be awkward, but it would be best if we could speak as frankly as possible."

"About . . . ?"

"Well, let's start with your academic background."

"Sure. Harvard."

Jackson smiled again but it was a different kind of smile, one that Anton thought contained an element of sadness. "Right," Jackson said. He stood up, smoothing imaginary wrinkles from the front of his suit jacket. "Well, we'll speak again about this soon. Did I hear a rumor that you're getting married?"

"End of August," Anton said.

"Congratulations. Are you going anywhere afterward?"

"Italy," Anton said. "Rome, Capri, Ischia."

"Ischia. Is that an island?"

Anton nodded. "In the Bay of Naples," he said.

On the way in to the office sometimes, in the days after the first conversation with Jackson, Anton closed his eyes in the subway train and tried to concentrate on everything that wasn't ruined yet. There was an idea he'd been thinking about for years now but especially lately, which was that everything he saw contained a flicker of divinity, and this lent the city a halo of brightness. Fallen, maybe, but beauty in the decrepitude, and it still seemed plausible in those days that everything might somehow fall back into place, that the background check might not have turned up anything of interest, that his original secretary might reappear at any moment. Easy to take refuge in the idea of holiness, with so much still possible and so much at stake.

The idea that everything might be somewhat holy had come originally from his mother, reading excerpts from a book on the philosophy of Spinoza on a Sunday afternoon. He was no older than twelve, and they were sitting together on the loading dock. She was reading him something impenetrable, he didn't under-stand half the words and she glanced up and saw the blank look on his face. "Look," she said, "I know the language is intense. None of the words are important, it's the idea that matters: he's saying God didn't create the universe, God *is* the universe. Do you un-derstand?"

"I do," he said.

Look at my holy fiancée in the mornings, pale and darting-eyed as she anoints her face with creams and powders. Look at my holy one-eyed cat, rescued two years ago as a sickly kitten from an unholy doorstep on West 121st Street. Look at the holy trains that carry us down into the depths of this city, passing through stations that shine like harbors in the deep. Look at the holy trees down the center of Broadway, the holy newspaper lying discarded on the sidewalk, the holy cathedral of Grand Central Station where we pass each morning under a canopy of stars. Anton glanced up every morning as he crossed the main concourse. Its ceiling was a chalky green-blue upon which stars were pinpointed in lights, the shapes of constellations etched in gold around them. The constellations were backward; the artist had been influenced, the sponsors claimed after the fact, by a medieval manuscript showing the stars as seen by God from above. It was impossible to stop and look up at the ceiling in the blazing crowd, everyone rushing in different directions to different jobs, but the glimpses were nearly enough. Anton was aware of no place more beautiful in the city. The color of the ceiling always struck him as being more ocean-like than sky-like, and the stars made him think of phosphorus, which he'd read about but never seen. There was one morning in particular when he wanted to ask Elena if she'd ever seen phosphorus, but it was Thursday and of course Elena had vanished four days ago, and he was waging a war of attrition with his new secretary. She ignored him as he walked past her into his office that morning.

He didn't look at her either, per their unspoken terms of engagement, but it occurred to him as he closed the office door that he'd had no occasion to ask her for anything yet, which struck him as odd. She had come to him for nothing; there had been no phone messages. As he sat down he noticed that his inbox was empty, for the first time in months. He remembered having reached the bottom yesterday afternoon, and he realized with a falling sensation that nothing new had been placed in it. He sat down at the desk, chilled by the air conditioning, and checked his voice mail. No messages. He had left his corporate cell phone in his desk drawer overnight. He tried to check his messages there too, but he couldn't get more than a fast busy signal no matter which combination of buttons he pressed. He logged on to his company email, or tried to, and then spent some time leaning as far back as his chair would go, contemplating the error message on the screen. *Access Denied.*

Jackson's card was on his desk. Anton hadn't really wanted to touch it since Jackson had left it there. He'd been moving his paperwork carefully around and over the card for the past several days in the hope that it might just disappear by itself. He looked at his screen another moment and then dialed Jackson's number.

"Anton," Jackson said, in a tone implying that Anton was absolutely the last person he wanted to speak with that morning. "What can I do for you?"

"Good morning, Jackson. Listen, I'm locked out of my company email account."

"I see," Jackson said.

"And my cell phone's not working."

"Really?"

"Since you were here a few days ago," Anton said, "I just thought you might be in a position to tell me what's going on."

"Well, I'm not a technical support person, Anton."

"Jackson, listen, my staff isn't reporting to me. Let's not pretend this is a technical issue."

Jackson was silent for a moment, and then Anton heard a soft click on the line.

"Anton," Jackson said very clearly, "have you thought any more about our conversation last week?"

"Am I being *recorded*?"

Jackson went quiet again, and then asked Anton if there was anything he'd like to add to last week's conversation.

"Nothing," Anton said. "Absolutely nothing, Jackson, but thank you for asking. Sorry to bother you."

Anton hung up, spent some time staring at the diploma on his office wall, and then dialed Jackson's number again.

"Jackson, I'm sorry to bother you again. But I wondered if you could tell me what happened to my secretary."

"Your secretary? She isn't at her desk?"

"I meant Elena," he said. "Elena James."

"Marlene is your secretary, Anton."

"Is that her name? My former secretary, then. She wasn't fired, was she?"

"Of course not. No. Her reviews were excellent."

"Yes, I know her reviews were excellent, Jackson, I wrote them. Was she transferred somewhere? A different department?"

"I'm afraid I can't divulge—"

Anton hung up again and spent the remainder of the day reading and rereading the *New York Times*, drumming his fingers on his desk and staring into space, walking back and forth across the room with his hands in his pockets, writing his letter of resignation and then crumpling it up and throwing it across the room, wishing he were in Italy already.

The stop before Ischia was the city of Naples. Anton and Sophie came in by train after sunset and emerged from the station into a broad curved cobblestone street where no one spoke English but the taxi drivers all insisted that they knew where their hotel was, and the streets glimpsed near the train station were dark and strewn with trash, ancient apartment buildings towering unlit. The driver took them at high speed through an intricate network of freeways, and the overpasses curving overhead had a futuristic and sinister gleam. As they sped around corners the city was fleetingly visible, a gray glimmering chaos of buildings clinging to the hillside as far as the eye could see, and then they were plunging down the hairpin turns of a narrow street, passing between buildings that appeared to have sustained some unrepaired shell damage during the course of the Second World War. The driver performed a harrowing U-turn and screeched to a halt before the Hotel Britannique. They checked in and ascended in silence to the room, where Sophie took a shower and Anton stood on the tiny terrace six stories above the traffic. He was looking out over a scattering of palm trees that stood across the street, down over the narrow section of city that descended from their street to the Tyrrhenian Sea, the Bay of Naples calm below. There were boats in the moonlight. He heard the bathroom door open in the room behind him and he realized that he and Sophie had barely spoken in hours, and not at all since they'd arrived in the city. Anton turned and through the gauze curtains she was a ghost in the steam, drifting across the room toward her suitcase, pulling a dress on over her skin. He parted the curtains and she stood barefoot and pensive before him, hair dripping dark water spots on the sky-blue linen of her dress. She looked at him and for an instant he thought he saw panic in her eyes.

"I'm just tired," she said quickly.

It took him a second to notice that her eyes were red. Three months ago, he thought, he would have noticed that instantly.

"That's why you were crying?"

"I just get tired sometimes," she said.

"I know you do. It's okay."

She smiled and twisted her hair up behind her head, secured it with a clip, seemed unaware of her beauty as a few strands escaped and fell over her neck.

"Sophie," he said. She looked up. "Let's go out and see the city."

On the street outside the night was subtropical, palm trees lit up against a deep blue sky. The sidewalk was narrow, cars and scooters passing so close that he could have reached out and touched them. Sophie clung to his hand. The street began a curve that didn't seem to end. They kept walking uphill, the road turning and turning ahead of them, until Anton thought they should have gone in a complete circle. There was no breeze from the sea below—it was as hot here as it had been in New York when they'd left—and his shirt was wet against his back. It was a long time before they came to a restaurant. He pushed open the wooden door, and Sophie moved past him into the room without speaking. The sign read *Ristorante,* but it was more of a lounge; a dim space filled with tables that terraced down toward a small stage where a girl in a sparkly dress was singing in English. Anton thought she was pretty and wished for a moment that he could share this observation with his wife.

"She's singing a New Order song," Sophie said suddenly. "Listen."

"I have this album," Anton said. "I used to listen to it all the time."

"I know, but she's singing it at half-speed. Like a *nightclub* song."

"Well," he said, "it *is* a nightclub."

"Do you hear an accent?" Sophie asked. She didn't seem to have heard him. "I think she's British."

"I think you're right."

"She's terrible," Sophie said after a moment.

A waiter had appeared. Anton got Sophie to order for him in her phrase-book Italian, and the song finished to surprisingly fervent applause. The singer's dress was very tight and seemed to be made entirely of sequins, so that she emitted shards of light with every movement. It hurt his eyes to look directly at her. Her hair was dark and pinned up elaborately. She wasn't terrible, he thought. Her voice was sweet and a bit too young for her body.

"Now she's singing old Depeche Mode stuff," Sophie said, in the tones of a girl watching a scandal unfold, and he forced himself to avert his attention from the broken-glass dress and listen to the song.

"I like it," he said. "I think it's interesting." He watched Sophie's face, but she didn't respond or look away from the girl. They were taking a ferry tomorrow to the island of Ischia.

"What I wish you could tell me," Gary said at the beginning of Anton's fourth week alone on Ischia, "is what you're actually doing there."

"I can't talk about it," Anton said. He'd been calling Gary almost every day since Sophie had left the island. He was bored and there was no one to talk to there.

"Are you waiting for something?"

"You know what's strange," Anton said, "and this will sound awful—but what I really miss is my cat. I miss my cat more than I miss Sophie."

"Your cat?"

"Jim. I know it probably sounds strange, in light of everything, but he's the one I keep thinking about."

"You're right, that sounds strange. Why don't you come back?"

"I can't. It's a long story."

"Is there some reason you're avoiding New York?"

"Well," Anton said, "now that you mention it."

"You kill someone?"

"Please. I can't even set mousetraps."

"Affair with your secretary? Unpaid debt?"

"Can you think of anything more banal," Anton said, "than having an affair with your secretary?"

"You *were* sleeping with her. Jesus."

"Things happen," Anton said. "Look, I'm not proud of it."

"Christ. Your *secretary*. How did it start?"

"The way I noticed her," he said. "It wasn't the way you're supposed to notice someone you work with."

Elena in the evenings: she stood by the window at six thirty P.M., watching as the evening reflection of their office tower appeared on the side of the Hyatt Hotel. The hotel was a reflective wall of square panels no more than fifty feet away, a mirror on which the bright windows of their offices began to appear at night-fall, before five in the winter. This was the time of day when, just by looking out the window, Anton could see the movement of workers on the floors above and below him. They walked across their offices from one lit square to another, wavering like ghosts in the reflection. The exterior of the hotel was composed entirely of glass and revealed nothing of its secret life except when a window was opened, which was rarely. Once Anton looked out and a man was leaning out the hotel window smoking a cigarette, and the sight gave him a shock—he was so used to thinking of the hotel as a mirror that he'd all but forgotten about the hotel rooms and suitcases and transient human souls on the other side of the glass.

Elena liked to pause by the floor-to-ceiling window in the

reception area on her way back from the water cooler and stand there for a moment, sipping from a paper cup. He knew this because he watched her through the window of his office, their reflections separated by an interior wall but side-by-side on the hotel's dark glass. Sometimes she waved at him and then he'd wave back, but more often she didn't seem to notice him at all and then he'd watch her unobserved. At the end of the day it sometimes made him sad to look at her. She was tragic in the way he found half the office girls he'd ever met tragic, especially the ones who didn't come from New York. She was one of millions of girls who'd come there from elsewhere and somehow gotten stuck in the upward trajectory, lost in the machine; making photocopies and fetching coffee for other people from nine to five or nine to six or nine to eight five days a week, exhausted at the end of a workday that far too closely resembled the workday before, and the workday before, and the workday before that; young and talented and still hopeful but losing ground; bright young things held up by their pinstripes on the Brooklyn- and Queens-bound trains every weekday evening, heading home to apartment shares in sketchy neighborhoods and dinners of instant noodles from corner bodegas.

The new secretary never stood by the window, and if she had Anton wouldn't have waved to her. When ten days had passed without Elena, without email access or an explanation or word from his supervisors, he called Sophie to tell her that some genius had called a six o'clock staff meeting and he'd be home late. He closed himself in his office with a bottle of water and a sandwich. It seemed at least possible that if Elena were elsewhere in the building, her new office might be on the side of the building that

faced the hotel, in which case he hoped he might see her reflection after sunset.

Sometime after seven his office window began to appear faintly
on the surface of the glass tower outside, like a photograph rising
out of liquid in a darkroom. An hour later the image was clearer,
and by nine o'clock—damn these endless summer evenings—
Anton could see almost every window of his building reflected on
the side of the hotel. He tried to watch every reflected window at
once, but the angle was such that he could really only make out
people on the two floors above and below him. Any higher and
he could see only the reflections of fluorescent lights. Any lower
and there were only windowsills and angled blinds, a potted plant
in an office four floors down. As time passed most of the lights
blinked out. Two floors above him a man was working late. The
man paced by his window once, twice, holding a cell phone to his
ear and gesturing with his other hand. Anton stood close to the
glass, looking from window to window, but none of the brightly
lit squares held Elena.

He called the company's main number at nine thirty. He listened to a recorded voice reading names, but Elena's name wasn't
in the directory. It was strange to think of her living off the company grid, invisible and out of reach. Typing somewhere under the
radar, making unrecorded calls.

On Monday morning Anton arrived at the office to find Jackson talking to the new secretary—Maria? Marla? Marion?—and
the new secretary looked away with an unsuppressed smirk as
soon as she saw him. Jackson smiled.

"Good morning, Anton."

"Jackson. To what do I owe the pleasure?"

Anton was moving past Jackson into his office, but he stopped just inside. The room was utterly empty, the desk and chair and sofa gone, his computer. Only the telephone remained, adrift on the carpet, plugged into the jack that had been behind his desk. He lifted his diploma down from the wall and held it to his chest. Jackson was watching him from the door.

"If you were planning on firing me," Anton said, "why didn't you do it on Friday?"

"Oh, we're not *firing* you. Can you think of any reason why we should?" Jackson's eyes flickered over the diploma. "I just came to show you to your new office, actually. We're reorganizing a little."

"Why can't I stay in my old office?"

"You're being transferred to a new division," Jackson said. "You're aware that we've taken over space on the twenty-third floor?"

"I remember hearing something about that."

"Well, we'd like you to head the new team up there," Jackson said. He inclined his head for Anton to follow him and they walked out together, through the open workspace where no one looked up as Anton passed, beyond the glass doors to the corridor by the elevators, where Jackson pushed the down button and stood avoiding Anton's eyes until Anton gave up trying to make eye contact and stared down at the carpet. When the elevator arrived Jackson pushed a button marked M between the lobby and the first floor.

"The mezzanine level," Jackson said when Anton looked at him.

"You said the new division was on the twenty-third floor."

"I'm afraid the offices up there aren't ready yet," Jackson said. "Still under construction. It will probably be a month or two before

we can occupy the space, so we're putting you in a temporary office space for now."

"On the *mezzanine* level? Is that even a floor?"

Jackson managed a pained half-smile but had nothing to say
to this. The elevator was descending. The corridor on the mezzanine level was unusually wide, and covered in linoleum instead of
carpet. Bare lightbulbs hung at intervals overhead and pipes were
exposed along the ceiling. Anton was struck by the white noise of
this place, an indeterminate rushing and whirring, the vibrating of
engines—were they close to the boiler room? Some sort of enormous central pump?—and the movement of air and water through
the pipes and the ductwork all around him. He thought it was like
being in the depths of a ship. The doors down here were older
than any he'd seen elsewhere in the building, battered wood with
scratched-up brass handles.

Anton heard a sound ahead, shuffling footsteps and a rhythmic squeaking; a woman came around the corner, pushing a plastic cart full of cleaning supplies. Her ankles were swollen as wide
as her knees, and she stared flatly at him through thick round
glasses as he passed. It occurred to him that he had seen her on his
floor a hundred times and that neither of them had ever said hello.
He said *Hello* this time, softly, experimentally, but she didn't answer
him and her expression didn't change. They passed doors marked
Security and Building Services and then a series of doors marked
Dead File Storage, one through three. Jackson paused at the fourth
one, Dead File Storage Four, fumbling with keys. Anton didn't
find the name of the room particularly comforting from a career
ascension standpoint.

"It's much larger than your old office," Jackson said.

This was technically true. The room was enormous and nearly empty, and Anton's footsteps echoed on the linoleum floor. His desk, chair, and sofa were marooned at the far end of the room, which was otherwise unfurnished and very bright. At the end of the room farthest from his desk, a line of decrepit filing cabinets stood unevenly against the wall. There were four large windows, none of which had blinds.

"This is a very strange office," Anton said.

"It's temporary," Jackson said. "Larger, though, isn't it?"

"I suppose that's one way of looking at it. What is this new division? What will I be doing?"

"I'm afraid I don't have the specifics. You should wait to hear from your supervisors."

"What do I do in the meantime?"

"That's between you and your supervisors," Jackson said, and left Anton alone in the room. Anton went to the nearest window. He was on the same side of the tower as his old office, but so far down that the reflective glass wall of the hotel was blocked by a line of colossal air vents. His new windows were only four or five feet above a gravel rooftop. Ladies and gentlemen of the jury, allow me to explain. I only wanted to work in an office, and some things weren't possible by normal channels. This is all I ever wanted. There were certain shortcuts I had to take.

He woke that night from a dream of the other Anton. The real Anton, or more precisely, the Anton who'd really gone to Harvard. In the dream he was the other Anton and he was walking down a street in a strange city, glancing at an unfamiliar reflection in a shop window, sitting down in an armchair and taking off his shoes, petting the head of an adoring golden retriever, moving to lift the receiver of a ringing telephone, hanging up his coat in a closet; all of the details, small and personal and utterly beautiful and mundane, that make up the fabric of a person's life.

2.

Time seemed to slow in the mezzanine office. Anton was chilled
by the air conditioning. For the first time since he'd proposed to
Sophie he found himself grateful for the impending wedding; he
had a little over two months to go and there were things to be
done, and having things to do gave the day some semblance of
structure. He could only spend so much time reading newspapers.
His inbox remained empty. He had a computer, but it was as marooned as he was; there was no access to a printer, the company
network, or the Internet. Messages left with the IT department

went unanswered. He played Solitaire for a few days and then stopped. There was a telephone on his desk, but it only ever rang when people called looking for a woman in Accounts Payable whose extension number differed from his by one digit. He sometimes tried to engage them in conversation, unsuccessfully.

Riding in the elevator was unpleasant. It was awkward boarding from the mezzanine, especially when there were people he knew in the elevator already and they said things like, "I didn't know you still worked here" and "What the hell are you doing on the mezzanine level?"

He started telling people he'd been transferred to a different division, which seemed to raise more questions than it answered ("You're trying to tell me you've joined the cleaning staff?"), so he started leaving at four, which largely eliminated the problem of running into people on their way out but raised a larger question: if he could leave at four without ramifications—he hadn't seen his supervisors since shortly before he'd been exiled two weeks earlier, and he had stopped leaving messages for them as a matter of pride—then it logically followed that he could leave at three. Or one. Or noon. Or actually never arrive in the first place. He was interested to note that he was still being paid for his time; his paychecks were deposited into his checking account with metronomic regularity. This made him think that the situation might still be salvageable in some way, that there might be some hitherto unnoticed angle of approach that would move him back up to the eleventh floor, that if he waited long enough things might become clear. Look at the holiness of this empty room. He was unsoothed by philosophy. His corporate cell phone remained dead, so he bought a cheap new phone and told Sophie he'd lost the old one. He brought books to work with him, but he was frequently too upset to read and so spent a great deal of his time pacing the room or doodling on a legal pad or thinking about how glad he was about his decision not to invite any of his coworkers to the wedding. He tried doing sit-ups but always ended up lying on his back staring at the ceiling. Nothing was clear.

At the beginning of his fifth week in the mezzanine Anton brought his basketball to work. It was strange carrying it in the elevator instead of a briefcase. When he disembarked on the mezzanine level he dribbled it down the corridor to Dead File Storage Four, past a cleaning woman who glared and muttered something in Polish as he passed. He closed his office door behind him, took off his tie and tied it around his forehead like a sweatband, and then ran and dribbled the ball back and forth across the room for an hour or so, maybe longer, until he threw it hard against the wall and it bounced off the floor and sailed through a closed window with the most satisfying sound he'd ever heard in his life. He went to investigate, broken glass crunching under his shoes. It was about a four-foot drop from the window to a lower rooftop of the Hyatt Hotel and the ball was nowhere. After a long time he saw it—a bright dot far off on the roofscape, like a lost orange. He untied his tie from around his forehead and draped it over the broken edge of the hole he'd made, and the part of the tie that hung outside the window fluttered in the breeze. He invented a new sport: when he'd finished reading the *Times* and didn't want to take a nap he sometimes wadded up sheets of newspaper and threw them through the hole in the window. The game was to throw them from as far back in the room as possible, ideally with one foot against the opposite wall. This worked reasonably well with several sheets wadded up together into a solid ball, less well with a single page. It was a question of weight; three sheets of newsprint seemed to be ideal. He'd been a decent pitcher as a kid but the hole was easy to miss even with the tie as a marker, and a snowdrift of crumpled paper rose up gradually over the broken glass.

Anton realized on a Friday that he hadn't used his stapler in a while, so he threw that out the gap in the window too. It sailed through perfectly. And then he heard a sound behind him, and when he looked over his shoulder Elena was watching him from the doorway.

"I've often wanted to do that," she said. "Throw my stapler out the window." She stepped into the room and closed the door behind her.

"It was a pretty good throw. I'm glad someone saw it. Where have you been?"

"The proofreading department. Twenty-second floor."

"The twenty-second floor," he said. "Do you ever hear construction up there?"

"Sometimes," she said. "I think they're renovating the floor above."

The idea that he might not be stuck in the mezzanine forever made him happier than he'd been in weeks. Offices were being constructed on the twenty-third floor. Jackson had been telling the truth: Anton was moving up there. It was a large company, his supervisors were busy on the New York City water project, and it was a well-known fact that the IT department was perpetually overwhelmed—the fact that he'd been languishing in the mezzanine for weeks might have absolutely nothing to do with his background check after all. He might have just been temporarily misplaced.

"Why are you grinning like that?" she asked.

"No reason. How'd you know where to find me?"

"I know a girl in HR." The way she said it made him imagine whole networks of assistants throughout the tower, names unmarked in the company directory, passing information silently from floor to floor. She sat down on his sofa. After a few minutes he came and sat down on top of his desk, a few feet away from her, but he couldn't think of anything to say. She leaned back on the sofa and looked around the room. He could see that she'd been crying, but he couldn't think of a way to ask what was wrong without embarrassing her. He thought perhaps she just wanted company—he couldn't remember if she'd ever mentioned a boyfriend—and so tried to silently convey the impression that there was nothing he'd rather be doing than sitting on top of his desk staring into space with her.

"What's in those filing cabinets?" Elena asked finally.

There were five or six old four-drawer filing cabinets in a far corner of the room. He had never opened them.

"I have no idea," he said. "We're just in storage together."

She smiled but had nothing to say to this. They sat in silence for a while longer before his phone began to ring. It was Sophie. He heard himself telling her that he was going to be home late again. "Yes, another staff meeting. I know, this evening staff meeting thing is completely unreasonable, but what can we do? We're right up against deadline for phase one of the—okay, sure, I'll call you when I'm on my way home. I love you too."

When Anton hung up Elena was watching him.

"I don't know," he said preemptively, "I just didn't feel like going home right now. What time is it?"

"A little after five," she said. "You could leave if you wanted to."

"I don't want to. Are you hungry?"

"Maybe a little." She made no move to get up.

"Come on," he said. "That lunch place in the Metlife Building lobby stays open till seven."

They ate expensive Metlife-lobby sandwiches picnic-style in the middle of the room, at the halfway mark between the desk and the broken window. It was the only part of the office that wasn't too air conditioned; a warm breeze came in through the hole in the window. Anton had closed the door against the empty corridor, and he moved the floor lamp to stand watch above them. In a circle of lamplight they ate turkey on rye and drank iced tea, almost without speaking. When the sandwiches were gone Elena lay on her back, legs crossed, hands clasped under her head, and gazed at the ceiling.

"It must be late," she said, after they'd been silent for a while.

"Where are you from?" Anton asked.

"You know where I'm from. I told you when we first met."

"I know, but it's a big country. Where exactly?"

"The far north," she said.

"That's not terribly specific."

"It's a town you've never heard of."

"Try me. I read travel books for fun."

"Inuvik," she said.

"Inuvik," he repeated. "You're right, I've never heard of it. How would I get there?"

"From New York?"

"Where else?"

"It takes five flights to get there from here."

"*Five?*"

"First you'd fly to Washington, D.C.," she said. "Then from Washington to Ottawa. From Ottawa you fly to Edmonton. Then from Edmonton you fly to Yellowknife—"

"Yellowknife?"

"A small northern city." She glanced at him; he made a motion for her to continue. "Then you fly from Yellowknife to Inuvik."

"How long does all of this take?" And later it seemed that there was no forethought, no planning and no doubt. He was clearing away the sandwich wrappers and iced-tea bottles between them, moving them aside, lying beside her on the floor as if this were something that had been planned and agreed upon beforehand. She closed her eyes. He reclined on his side to look at her, so close that he could see the texture of the violet powder that she'd dusted over her eyelids that morning, the faint dark smudges around her eyes where her mascara had been washed from her eyelashes by tears that afternoon.

"A long time."

He saw for the first time that she'd aged slightly in the two and a half years since he'd met her, or perhaps it was only that he'd never seen her so close before. The finest of lines fanned outward from the corners of her eyes. "How long?"

"Twenty-four hours," she said. "Sometimes longer in winter."

"How much longer?"

"Days. The northern airports close sometimes when the weather's bad." As she spoke she was drawing her skirt slowly up her legs, the material loose between her fingers. He reclined beside her, not breathing, looking at her pale blue underwear and the white of her thighs. She pulled the skirt up over her waist and then slowly, almost lazily, began unbuttoning her shirt. She didn't open her eyes.

"A distant northern land," he said. Her shirt was open; her fingers were unclasping her bra at the front. He rested the palm of his hand flat on her stomach. Her breath was rapid. "How long since you've been back there?"

"I haven't," she said.

"Haven't what?"

"Haven't been back." His hand traveling lightly over her skin.

Anton said, "This place you're from." They lay side-by-side, no longer touching. He had turned off the lamp and a pale light came in from the night city outside. There was a breeze through the broken window.

"Inuvik," she said.

"Why haven't you been back?"

"I can't afford the ticket."

"How did you get from there to here?"

"Sheer willpower." He laughed and rolled onto his side to stroke her hair away from her forehead. "Where are you from?" she asked.

"Brooklyn," he said. "I'm nowhere near as exotic as you. Elena, are you with someone?"

"Caleb," she said.

"I'm sorry," he said. "I shouldn't have . . ."

"No apologies. I'm breaking up with him anyway."

"Why?"

"Because it's almost over." She was sitting up, reaching for her bra. "Because all living things have a natural lifespan, and relationships are no exception. Because I don't understand the way he thinks, and vice versa."

Anton wasn't sure what to say to this but felt it would be impolite to say nothing. "I'm sorry," he repeated uselessly.

She laughed softly. "Stop saying that," she said. "Anyway, getting back on topic, Brooklyn *is* exotic."

"Not if you grow up there, believe me."

"What was it like when you were growing up?" He couldn't quite see her face in the dimness.

"You mean Brooklyn?"

"No," she said. "I mean everything."

And it struck him instantly as the most obvious, possibly even the most important question you could ever ask anyone—*How were you formed? What forged you?*—but no one had ever asked him that before, and for a second he found himself flailing in the dark. It was corrupt. It was beautiful. My parents were the best parents anyone could hope for, and also they were dealers in stolen goods. I was in love with my cousin. I was raised by thieves. I was often happy, but I always wanted something different. I used to walk down the street with my best friend Gary when we were nine, ten, eleven, twelve, not going anywhere in particular, just surveying our kingdom. Everyone in the neighborhood knew us and we sucked on popsicles that turned our tongues blue and all was right with the world. On Sundays my mother sat with me on the loading dock and we drank coffee together. There were over a thousand books in my childhood apartment.

Over a thousand books, shelved in no particular order. The shelves were a chaos of genres: the Oxford Italian-English dictionary stood alongside a biography of Queen Elizabeth I, poetry was mixed in with cookbooks, and a random sampling of twentieth-century fiction was interspersed with a fantastic collection of travel guides. Travel guides were his mother's particular passion. Before Anton was born his mother had traveled the world, as she liked to put it, although technically she only saw as much of the world as could be reached by car from Salt Lake City. She drove due south at sixteen and didn't stop moving for a decade: Mexico, Guatemala, Honduras, all the way down through Brazil and Argentina to the southernmost bit of Chile (this was where she met Anton's father, an American working for a fly-by-night scuba-diving outfit that salvaged bits of shipwrecks off the rocks of Cape Horn), and she collected travel guides for every country she passed through. Later she began collecting travel guides for everywhere: Albania, Malawi, Portugal, Spain. She had a special passion for the places that no longer exist on maps: Czechoslovakia, Yugoslavia, the USSR. The Belgian Congo, East Germany, Gran Colombia, Sikkim.

"Why do you have so many?" Anton asked her once. He might have been ten.

"It's important to understand the world," she said.

After that he read through all of her travel guides, made a serious study of them, but later he remembered almost nothing except a few random phrases. *The history of the Congo can best be understood as a series of catastrophes. While Gran Colombia is a hospitable nation, care should be taken to avoid certain sections of the countryside. Yugoslavia is a temperate country.*

Elena laughed softly and stood up from the floor. She put on her underwear and skirt, sat down again to button her shirt. When it was buttoned she stayed on the floor for a moment, combing her fingers through her hair in an effort to tame the disorder, and then began casting about for her shoes.

"It's all right," she said, "you don't have to answer me if you don't want to. It's an enormous question."

"No," Anton said, "let me try to answer it, no one's ever asked me that before. What was it like when I was growing up? It was wonderful, mostly. But I always wanted something else."

"What did you want?"

"The same thing I want now," he said. "A different kind of life."

There were soldiers on the trains that night. He didn't know what had made him open his eyes so suddenly, but he looked up just as the nineteen-year-old with the M16 met his eyes, and then they both looked away quickly. There were fifteen or twenty of them, standing quietly among the rush-hour crowd. They left the train at 59th Street, a flood of green camouflage between blue-painted pillars. What was stirring to him was the way they left all together without speaking, the way a flock of birds will sometimes rise all at once from a field.

Anton opened the door to his apartment on West 81st Street, his undershirt soaked through with sweat, and Sophie stood up from the sofa where she'd been reading and came to him. He was carrying a few shirts from the dry cleaners, and she took them from his hands before she kissed him.

"How was your day?"

"Overheated," he said. He kissed her lightly and held her

against him for a moment in the cool of the apartment. The air conditioner in the window rattled and hummed and spat a sporadic mist of water through its gills. He had changed his shirt before he came home; the one he'd worn all day smelled like the perfume Elena had been wearing. Fortunately, there had been dry cleaning to pick up. He'd retrieved his shirts from the cleaners on Amsterdam Avenue, doubled back a block, changed into a clean shirt in the restroom at Starbucks and shoved the old shirt into the bathroom trash with all the used paper towels. "How about you?"

"Fine," she said. "Long rehearsal, but I think the pieces are coming together. How was the staff meeting?"

"Tedious. Sorry I'm late." It was surprisingly easy to lie to her; he didn't feel particularly guilty, which alarmed him. "What shall we do for dinner?" He kissed her again, she moved back toward the sofa, the conversation turned to whether it was a good idea to go to a sushi place when the temperature was in the 90s. He had certain concerns about raw fish in hot climates. He listened to their conversation as if from some distance, and was interested to note that his voice was utterly calm.

The worst thing about having an affair was that he was naturally good at it.

The afternoons assumed a particular rhythm. He waited all day for the sight of her: Elena arrived without fail a few minutes after five o'clock, pale and crisp in her summer work clothes. She stepped into the room quickly, she locked the door behind her and then she came to him smiling, removing her clothes as she crossed the floor, kicking off her shoes when she was close to him. He didn't think he could regularly stay later than six without Sophie becoming suspicious, so his affair transpired every day in that delirious last hour that began at five o'clock. At six he put his clothes on and kissed her goodbye and went home to his fiancée. When he arrived at the apartment Sophie was usually in her study, and the notes of her cello swelled out through the closed door. He sat on the sofa and the cat jumped up on his lap. He closed his eyes and sat unmoving, dreaming almost, listening to his fiancée's music. Filled with admiration at the extremity of her talent, this woman who came from nothing and rose to the level of the New York Philharmonic. Thinking of Sophie and Elena at the same time until one bled into the other, stroking the cat's white stomach when it flipped over on its back in purring ecstasy. When Sophie came out of the study he tried to lose himself in her beauty at the instant she opened the door, but Elena skirted the horizon of his thoughts. She had seeped into him, she permeated the tissues of his body, he couldn't think of anything without also thinking of her.

Sophie's wedding dress hung in the bedroom closet. It was a white, enormous thing, voluminous under plastic, and he saw it every morning while he was getting dressed for work. He stared at it while he put on his tie. It hung still and heavy, a presence, a ghost.

3.

Life on earth, as far as anyone can tell, arose only once. A little before Christmas, toward the end of Elena's first and last semester at Columbia, a professor was explaining about the search for the holy grail of astrobiology: *LUCA*, he wrote on the board, and stood back for a moment to look at the letters. He leaned in again, punched a staccato period after every letter and then underlined the whole thing. He let the chalk fall to the floor and then turned to the class. A girl in the front row raised her hand.

"The Last Universal Common Ancestor?"

"The Last Universal Common Ancestor," he said.

The Last Universal Common Ancestor: one cell that appeared four or five billion years ago, from which all life on earth is descended. The ancestor we have in common with violets, with blue whales, with cats and with ferns. The cell from which we and the starfish and the pterodactyls and the daffodils originated, DNA mutating and spinning out in all directions over the passage of millennia and becoming elm trees, goldfish, humans, cacti and dragonflies, sparrows and panthers, cockroaches, turtles and orchids and dogs. We evolved from the same cell that spawned the daisy, and Elena had always been soothed by this thought. Two days before the first time she went to see Anton on the mezzanine level, she was waiting in the lobby of an office suite on the twelfth floor of the new World Trade Center 7. She was staring into space thinking of daisies and starfish and birds when she heard her name.

"Elena," said the investigator, "I'm Alexandra Broden." She was a calm woman in a gray suit, with extremely blue eyes and short dark hair. Her office had a temporary, rented-by-the-hour look about it, generic photographs of sunsets and black-and-white forests on the walls and two stiff-looking little armchairs by the window, and there was nothing on the desk but a telephone and a banker's lamp. Broden retrieved a pad of paper and a pen from a desk drawer, sat down in one armchair and gestured Elena into the other. It was no more comfortable than it looked. "Thank you for coming in to see me this afternoon."

"You're welcome," Elena said. It wasn't at all clear that she'd had any choice in the matter, but she decided not to bring this up. She sat on the edge of the seat, fiddling with the pearl ring she wore on her right hand. The investigator leaned back in her chair and watched her. "I wasn't sure I was in the right place. There's no sign on the door."

"We're just moving into the space."

Elena nodded and looked at her ring. Eventually Broden flipped the first page of the legal pad over—it was already filled with notes—and said, "You were Anton Waker's assistant?"

"I was, yes. For two years or so."

"Until when?"

"Until just recently. I guess it's been a couple of weeks."

"You liked working for him?"

"I did." Elena had the impression that Broden was writing more words than she was actually saying, but it was impossible to verify this. The notepad was tilted away from her.

"Why?"

"He was nice to me. Most people you work for in your life aren't."

"I hope you don't mind," Broden said, "but I'd like to just get a little more background on you before we move on to Anton. I believe you did a semester at Columbia?"

"I was an astrobiology major."

"Why did you drop out?"

"It was too much," Elena said. "I'd never left the Canadian arctic before, and then all of a sudden I was in New York on a full scholarship, and it was just, I guess it was too much all at once. I'm sorry, it's hard to explain. I was eighteen and I was alone in the city. I did badly in my first semester, so I thought I'd take a semester off."

"But you never went back, did you?"

"No. I didn't go back."

"I see. We'll just go through this quickly. So you left Columbia five years ago now? Six? And you began working in a restaurant, if memory serves. Was this immediately after you left school?"

"Yes," Elena said.

"Was the restaurant your first job?"

"I was a waitress in my hometown back in high school. Then I went to Columbia, then I worked in a restaurant and posed for a photographer, and then I came here. That's my entire employment history."

Broden turned the page and continued to write. "And are you on a work visa, or do you have a green card?"

"My father's an American," Elena said. "I have dual citizenship."

"How fortunate for you. Where was your father born?"

"Wyoming."

"Nice state." Broden kept writing. "Now, I know HR's likely gone over this with you, but if you'll just bear with me, I do need to ask you a few questions about Anton."

"Do you work with them?"

"With . . . ?"

"With HR," Elena said.

"I'm sorry, I must not have been very clear when we spoke on the phone. I'm a corporate investigator. I work in conjunction with the HR departments of various companies, but I'm a third-party consultant." Broden looked up briefly, then returned her attention to the pad of paper. "Did Anton ever mention anything to you about his background?"

"You know, a guy from HR asked me that exact same question. Three times."

"And what was your response?"

"That the extent of my knowledge of his background was the Harvard diploma on his wall, and no, he never talked about it."

"He never spoke about his family at all? His cousin?"

"No, nothing about that. He never mentioned a cousin."

"I see. And you never met his family, I assume."

"I met his fiancée once at a company Christmas party. Does that count?"

"When did you first meet him?"

"Anton? A little over two years ago. At my job interview."

"You're certain that was the first time you ever met him," said the investigator. "At your job interview."

"Yes," Elena said.

When Elena returned to her desk an hour and a half later a stack of interoffice envelopes had accumulated, but she didn't open them. She stared at the cubicle wall for a while, and when she looked at her watch it was four fifteen.

"Slipping out early?" Graciela asked. She was a company messenger, one of two; she stood by the elevator with an armload of envelopes.

"Coffee break," Elena said dully.

"You look pale. Maybe take the day off tomorrow. Call in sick."

"Maybe." The elevator arrived. Graciela pressed the lobby button. Elena pushed the button for the third floor.

"What're you doing on the third floor?"

"Just wanted to say hello to someone who works down there," Elena said. When the door opened she said goodbye and walked down the corridor quickly, turned a corner, looked both ways and slipped through an exit door. In the cold gray light of Stairway B, a man was sitting on the cement steps with his eyes closed.

"Excuse me," Elena said.

He nodded wanly as she stepped around him, and when she looked back he had closed his eyes again. She heard the sounds of the mezzanine as she pushed open the door: the rush of water through exposed pipes overhead, the rattling of vents, the movement of air—an industrial hum with no beginning or end, constant as the ocean. The corridor was wide and empty with a drifting population of dust bunnies, dimly lit. She passed a number of doors before the file storage rooms began: Dead File Storage One, Dead File Storage Two, Dead File Storage Three. She stood for a moment in front of the closed door to Dead File Storage Four and then backed silently away and walked back toward the stairwell. The office worker was still sitting on the stairs. He nodded again but didn't speak as she stepped around him. On the elevator between the third and twenty-second floors she closed her eyes and leaned her forehead against the wall.

"Took another unscheduled break?" her coworker asked. Nora occupied the desk closest to the elevators, where she took apparent pleasure in observing and commenting on the comings and goings of the department. Elena ignored her and went to her cubicle. The number on Broden's card was apparently a cell phone. There was a shaky, staticky quality to the rings.

"I'm sorry," she said when Broden answered. "I know your investigation is important, but I don't think I can do this."

"Why's that?" Broden's voice was mild.

"I know it's a serious thing to lie about your credentials on your résumé, I know it's fraud and I don't agree with it, it's not that I approve, it's just that he was my boss for two and a half years and I almost consider him a friend, I can't just spy on him and try to get him to say something and report back to you, I just—"

"Tell you what," Broden said, "why don't you come in tomorrow and we'll talk about it. I think it might help if I explained the situation more fully."

When Elena had hung up the phone she stared at the document she was supposed to be proofreading, but her eyes kept skipping over the same paragraph over and over again. She closed her eyes, rested her elbows on her desk, and pressed her fingertips to her forehead. She wanted it to appear to any casual observer that she merely had a headache or was perhaps resting her eyes for a moment. The problem was more serious: she had forgotten how to read.

This happened almost daily and she was used to it—she understood it to be a side effect of being unable to stand her job—but lately it had been happening earlier and earlier in the day. The mornings went quickly but the afternoons were deadly. Time slowed and expanded. She wanted to run. By four P.M. she sometimes had to correct the same paper three times. She reread words over and over again, she broke them down into individual syllables, she stared, but if you stare at any word for long enough it loses all meaning and goes abstract. She had had this job for two or three weeks now, ever since she'd been exiled without explanation from Anton Waker's research department, and it was becoming gradually less tenable each day.

"Elena?" Nora had a strong clear voice, like a singer's. "Could you come here for a moment?"

When Elena went to her she had a document Elena had labored over that morning, lying on her desk like a piece of evidence. Nora weighed well over three hundred pounds and had beautiful long dark hair, but what was more notable about her was that she loved mistakes. Here in this dead-end department in the still brackish backwaters of the company, her power and her happiness lay in the discovery of errors. "Elena," very patiently, as if addressing a child, "I'm not sure why you didn't correct the spelling of this word. Were you under the impression that there's a hyphen in 'today'?"

"Oh. The writer's British, he does that sometimes. Give it back to me, I'll mark it."

"Oh, I mark *all* the errors that I find." The pleasure in Nora's voice was unmistakable. Her eyes were alight; she was in her element. "I've told you that *many* times."

"Okay, well, thanks for pointing it out. I'm going back to work."

But Nora disliked having the game cut short. "If you'd ever like to borrow my dictionary, Elena," she said sweetly, "you're welcome to look up *any*thing you need."

"I don't need your dictionary. Thanks."

"Well, but the thing is, Elena, you thought there was a hyphen in 'today.' " All wide-eyed innocence now, the malice vanished like a passing cloud.

"No, I didn't."

"So what you're telling me is that you *saw* it," her voice incredulous now, "but decided not to *correct* it, even though you knew it was *wrong*?"

"Look, obviously I just missed it," Elena said. "Are we done?"

"Elena," spoken very seriously and reproachfully, like a CEO on the verge of firing a disobedient minion, although as far as

Elena was aware Nora's supervisory role was so nominal that she didn't have the ability to fire anyone, "I know you haven't been in your position for very long, but one thing that might not have been made clear to you is that it is our responsibility to correct *every* error that is made. That includes the errors that we don't think are important enough to correct."

"That's cute, Nora. If you'll excuse me, I'm going back to work."

"Elena, just because I pointed out your mistake doesn't mean that you have to get all pissy with me. I find it annoying."

Elena went back to her cubicle, and some time passed in which she did no work whatsoever.

"What are you doing? Are you okay?"

"Oh, I'm fine," Elena said. A coworker was standing at the cubicle entrance. She realized she had been sitting for some time with her head in her hands. "Just a headache."

"It's five o'clock," Mark said. "You could probably leave if you wanted to."

"Right," she said. "Thanks." She was unsure what she was thanking him for, and Mark didn't seem to know either. He stared at her for a moment through glasses so thick that his eyes were magnified, shook his head and turned away. It was the most he'd ever said to her. She picked up her handbag and left her desk in disarray. She descended to the marble lobby and down the steps that connected the tower to Grand Central Station, walked across the main concourse with its ceiling of stars. She stood packed in among strangers on a series of subway trains until one of them deposited her on a hot street in Brooklyn, the air still bright but the shadows slanting now, children drawing pictures of people with enormous free-form heads and stick arms on the warm sidewalk and men playing dominoes at a folding card table, speaking to each other in Spanish and ignoring her as she passed. Three keys were required to get into her apartment building. A metal grid door slammed behind her like a cage and there was a regular apartment-building door just behind it, then a little foyer with dusty archaeological layers of takeout menus and unclaimed mail rising up under the mailboxes, then another door after that. At the top of the stairs a fourth key was required to open the door to the apartment, where the first thing she saw when she came in was the tank of goldfish that Caleb kept on a table in the hallway, the five fish bright and perfect, the tank impeccably maintained.

"You know," her mother said, "I wish your sister had your kind of ambition."

"I don't know that it's *ambition*, exactly." Elena was filling a kettle with water, the phone held between her shoulder and her ear. She hadn't spoken with her mother in two or three months, and she was surprised by how much she'd missed her voice. "I'm not sure what it is. It's more like a gene for escape. You're either born with it or—" She placed the kettle on the stove and stood watching the blue gas flame as she listened. "No," she said after a moment, "I think ambition makes you accomplish things, see things through. All I've done is leave and quit."

"That isn't a minor accomplishment," her mother said. "The leaving part, I mean. All I'm saying is, when I look at your sister . . ."

"I don't know, it's hard to think in terms of having accomplished anything at this point." Elena listened for a few minutes, looking at her reflection in the darkened window. In the Northwest Territories it was two hours earlier, five o'clock in the afternoon, and her hometown was so far north that at this time of year the sun wouldn't set at all. She imagined her mother sitting by the window in the blazing daylight, flecks of dust in the sunbeams and the dog sprawled out on the carpet, until the whistle of the kettle snapped her back to New York. Elena turned off the flame and poured hot water into an open container of instant noodles on the countertop. Her mother was still talking. "You don't understand what my job's like," Elena said when her mother stopped to take a breath. "It isn't really bearable. I was supposed to be a scientist, and now I'm just here working. My only accomplishment is that I left."

"You've survived in that city," her mother said, "for how long now? Eight years?"

"Eight years. Don't say 'that city' like that. You make it sound like Baghdad. Is Jade home?"

"Your sister's not feeling so well, actually."

"She doesn't want to talk to me."

"No," Elena's mother said mildly, "she doesn't. She never tells me why not. Don't take it personally, love, she's been moody lately. How's Caleb?" Elena's mother had never laid eyes on either Caleb or New York City; both entities were the subject of frequent speculation and perpetual concern.

"Caleb's fine. He's studying."

This provoked a brief silence, because the question of why Elena wasn't studying too had never been resolved to anyone's satisfaction. Elena's mother cleared her throat.

"Well," she said, "take care, now."

"Goodnight."

The line went dead. When Elena's mother ran out of things to say she signed off without preamble. There had been a time when

Elena had been annoyed by this, but tonight she found herself admiring the decisiveness of the ending.

Outside the sky was growing dark. There was thunder, and when the rain began Elena opened the window as wide as it would go. The sounds of the storm filled the kitchen. She stopped thinking about Broden for a moment and picked up the newspaper, and she was eating noodles and reading the news when Caleb came in. She heard him stop by the goldfish tank and murmur something approving to the fish. His glasses fogged quickly in the warmth of the kitchen; he took them off and blinked at her from the doorway, his hair dark with rain.

"You had no umbrella?"

"It broke," he said. He was smiling in a far-off distracted way that meant the research was going well. She raised her face to him when he approached her, but he kissed her forehead instead of her lips.

"Have you eaten?"

"I had a sandwich up at Columbia," he said. "Instant noodles again?"

She nodded.

"How was work today?" He was taking off his rain-soaked shirt and hanging it over a kitchen chair. His naked back had an unearthly pallor.

"Oh," Elena said, "you know, an average workday . . ." and realized that of course he didn't know. Caleb didn't hold a regular job, and to the best of her knowledge never had. "Well," she said. He was staring at her, half-smiling, hoping for a punch line. "I guess you wouldn't know, come to think of it." She laughed quickly to make this last comment as joke-like and unresentful as possible. Caleb smiled back and retrieved a carton of orange juice from the refrigerator. "Are you cold from the rain? I was just going to take a hot shower."

"Oh?" He was pouring himself a glass of juice.

"You're welcome to join me."

"Oh," he said again. He was quiet for a moment, looking into his glass. "No, you go ahead. I was actually going to do a little more work before bed." He kissed her quickly on the lips, not insincerely, and left her sitting alone in the kitchen.

When Caleb left the room she threw the rest of the noodles away and drank a glass of water standing by the sink. The rain had stopped and the heat was again subtropical, moths beating soft wings against the window screen. Elena took the telephone into the bedroom, opened the top right-hand drawer, and extracted a scrap of paper from inside a blue sock. The paper had been folded years ago and was soft along the crease lines. On the piece of paper she'd written a phone number and also the address of a café on East 1st Street. She dialed the number quickly, refolded the paper and put it back in the sock and put the sock back in the drawer in the interlude before a woman's voice answered.

"Aria," she said, "I'm not sure if you'll remember me. It's Elena James."

"Elena James," Aria Waker repeated. She was quiet for a moment, and then said, "You're the Canadian."

"Yes. Listen, I just—"

"Before you say anything," Aria said, "I'm on a cell phone, and I don't discuss business on cell phones anymore. Give me a land-line number where I can call you back."

Elena gave her the number and the line went dead. The phone rang twenty minutes later.

"Yes," Aria said, when Elena answered. The sound quality was tinny, and there was background noise. Elena thought she might be calling from a pay phone in a bar.

"There's someone interviewing me," Elena said. "Some kind of consultant, a freelance corporate investigator—at least, she says she's a corporate investigator, but I don't . . . listen, I don't know who she is, and she's asking me questions about your cousin. About his background."

"What kind of questions?"

"His family. Where he went to school. I don't know anything about the school thing, it's none of my business, but she's asking questions about me too. My employment history."

"You knew there were no guarantees," Aria said, but her voice was gentle.

"Oh, it isn't that. That's not why I'm calling. I don't . . . Listen, I appreciate what you and Anton did for me, and I just thought you should know. She also asked me where I met him. Of course I told her I met Anton at my job interview, but she was insistent, she repeated the question twice. Am I being clear? She's asking me about my employment history, she's asking me about my immi-gration status, and she asked me when I met Anton."

The line was quiet for a moment.

"I'd appreciate it if you wouldn't say anything to Anton about this," Aria said. "I'd like to bring it up with him directly."

"Okay."

"Thank you for calling me," said Aria. She hung up the phone.

In the morning Elena woke before the alarm clock rang and lay for a while staring at the ceiling. Caleb was asleep beside her with his back turned. She couldn't remember him coming to bed and realized she'd fallen asleep alone again. It was too hot in the room; the ceiling fan stirred warm air over the bed. She showered and dressed quickly, all in black (there was a feeling of dread), bought the daily croissants and coffee at the bakery by the Montrose Avenue L train station, and sat staring at her reflection in the window of the train. Somewhere under the East River she imagined the weight of the water over the tunnel, boats moving on the surface far overhead, and she closed her eyes. She didn't open them until she heard the announcement for Union Square, where she switched to a train that took her north to Grand Central. She walked quickly across the main concourse, feeling lost in the crowd, and another day passed like a tedious dream.

At five o'clock Elena took the subway downtown to the World Trade Center area. She was early for her appointment; she stood looking down at the construction site for a few minutes before she crossed the street to the newly rebuilt Tower 7 and took the elevator up to the twelfth floor.

In the cool still air of the waiting room she turned to the magazines, and found a battered copy of the *New York Review of Books* in the pile. There was an article about trees, and she almost forgot about Broden for a moment. The oldest living thing in the world is a bristlecone pine tree. It grows somewhere in the western United States. She read this while she was waiting for Broden to appear, but even as Broden was opening the door to her office the details were growing hazy, and by the time she sat down on the same stiff chair she couldn't remember where exactly the tree was—Utah? California?—and the fear was awful. Broden was sitting down across from her, flipping through notes. But location aside, Utah or California, the oldest known living thing on earth has been alive for four thousand six hundred years. Elena had paused when she read this in the waiting room, stared out at nothing for a moment and thought of that great expanse of centuries stretching halfway back to the end of the last ice age.

"Elena," Broden said, "how's your day going?"

"Badly," said Elena. Nora had called her over to her desk four times and finally made her cry, and the thought of returning to the office the next morning made her want to go down to the street and hail a taxi and ask to be taken anywhere. To any other destination, any other life.

"Badly? Well, I'm sorry to hear that. Thank you for coming to see me again. Is it still hot out there?"

"Extremely," Elena said.

The oldest living thing in the world is a bristlecone pine tree, but the tragedy of the story is that there was one even older. A geology student in Utah, determined to find an even more impressive specimen, went up into the mountains and staked out the biggest tree he could find. He had borrowed a corer, a tool used to take a pencil-sized core sample at the base of the trunk. He began drilling, but the corer snapped, and a park ranger gave him permission to cut down the tree to retrieve it.

When the rings were counted, the tree turned out to be four thousand nine hundred years old. In order to retrieve a broken measuring tool, a student had killed the oldest living thing on earth. Elena's mind wandered. Four thousand nine hundred years ago, glass had just been invented in western Asia. The first cup of tea was being brewed in China. A band of wandering tribesmen at the eastern end of the Mediterranean was developing the first monotheistic religion, although some time passed before they came to be known as the Jews. An unknown Sumerian writer had just composed *Gilgamesh*. A pine cone fell to the ground and produced a minute sapling in the mountains, and you can count the rings yourself—four thousand nine hundred years after the pine cone fell, a thin dusty slice of the trunk hangs in a bar in Nevada.

"So," Broden said, "let's get down to business."

Elena looked up, startled out of her thoughts. She couldn't think of anything to say and so smiled weakly and said nothing. The office had changed slightly. A child's drawing of a ballerina was framed on the wall behind the desk, and there was a pot of geraniums on the windowsill behind Broden's chair with a little plastic flag reading "Happy Birthday!!" sticking out of the dirt.

"Was it your birthday?" she asked.

"It was. Listen, I didn't mean to stress you out. I just wanted you to go down to the mezzanine level, say hello to Anton, engage him in conversation, ask what he's doing down there. I was hoping he would volunteer something. An admission of guilt would make things much easier for us."

"I'm sorry," Elena said. "It isn't that I don't think it's important, your investigation, it's just that I'd feel like I was betraying him, spying on him like that, and we worked together for years, it just doesn't seem . . ."

"Doesn't seem right?"

"To be honest, it doesn't."

Broden nodded. "I appreciate your candor," she said. "Still, I can't help but wonder if it's not a question of motivation. What if there were more at stake than just a fraudulent résumé?"

"Are you saying that he's committed a crime?"

Broden looked at her for a moment, and then smiled. Elena shivered.

"Cold?"

"A little. The air conditioning in this building . . ."

"It *is* a little cool in here," Broden said. "I'd just like to go through your background one more time. Just to clarify a few points, and I believe that will bring us naturally back to the question at hand. After you graduated high school, you moved to the United States to go to college."

"Exactly. Yes."

"You were eighteen?"

"Yes."

"You had a scholarship to Columbia?"

"And an offer of one at MIT. But I wanted to live in New York."

"Quite an accomplishment," Broden said. "Did you work while you were in school?"

"No. I worked after I left school," Elena said.

"Tell me about that time," said Broden. "After you left school."

"Well, there's not much to tell. I was washing dishes at a restaurant. Then I was a photographer's model, and then I came here."

"Uh-huh. Let's go back a step. The time when you were posing for the photographer. What made you start doing that?"

"The posing? I don't know, it's hard to find a decent job without a bachelor's degree. I didn't make a lot of money at the restaurant. It was just extra income."

"I understand," Broden said. "It was something you could do without being legal in the United States."

"Oh no, I, wait—I beg your pardon?"

"Did you mishear?"

"No, but perhaps you misunderstood. My father was born in Wyoming. I was born and raised in Canada, but I'm an American citizen." Elena was flailing. The waters were rising and there was nowhere to go.

Broden sighed, and set the pad of paper down on the desk. "Do you ever get headaches?" She was examining her fingernails, which were cut very close and unpolished.

"I—"

"I get them in the evenings sometimes. After work, when I come home at night. My husband thinks it's stress, but I think it's deception."

"I don't—"

"And listen, let's be frank for a moment, it's not that the job itself isn't stressful." Broden stood up from the chair and moved behind it to the window, where she gazed out at other towers and the sky. "Believe me, it is. You've no idea what's at stake here. But it isn't the stress that wears at me, it's the deception. This endless, juvenile, pathetic deception, when the facts of your life were so easily verified, when a copy of your father's birth certificate was obtained so easily from Canada. And believe me, it's not just you, everyone thinks they've somehow moved through life without leaving any kind of a paper trail. It's frankly baffling to me." She clasped her hands behind her back and craned her neck to look up at the bright blue sky between towers. "Is there any part of a person's life that isn't recorded? The major events require certificates: births, marriages, and deaths are marked and counted, and the rest of it can be filled in with a little research. Your country of residence and citizenship is a matter of public record, as is your education, the identities of your parents, and their countries of citizenship and birth. So tell me, Elena, has this American father of yours ever even set foot in the United States?"

"No, listen, there's been some kind of a . . . I'm not . . . I'm an American, my father's an American, we—"

"And yet both your parents were born in Toronto, and you attended Columbia University on an international student visa. Which would have become null and void, of course, once you dropped out of school." Broden spoke without malice. She was stating a fact. "Everyone leaves a paper trail, Elena, even illegal aliens who can't afford immigration attorneys. Do you think you're invisible?"

"I don't know what you're talking about." Elena was having trouble breathing.

"It isn't easy being illegal here. I do understand that. It isn't exactly easy immigrating here legally, either, especially if you're a shiftless college dropout from some frozen little town north of the Arctic Circle. It isn't quite 'Give us your tired, your poor, your huddled masses yearning to breathe free' anymore, is it?" Standing in the late-afternoon sunlight with her hands clasped behind her back, looking up at the sky above Lower Manhattan, Broden looked perfectly serene. "It's a little more like 'Give us your wealthy, your well-connected, your overeducated and your highly skilled.' I don't like what you did, but I understand your difficulty." She was quiet for a moment. "But at any rate," she said, "we have something in common."

"What's that?" Elena's voice was a whisper.

"We've both misrepresented ourselves." Broden reached into the inside pocket of her jacket and held up a yellow-and-blue badge in Elena's direction without looking at her. *U.S. Department of State, Special Agent.* "I'm not really a freelance corporate investigator, and you're not really legal to work in this country."

Elena's hands were shaking. She clenched them together in her lap until her knuckles went white and when she tried to remember the conversation a few hours later this was the point where her memory faltered. What did she say then? Difficult to recall: something stammering and unconvincing along the lines of "There's been a mistake" or "I think you're mistaken," something utterly inadequate to the catastrophe at hand.

"I work with the Diplomatic Security Service. We're an enforcement arm of the State Department, and my specialty is passport fraud." Broden turned away from the window and stood watching her. "It isn't that I'm all that interested in you, to be perfectly frank. What I'm interested in," Broden said, "professionally speaking, are your dealings with the syndicate from which you acquired your Social Security number and that gorgeous fake passport of yours. It's the syndicate I'm interested in prosecuting, Elena, not you. So answer me honestly when I speak to you, cooperate fully in our efforts, and I'll put you on track for a green card. You won't be deported. Otherwise I'm afraid all bets are off in that department." Broden was silent for a moment, watching her. Elena felt anchorless, as if she might float upward toward the ceiling. She was painfully aware of her heartbeat. "A response might be appropriate at this point," Broden said. "Do you understand your choice?"

"It's just," one last attempt at deflection, "that I have no idea what you're talking about. I don't know what you're referring to."

Broden sighed and glanced briefly at the ceiling as if hoping for divine intervention.

"I'm referring to the time," she said, very patiently, "when you purchased a Social Security number and a fake passport from Anton Waker at a café on East 1st Street."

Elena remembered this part of the interview very clearly, and the part immediately afterward when they talked about recording devices, but later she couldn't remember how she got home after the interview was done. She closed her eyes in her cubicle a day later and pressed her fingertips to her forehead, wishing herself almost anywhere else. There were tears on her face. Soon she would go down to the mezzanine level, where at that moment Anton was contemplating throwing his stapler through the window. In a moment she'd step through the door of Dead File Storage Four with a recorder in her handbag, and smile, and ask him questions about his life. It was Friday, and it was nearly five o'clock.

4.

Aria at twelve: she walked fast under the bridge with her hands in her pockets, a sheen of black hair falling to her waist, dressed in one of her father's shirts with the sleeves rolled up, wearing pants a few sizes too big that had been left behind by a cousin on the other side, the Ecuadoran side that used to come up for long contentious visits before her mother was deported, and Anton's mother murmured in his ear as Aria approached, "Be nice to your cousin, she's having a rough time of it." But the departure of Aria's mother hadn't changed her. Except for her clothes, except for her general air of neglect and the way she winced at even a passing reference to her mother, she retained an inner core unchanged from the one Anton had always known. She was infinitely confident. She was an expert thief. She shoplifted candy, bags of chips, fashion magazines. She wasn't kind and she tolerated nothing, but she was capable of friendliness. She exuded courage and malice in equal parts.

Anton was eleven. Aria was only six months older, but there were times when the space between them felt like years. He sat with his mother on the loading dock with a mug of coffee in his hands, watching his cousin approaching from the other side of the bridge.

"Ari," his mother said, in greeting.

"Hi." Aria ascended the loading-dock stairs, reached into her pocket and gave Anton a chocolate bar. He took it, knew it was stolen and was swept through with resentful admiration. He knew she didn't give him chocolate bars because she liked him; she gave him chocolate bars to remind him that he was too chicken to steal his own.

"Did you walk here alone?" Anton's mother asked.

Of course she had walked there alone. She lived a mile away, in a deeper part of Brooklyn that was less pleasant, farther from Manhattan, where the apartments were cheaper but had bars on every window and sometimes there were gunshots at night. Anton ate his chocolate bar and watched her surreptitiously in glances.

"*Sí*," she said casually, instantly widening the distance between them. Her Spanish was a sword that kept Anton at bay. When they were little he used to tag along behind her and beg for a way in, *Teach me a word, teach me a word,* but all he remembered at eleven was *sí* and the words for butterfly and dreamer (*mariposa, soñador*) and he wasn't even completely sure about the word for dreamer anymore; he had moments when he thought it might actually be something else.

"Where's your dad?" Anton's mother asked.

Aria shrugged and sat down on the edge of the loading dock with them.

"Are you hungry, love? You want some breakfast?"

"Can I have some coffee?"

"Of course." His mother set her half-empty mug down beside Anton and stood up in one easy motion, disappeared into the shadows of the store. Alone with Aria, he stared out at the river in silence until his mother returned with a cup of coffee. Sunday mornings were the only time when his mother was all his, and he was frankly annoyed by the intrusion.

They were quiet for a few minutes, drinking coffee in the May sunlight, and then Aria asked, "Can I have a job?"

"You want to work here at the store?" His mother sounded startled. She expended an enormous amount of energy trying to get Anton to work in the store, and succeeded only to the extent that he grudgingly pushed a damp cloth around for an hour after school and complained almost continuously while he was doing it.

Aria nodded.

"What about school?"

"After school. I meant part-time."

"Why do you want to work here?"

"I just want to work."

"Why do you want to work, though, sweetie? You're young."

"Independence," she said. "It's what I want."

The torment of the afternoons. Aria arrived around four, a half-hour after Anton got home from school, and swept the store. The store was more properly a warehouse, a vast dim space filled with fantastical objects: fountains, clocks, antique furniture, ancient oak doors, ornate mirrors and enormous picture frames, old claw-foot bathtubs restored to pristine cleanliness, delicate wooden birdcages from the century before last, wardrobes, an old iron spiral staircase that ended in thin air. Sweeping the store was an immensely tricky operation that could easily take upward of an hour. He watched her while she swept, while she polished the furniture, and he was seized up by a wild inarticulate longing to touch her hair.

When Aria was done sweeping the floor and polishing a few pieces of furniture Anton's mother always gave her twenty dollars, which was overly generous but no one had the heart to say anything about it (*it's Aria, for God's sake, she has no mother*), and in the beginning Aria always left after that, but then she started bringing her homework and staying later and later until it was impossible not to invite her to stay for dinner, and then Anton's father always walked her home in the dark. Or sometimes she stayed over, on a foam mattress on the living room floor, until gradually she established an outpost in the room next to Anton's that had previously been used for storage, and then days and even weeks passed when she didn't go home at all. His mother fussed over her, insisted that she eat breakfast, bought her clothes that fit properly. He heard his parents talking late at night, their voices a soft murmur on the other side of the thin adjoining wall to the kitchen. He gathered that Aria's father didn't go home very often either. Aria's father spent all his money on long phone calls to Ecuador. Words heard through the wall: *He's come undone.* Anton didn't know exactly what this meant, but he could imagine it as he lay still in the darkness of his bedroom. He had a nightmare about a man walking down the street toward him from a great distance away; as he drew near Anton saw that he wasn't a man at all, just an empty suit walking by itself, and then the suit started unraveling around the edges until it fell down on the pavement in a pile of shredded fabric and thread at his feet, and Anton woke up gasping and tangled up in the sheets.

A memory of his aunt: Aria's mother, Sylvia of the silver earrings and the long silk skirts. A family dinner, Thanksgiving perhaps, less than a year before her deportation. She was drinking too much and getting louder, lapsing in and out of Spanish. Aria's father had his arm around her; every now and again he whispered urgently in her ear but she ignored him. Anton was ten and unsure of what to do with himself. He tried to meet Aria's eye across the table in sympathy, but Aria was closed in on herself and mortified well beyond the point of eye contact. Sylvia slammed her glass down on the table, making a point; the sound made Anton jump. The other adults were trying to accommodate her, giving her space in their conversation, not pointing out how much wine she was consuming. She turned to Anton at a moment when everyone else was talking, and he was overcome by her. The wine on her breath, her perfume, dark hair. She was beautiful.

"You think I'm a drunk," she said confidentially.

Anton stammered something, at a loss.

"Well, I'm not." She was already turning away from him, already lifting a glass to her lips. "I only drink in this desolate country."

Anton's parents owned the store long before they had a child. Their apartment was in the back, and Anton's life transpired in the vastness of the store's interior. Playing under antique tables, standing on chairs to talk to marble statues who wouldn't meet his gaze, hiding behind sofas with books when he was supposed to be sweeping or polishing. But at eleven his life was changing so rapidly that he sometimes closed his eyes in the privacy of his bedroom and gripped his desk with both hands to steady himself. That was the spring when his aunt Sylvia was deported; pulled over for drunk driving in Queens on a Monday afternoon, blinking in the Ecuadoran sunlight on Tuesday morning of the following week. That was the summer when Aria arrived, circling the outskirts of Anton's small family and then slipping in and half-stealing his parents. He would have hated her if he hadn't already been half in awe, half in love. This was the year when certain aspects of his family's business were gradually becoming clear to him, and it felt like waking slowly from a dream.

There were the shipments, for instance, that arrived at three in the morning in unmarked vans. The vans pulled up to the loading dock in front of the warehouse and yielded their treasures: old furniture, entire marble fireplaces torn from walls, elaborate clocks. There was a crew that went out at one A.M. with wire cutters and crowbars and returned before dawn with ornate wooden railings from abandoned houses, 1920s-era school drinking fountains pried from the walls of condemned yeshivas, entire leaded-glass windows from boarded-up churches. Statues, chandeliers, mosaics pried meticulously from walls. And he'd been aware of all this forever, there'd never been a time when he hadn't half-woken in the darkness to the sound of men moving heavy objects on the other side of the thin wall separating the apartment from the store, but at eleven he found himself thinking about the question of provenance. That was the year when he realized that the practice of receiving shipments at three A.M. was somewhat unorthodox; his best friend Gary's father owned a small grocery store nearby, and he was aware that Gary's father's shipments arrived after the sun had come up. Anton and Gary discussed the matter at some length, sitting on the sidewalk outside the store sucking on popsicles.

"Deliveries come in the mornings," Gary said.

"But three A.M.'s still the morning," said Anton. "Just earlier."

"Three A.M.'s not the morning. My dad said morning's when the sun comes up."

"Why would they call it three in the morning if it wasn't the morning?"

"It's still dark outside. Everybody's sleeping."

"Well, why can't a delivery come early?"

"I don't know." Gary was looking at his popsicle, considering the problem. "If it comes in the middle of the night I think it's maybe not a regular delivery. I think then it's maybe something else."

Later that day Anton sat on a crate at the back of the store, watching his father working on an old fountain, and it didn't seem like an unreasonable question—"Dad, why do so many deliveries come at night?"—but his father didn't seem to like it. The fountain was an enormous white stone basin with stone birds perched everywhere, and his father kept scraping the grime from delicate stone feathers and didn't answer. The muscles in the back of his neck tensed up.

Anton persisted. "The stuff we sell," he said, choosing his words carefully.

"What about it?"

"Is it possible . . . is it ever . . ."

"What? Is it ever what?"

"Is it ever stolen? I mean *earlier*," he said quickly, as his father set down the chisel and turned to him. "I mean not by us. I mean before it *gets* to us."

His father's face was expressionless. He looked at Anton for a moment, turned away from him and resumed his careful work.

"Sometimes you need to improvise," he said.

"What do you mean?"

"I mean that sometimes regular channels aren't open to you, and then you have to improvise. Find your own way out. Think about it, Anton. What does it take to succeed in this world?" It was clear that he expected no answer from his son. "Finishing high school? A college degree? What if you had to leave high school to work? Money? Connections? What if you have none? Hard work? When everyone else in this frantic city is working just as hard as you are?"

Anton was silent, watching him.

"All I'm saying is, it isn't easy," his father said. "It's never easy. You have to be creative sometimes. You have to make things happen for yourself."

Anton watched him for a while longer and then drifted out to the front of the store. There was a hundred-year-old bicycle there that he liked, leaning up against the doorframe. He didn't dare ride it but he spent some time running his fingers over the rough texture of the metal, the dusty crossbar and the damaged seat, imagining someone else riding it a long time ago. He could see the river. He stood on the loading dock looking out at the water and the looming bridge above and the brightening spires of Manhattan on the other side, so close, so close.

That night his father came into his room to say goodnight. He kissed Anton on the forehead, as he had every night for as long as Anton could remember, and then he sat on the edge of the bed for a moment longer before he spoke.

"Everything I do," he said, "all of this, it's all for you and your mother. This is how I provide for you. Do you understand?"

Anton nodded.

"I love you," his father said, and then he stood up quickly and left Anton alone.

"You just take it from the shelf," Aria told him, in the summer when they were simultaneously thirteen. She was using the voice she reserved for small children and idiots. "You take it when they're not looking, and then you don't have to pay for it."

"I don't want to. I don't want to." They were standing under an awning across the street from the bodega. Anton's knees were shaking.

"You don't have to *repeat* yourself," she said disgustedly.

"I just think . . ."

"That stealing is *wrong*," she said, with exquisite contempt. "I know, you've told me. Wait here." She walked away from him across the street in the sunlight and came out of the bodega a moment later with a chocolate bar for each of them, just as casually as if she'd paid for them. Just as if it wasn't Gary's father's store.

At fourteen Anton passed by Aria's room one night and her door was open a crack, just enough to spill a wedge of light out into the corridor, and he found himself waiting there, listening, stilled, but all he could hear was a rhythmic sound like scissors closing.

"I know you're there," she said. "Can you come in here?"

He froze for a moment but there was nothing to be done but push open the door and find her there in her nightgown, sitting cross-legged in a dark pool of hair on the floor.

"Help me with the back," Aria said, and held out the scissors.

Anton closed the door behind him and stood perfectly still. She was destroying something beautiful, and he felt that he should say something but he didn't.

"I'm serious, Anton. Take the scissors."

He took the scissors from her outstretched hand and knelt on the floor behind her. She had attacked her hair unevenly, from a number of angles, but at the back a section still hung straight and shining almost to the floor. He lifted the sheen and carefully cut it away in pieces, until her neck was visible and hot to the touch when his hand brushed accidentally against her skin. He swallowed hard.

"You're ogling my neck," she said pleasantly. "Pervert."

"I'm sorry." His voice was hoarse. He tried to even out her hair as best he could, but it still looked ragged when he was done with it and he was afraid to make it any shorter. He set the scissors down on the floor and they sat in silence for a moment, almost not breathing, so close that her nightgown touched his legs. Until he whispered, strained, "I'm not sure what you want me to do."

"Nothing," she said, the spell broken. She smiled over her

shoulder, and then stood up and brushed pieces of hair from her nightgown. "I just wanted shorter hair. Goodnight."

Anton closed the door behind him and then spent a fevered hour in his bed entertaining an alternative version of events in which she turned to him and pulled her nightgown off over her head.

"What is there to think about?" Aria asked. "We have both supply and demand."

Anton was sitting on the loading dock of his parents' store looking out at the river, eighteen years old. Aria stood nearby smoking a cigarette and explaining a business proposition. He had graduated high school the previous spring and his grades were superb but he'd applied to no colleges, and now summer was over and he was tired and trapped. He'd stopped smoking, which seemed like his only accomplishment in a while. He had grandiose ideas with no clear structure to them. He had no long-term plans but he found himself anxious for the future to start, whatever the future might entail. Aria had graduated a year earlier and it seemed implicitly understood that she wasn't going to college either, although she spent most of her time rereading Machiavelli and it was obvious to Anton that she was smarter than him. What he wanted was to be an executive of some kind, to work in an office, but he wasn't sure he wanted to go to school to achieve this. He had an idea that there had to be some easier, less expensive way, a different approach that might somehow be faster. He'd spent a lot of time trying to explain this suspicion to Gary, who was going to Brooklyn College next month and didn't really understand what he was talking about.

Aria did understand. A part of her was always scheming.

"I don't know," he said. "It sounds insanely dangerous."

"As opposed to what, exactly? Dealing in stolen antiques?" A movement of her hand expressed her contempt of the warehouse behind them. Anton sighed. He wasn't really sure about anything these days, especially how he felt about his parents' business. His parents had recently started a new side business that he wasn't supposed to know about. There was a new climate-controlled room behind a hidden door in the back of the warehouse basement where the fruits of far more serious salvage operations were sold: strange objects from protected archaeological heritage sites, paintings with missing paper trails, statues that had disappeared years earlier from looted museums in war zones.

"You grew up in the business," she said. "You'd be fine."

"You mean I have dishonesty in my blood? Thanks, Ari."

"What, you think you don't?"

"I don't know," he said. "Does it have to be hereditary? I think I want something different."

"You poor sweet incorruptible soul. How are you going to earn the money for college?"

"I'm not sure I'm going, actually."

"Well," she said, "why don't you just make some money, then, and decide whether you're spending it all on tuition once you have it?"

Anton had no immediate response. He lay on his back to look up at the underside of the Williamsburg Bridge, dark steel bisecting the left side of the sky. Beyond the bridge clouds floated inscrutably over blue. Aria had become harder and harder to talk to lately, not that talking to her had ever been particularly easy. "Where did you get this idea, anyway?"

"From Jesús," she said.

"The Jesús who used to work for my parents?"

"Yeah, him. I knew him my whole life. Anyway, he comes up to me right before he moves back to Mexico, asks if I know anyone who might want to buy his Social Security number from him. Says he bought it himself fifteen years ago and figures he doesn't really need it anymore, and he thought someone else could use it. That's where I got the idea. Think about it, Anton: there must be a million immigrants in this city whose chances of becoming legal are slim to none. Green cards are difficult. There are fees involved, you need a lawyer to make it all happen, the waiting list can be twenty years long depending on which country you're from, and how are you going to survive in the meantime? Even marrying an American offers no guarantee—if you entered the country illegally, they can still break up your family and deport you. So they buy a Social Security card, they can then get a better job because they're plausibly legal, we make a profit, and everybody wins."

"And everybody wins!" Anton said. "I never knew you were such a philanthropist. Where do we get the numbers?"

"We make them up. I've done some research. The first three numbers correspond to the state in which the card was issued, and for New York State, that's any number between 050 and 134. It's a little more complicated, but the rest is more or less random."

"I don't know," he said. "Let me think about it."

The business was a success from the first month and Anton loved his job for years. There was no career he could possibly have been better suited to, he thought at first, than the sale of fraudulent Social Security cards to illegal aliens in the city of New York. They were interesting. They came from everywhere. They were polite, as people on the margins of the world often are, and grateful for his services. The transactions were never boring, because every transaction carried the possibility of prison time, and they were never impersonal, because he was selling each and every one of his customers a future. He thought of himself as the last step before their new jobs, the last step before an office where a manager would glance at the Social Security card—the forgery flawless; Aria bought an expensive printer and acquired a credible facsimile of the official card paper from somewhere—before the employment forms were pushed across the desk.

Within a year they had expanded into the sale of American passports. Aria would tell him nothing about this side of the business. Anton understood that the passports were manufactured elsewhere, but he didn't know where or by whom. Aria told him it was none of his concern and they had a series of unpleasant fights about it. The thought of unknown people being involved with their business made him profoundly uneasy.

"The less you know, the less risk there is for you," Aria said reasonably. "The only people you'll ever meet are our clients."

Of all the people Anton met, all the Hungarian strippers and Chinese factory workers and Jamaican nannies, there was only one who ever scared him: Federico, a Bolivian architect with a high-pitched laugh who rambled for an hour about his tormented and visa-dependent love life ("But turns out she's on a six-month visa, so back to Brazil at the end of June, bye-bye, and no more girlfriend! Just like that!"), then beckoned Anton close across the table and joked that he might just shoot him and run off without paying, ha ha! But this was Anton's last week in the business, and the system had been perfected years ago: Anton ordered a ginger ale, which was code for catastrophe. The waitress, Ilieva, nodded and moved quickly behind the counter to make a quiet phone call. Anton listened to Federico talk about his girlfriend and wondered if Aria was back from Los Angeles yet. She'd been renting an apartment in Santa Monica under an assumed name and going out there every three or four weeks for reasons that seemed vaguely business-related, although she wouldn't discuss her activities in any great detail.

"So when do I get the documents?" Federico asked, but Aria had already pulled up outside. She tapped her horn three times lightly as Anton stood up from the table.

"This is a sting," Anton said softly. "Leave now and you won't be deported."

"What the . . . ?"

"Seriously, take off. You'll be arrested in three minutes if you don't."

Federico went pale and left quickly. Anton gave a hundred dollars to Ilieva and got in Aria's car and she berated him all the way back over the Williamsburg Bridge while he fiddled with the radio and the heat knobs. It was snowing. She was living near the store in those days, dressing the same way every other girl in the neighborhood dressed in the first few years of the twenty-first century: shapeless dresses made out of t-shirt material in eye-popping colors, low-slung leather boots and an asymmetrical haircut. He understood this to be a uniform; none of her income came from legal sources, and she didn't especially want to draw attention to herself.

"Anton, answer me. Seriously, what happened? Why did Ilieva call?"

"I told you, he made a joke about shooting me. I couldn't tell if he was serious or not."

"Christ," she said. "This was one of yours, wasn't it? I didn't screen this guy. So tell me, was there any screening involved whatsoever? You didn't ask him anything before you met with him, did you?" Anton decided not to dignify this with a response. "Stop fucking with the radio," she said. "All I'm saying is that if he was crazy enough to shoot you, he could just as easily have been FBI."

"He wasn't FBI. He was just some lunatic with a fucked-up sense of humor."

"Are you even *listening* to me? You're lucky I was in town. I've been out in LA half the week."

"Where are we going?"

"The store. I have a new batch of cards for you." They were leaving the bridge under a deep gray sky.

"No passports?"

"One passport. The rest just want cards, because they're fucking cheapskates. Anton, seriously, I think you should carry a gun."

"*What?* I'm out of the business anyway. You know this is my last week."

"For your own protection."

"Do you carry one?"

"Not on a regular basis," she said.

"You own a gun. Are you kidding me?"

"We're gangsters, sweetheart."

"We're a gang of *two*, Aria. You watch too much television."

"We're not a gang of two. You know other people work with us on the passport side. Anyway, all I'm saying is, we're selling an illegal product to illegal people, and things get a little sketchy sometimes. It might not be a bad idea."

"Illegal people. *Illegal people?* Did you actually just say that?"

Aria ignored him. She had pulled up behind the warehouse; he got out of the car and followed her around through the side entrance into the shadowy interior, where his father was polishing a bronze sculpture of an angel in a 1920s flapper dress. Aria disappeared into his parents' apartment in the back.

"Surprised to see you during the day," his father said. "Doing well?"

"I'm great. Some crazy Bolivian just threatened to shoot me."

His father whistled softly. "Rough business."

"Yeah, that's why I'm getting out."

His father grunted, but didn't respond to this.

"Dad, have you ever owned a gun?"

Aria was emerging from the back with a ziplock bag.

"There she is," his father said.

"Dad? Have you ever owned a gun?"

"Here you go. Five cards," Aria said, "and one card-passport combo. They're all scheduled for this week."

Anton gave up on the gun question. "What times? You know I'm nine to five at the company."

"Yes, I know you're nine to five at the company, you poor corporate drone. Here's your schedule."

He glanced at it quickly and folded it into his pocket. "So much for my weekend," he said.

Aria gave him a smoky-eyed glare—every hipster girl in the neighborhood was wearing eye shadow the color of gunpowder that season—and turned away from him. She was furious, and had been for some weeks now. It was in the lines of her shoulders, the angle of her head, the way she leaned with exaggerated calm against the counter to look over the store's order books, the efficient flick of her pen over a completed delivery.

"You sure have left her hanging," his father said, without looking up from the bronze. He was buffing a tarnished wrist. The sculpture was half-dark and half-shining from his efforts, like a woman stepping out of shadow. "Walking out on your business partner like that."

"I don't want to live like this anymore. I'm sick of doing illegal things."

"What we do for a living bothers you that much?"

"It has nothing to do with you. It has nothing to do with my *family*, Christ, haven't we been over this enough? It's just me. It's just me. And another thing," Anton said, on his way out the door, "I will never carry a fucking gun. Both of you, you hear me? I'm not stooping that low."

His father didn't respond to this. Aria was pointedly not looking in his direction. Anton walked out and headed for the subway station. It was the middle of the day and the platform was mostly empty. Alone near a pillar, he glanced at the schedule again and then thumbed quickly through the cards. He opened the passport. It was perfect, as always, and he wondered for the thousandth time how Aria acquired her passport blanks and how the passports came out so perfectly, who else worked on the passport side of the business and whether or not they could be trusted. There were parts of the business that were closed to him and always had been. The girl in the picture stared solemnly back at him. She was pretty, with short blond-brown hair and gray eyes. *Elena Caradin James. Place of birth: Canada. Citizenship: United States of America.*

Elena Caradin James. Two and a half years later she lay on the floor of his office in a fever, a sheen of sweat on her skin. He touched her, her eyes closed, and he was brought back to that moment on the subway platform with such force that the memory rendered him breathless. He realized suddenly who she reminded him of. A photo of a girl on the front cover of one of his parents' books. *What Work Is*: a collection of poems. He read the poetry once and liked it, but he was less taken by the poetry than by the cover: a photograph of a girl of about ten, with Elena's stillness and Elena's eyes. She stood between an enormous machine and a factory window, and you could see this in her face: she knew what work was, and she knew she wouldn't escape it in this lifetime. She was facing the camera, half in shadow. When Anton was ten and eleven and twelve and even fifteen he sometimes took the book down from the shelf just to look at her face.

"It can't have been an easy business," Elena said.

"It was an easy business. I was good at it. It was the easiest thing I ever did in my life."

"Then why did you get out?" She was naked, resplendent in the August heat. A current of warm air moved through the broken window and passed over her skin.

"I don't know, I just gradually didn't want to do it anymore."

"Why not? What changed you?"

"I don't know. It was gradual."

"If you could name one thing."

"Well, there was a girl. Catina. I'd been thinking about getting out, but it was meeting her, it was talking to her . . . I didn't know before her that I was really going to do it. Get out, I mean."

"A girlfriend?" Elena asked. The recording device in her purse listened silently.

"No, not a girlfriend. I sold her a passport."

Catina was reading a magazine when Anton came into the café. She looked up and smiled when he said her name, and he caught a glimpse of the page she'd been reading as she closed the magazine—the headline, "Who Was the Falling Man?" and a famous photograph. He'd seen it years earlier, and he recognized it at a glance. The picture was taken on September 11, 2001, at fifteen seconds past nine forty-one A.M.: a man, having jumped from one of the North Tower's unsurvivable floors above the point of impact, plummets toward the chaos of the plaza below. He is falling headfirst. He will be dead in less than sixty seconds. One knee is bent; otherwise his body is perfectly straight, his arms close against his sides. He is executing a dive that will never be replicated.

"Did they figure out the guy's name?" Anton asked. Catina looked blankly at him until he gestured at the magazine.

"Oh." She shook her head. "They thought they knew. But the family wouldn't concede it."

"The family doesn't think it's him?"

"They don't want it to be him. The guy in the picture's jumping before his tower falls, so I guess they see something unheroic about it. They say their son wouldn't have jumped."

Anton shrugged. "Doesn't seem like an unreasonable thing to do," he said. "I might've jumped."

"I think the falling man's . . . admire-able?"

"Admirable."

"Admirable." Catina spoke with a Portuguese accent; she had been in the country for four years now, working as an assistant to a Portuguese businessman, and her English was good but traces of

Lisbon remained. "There was no way out, and he made a choice. The air was all flames. On flames?"

"On fire."

"The air was on fire. He could pause . . . no, hesitate. He could hesitate and burn to death, or he could take control in those last few seconds and dive into the air. I like to think I would have done the same thing."

Anton nodded and found suddenly that he couldn't breathe. He excused himself and went to the bathroom and spent several minutes staring at his face in the mirror, trying to think about what he would do if he were marooned a hundred stories above the surface of the earth with the air on fire all around him. He went back out into the Russian Café and completed the transaction as quickly as possible. Outside in the sunlight he stood still on the sidewalk, watching Catina depart with the magazine rolled up in her hand, and then he walked away slowly in the opposite direction. He locked eyes with everyone he saw on the sidewalk. Some stared back at him, some ignored him, others glanced quickly and then looked away. At dinner with his parents a few hours later he pushed food around his plate and didn't eat until his mother put her fork down and asked what was wrong with her spaghetti.

"No, the food's good. I'm sorry. I've just been thinking a lot about the business."

"What about it?" his father asked.

"Not *your* business. This thing with Aria."

"Really," Aria said.

"Oh," his mother said, visibly relieved. She preferred not to discuss the family business in any great detail, but her niece's forged-documents venture was fair game. "What about it?"

"I was thinking about this earlier in the day. Do you mind if I ask a hypothetical question?"

"I love hypothetical questions," his mother said.

"How would a terrorist get into the country?"

"Well, he'd come in on a tourist visa, I imagine."

"Or he'd get a friend in the country to come to me and Aria and get him a passport, and then he'd enter as an American citizen. Or if he were already here on his tourist visa, he'd buy a Social Security card directly from us and use it to get a job. You know, guarding a seaport. Or driving a truck that he could then pack with explosives. Or whatever."

His father shrugged.

"So then what are we doing? What are we doing here? We—"

"Think of your aunt," his mother said. "Don't get worked up, sweetie. You're helping people like your aunt."

"Yes," Aria said, "my dear departed mother." She liked to say *departed* instead of *deported*, which was disconcerting, because as far as anyone knew her mother was alive and well and living in Ecuador.

"Yeah, I am. Hardworking illegal aliens who have no chance of getting citizenship, I know, I get it, but who else? Who else besides them?"

His parents were quiet. Aria watched him silently over the table.

"It was just something I was thinking about today. Actually, not just today, it's been ... it weighs on me," Anton said.

"You have to do things that are a little questionable sometimes," his father said. "It's all part of making a living."

"Yeah, but maybe it doesn't have to be. I keep thinking there's maybe something else I could be doing. I've been putting my résumé together."

"Your résumé," Aria said. "Your *résumé*? Really? You've only ever had two jobs in your life: selling stolen goods in your parents' store and selling fake documents to illegal aliens." His father's jaw was tensing again; he didn't like the word *stolen*. Anton's mother was immune to accusations of theft, but disliked any suggestion of disloyalty; she was sipping water, watching Anton, her eyes cool over the top of her glass. Aria pressed onward: "Are your jobs on your résumé, Anton?"

"My education's on my résumé."

"Our high school's on your résumé? Are you serious? If it weren't for social promotion, you'd have been the only student in your graduating class."

Anton extracted his wallet from his jeans. Folded behind the bills was a newspaper clipping; he had been carrying it around for months and it almost fell apart when he unfolded it. He passed it to his mother, who looked at it and frowned.

"A story about an alumni association meeting, Anton? You wanted me to read this?"

"Look at the end. There's a quote from an Anton Waker, who just graduated Harvard. I was surprised, I mean, the name can't be that common. And I was looking at it and thinking, you know, what if I'd gone to college? What opportunities, what jobs would be open to me that aren't open to me now? I always thought I wanted to work in an office somewhere, be an executive of some kind."

His mother was smiling. "You applied to *college*," she said, and he almost winced against the delight in her voice.

"No," he said, "I did something different. The guy they quote there, the other Anton—how old are you when you graduate college? Twenty-two? Twenty-three? He's a little younger than me, but it's close, it's close. I could've taken a year or two off after high school—"

"Or four or five years off after high school," Aria said. "I'm looking forward to hearing the explanation for that one."

"So I just wrote a letter to Harvard," Anton said, ignoring her, "requesting a copy of my diploma."

There was a bad moment when he thought his mother might cry, but then she smiled and raised her glass to him instead. His father raised his glass too.

"To improvisation," his father said.

5.

"That's horrifying," said Caleb, when Elena told him the story about the four-thousand-nine-hundred-year-old pine tree. "They just let him cut it down?"

"For a broken measuring tool. I can't stop thinking about it. It was in a magazine I read today."

"Christ." He sounded genuinely moved. She had lit two scented candles in the bedroom while he was still at his desk: vanilla and jasmine, sweet and dizzying in combination. When the candles were lit she had taken her clothes off, but he was still fully dressed when he came to lie down beside her and didn't seem to notice that she wasn't wearing anything. He wanted to hear about her day.

Elena didn't want to talk about her day. She didn't want to tell him about Broden. She could hear Caleb's heartbeat through the fabric of his shirt.

"So, I found out about my grant," he said.

She sighed and pressed herself against him. He shifted away from her almost imperceptibly, ran his hand through her hair and turned his head briefly to kiss her forehead.

"Good news?"

"Very good." He kept talking. She pressed the length of her body against him again, but so gently this time that it could easily have been mistaken for an accidental shifting of weight. He didn't notice, or chose not to.

"Was that a no?" he asked finally.

"I'm sorry, what?"

"The party," he said. "To celebrate the grant renewal. Tomorrow at my professor's house. You want to come?"

"Absolutely. Of course. I'm sorry I was distracted, it's not that I wasn't interested."

"Has your job gotten any better?" he asked gently. "The proofreading?"

She didn't want to think about work; she began stroking his arm instead of answering him. His arm tensed very slightly under her fingertips. Haptics: the science of studying data obtained by touch.

The slow agony of morning, cubicle life. Elena tried to concentrate on the documents she was reading, but she'd slept badly the night before and her exhaustion was a weight. She was on her third cup of coffee when Nora called her name.

"It isn't that I think your work is bad," Nora said. She was in the habit of offering unsolicited performance reviews. She held the document Elena had been proofreading the previous afternoon. "It's just that I notice a certain lack of attention sometimes."

A certain lack of attention. Elena's hands were shaking when she went back to her desk, but she wasn't sure if it was from the coffee or because she had to see Broden over the lunch hour. Broden had told her to acquire as much information as possible but all she had acquired so far was guilt. And fears as strong as memories, as if the deportation had already occurred: the walk through the airport in handcuffs, an FBI agent on either side. The sequence of flights, New York to Washington, D.C. and then northward, the hours in Customs on the other side of the border before being released into the shadowless arctic summer with people whispering on every street.

At one o'clock she went back to World Trade Center 7, sat in Broden's office while Broden took notes. She found herself staring out the window at the blue sky and glass towers outside. Thinking of the far north, of exile and snow. Elena had been on the front page of her hometown newspaper when she'd made it into Columbia on full scholarship; imagine the stories if she came back in handcuffs. But would they bother to take her as far as Inuvik? Of course not. It was a two-thousand-dollar ticket. A shorter flight, then, hauled over the border to the closest major Canadian city. Abandoned in Toronto or Montreal at nightfall, still three thousand miles from home and New York City lost forever on the other side of a closed border, her name on a list at Customs, oh God.

"Elena." Broden was leaning forward in her chair, and Elena realized from her tone that she had said Elena's name more than once.

"I'm sorry."

"Do you have the tape?"

"Yes," Elena said. It was in her handbag. She fumbled about until she felt the hard plastic edge of the case under her fingertips, and she unexpectedly burst into tears. "I'm sorry," she said. "I'm sorry, I never do this. I never cry in front of people."

Broden had produced a box of tissues from somewhere, and she passed it to Elena without a word. Elena pressed two tissues to her face and forced herself to be still. She stood up, straightened her skirt, and placed the tape on the desk on her way out of Broden's office. She didn't look back, but she felt Broden's eyes on her as she left.

Strange to go back to the office, after such a meeting. Her reflection in the darkened window of the subway car, staring back at herself. At Grand Central Station she walked very slowly across the main concourse, the vast space filling up already even though it was only three in the afternoon, executives rushing to catch their trains home to Westchester County. In the elevator Elena pressed every button to buy time and the doors opened and closed on other people's working lives; glimpses of beige carpets, white marble, dark wood, glass walls, a woman walking with a cup of coffee. On the twenty-second floor she left the elevator and opened the door to the office, walked past Nora without looking at her and went to her desk. The paper she was supposed to be proofreading blurred before her eyes. Nora's voice was distinct over the top of the cubicles—"You know, Mark, when I write you a memo, you should *probably* read it"—and the fluorescent lights hummed softly overhead.

Elena put down her red pencil and closed her eyes. All her life she'd paid attention to last moments—the last moment before a catastrophe, the last moment before a surprise, the last moment before you open the envelope from Columbia University in the living room in your arctic hometown with your parents standing breathless in the doorway—and she'd come to recognize last moments when she saw them. This was the last moment she could stand to go on like this.

Elena took a page from her inbox, wrote *I QUIT* on the back in block letters, signed her name, and slung her handbag over her shoulder. She walked past Nora's desk and dropped the piece of paper in Nora's inbox, but Nora was preoccupied with insulting someone else and didn't notice. By three forty-five P.M. she was outside in the haze of midtown Manhattan, as free and as lost as she'd ever been.

The party was in a brownstone on a tree-lined block off Broadway, high up on the island near the university gates. It was miles from the office but Elena walked there anyway, a slow northwestern movement across the span of a city and an afternoon. She would walk until the heat was overwhelming and then step into a Starbucks—there seemed to be one every three and a half blocks or so—and walk out of the air conditioning with a plastic cup of something sugary and frozen in her hand. The air was dense and heat waves shimmered over the street. She alternately sipped iced coffee and pressed the cold cup to her forehead as she walked, thoughts of Broden and Anton and the job she'd just quit and Caleb drifting together and sifting to white. The walk through Central Park was the hardest stretch; a few steps in and the sound of traffic vanished, the landscape closing in around her like an implosion. There was a weighted quality to the park, a hush, footsteps almost silent and her heart beating too fast, dragonflies gliding on imperceptible breezes under the pressing canopy of trees. There were few people here at this hour, in this heat: a woman pushing a red-faced child in a stroller; a runner almost staggering, streaked with sweat; a man sitting alone on a bench with his possessions in plastic bags around him, singing quietly and scattering seeds to a congregation of pigeons. Day fell into twilight, but twilight brought no relief.

When Elena emerged from the park at 110th Street her head was light and there was a confused shifting darkness at the center of her vision. She bought plantain chips and Gatorade in a tiny bodega and pressed on against the air. She was dizzy. Her breath was ragged. Caleb had given her the address but it took her a while to find the place, walking somnambulant along a tree-lined street until she saw the number, the door ajar. There were voices coming from inside. It took a few minutes to make it up the steps.

She pushed the door open and slipped into the foyer. The crowd was larger than she'd thought it would be, but she recognized no one. The living room looked more or less the way she would have expected a professor's living room to look: deep red walls hung with African masks, bookshelves overflowing their contents onto side tables and chairs. Caleb was nowhere. Elena wanted to sit down, her legs were aching, but every chair and sofa seemed taken. She settled for leaning against a wall in dazed silence. The room was well air conditioned; her sweat dried on her face. She thought she recognized a face or two in the crowd, old classmates from her astrobiology days, but no one she'd been close to or whose names she remembered—had she been close to anyone besides Caleb at school? It was unclear in retrospect, and no one here seemed to see her. More people were coming in from outside, and everyone seemed to know each other. The room was becoming more crowded and she was becoming more alone.

"Ellie?"

The photographer was grayer than she remembered, but with the same appraising eye. Her initial impression, when she'd met him for the first time three years earlier, was that he had the look of a man who'd seen too many naked women in his lifetime.

"Leigh," she said. "What are you doing here?"

"My wife teaches up at Columbia. We're friends of Dell's. Are you okay? You're a little flushed."

"Fine. A little hot. The temperature out there . . ." She gestured weakly.

"I know, it's brutal. Here's to air conditioning." He raised his glass. "What brings you to the party?"

"My boyfriend's working on the plant genome thing."

"You're dating a professor?"

"He's a Ph.D. candidate."

"What's his name?"

"Caleb. Caleb Petrovsky."

"Tall, kind of lanky? Light brown hair, falls in his eyes a little?"

"You know him?"

"We were just introduced. Didn't realize he was yours."

"Is he here somewhere?"

"He's talking to Dell in the kitchen."

Elena nodded and sipped her Gatorade, suddenly not at all sure that she wanted to see Caleb after all. He would ask how work was, she would tell him she had quit her job, he would look at her strangely and they'd fall into an awkward silence, et cetera. She contemplated slipping out. Across the room, a girl she remembered from a long-ago biology class was holding court in a circle of men; she caught "—but if you focus just on the chloroplast—" before Leigh cleared his throat.

"Not to be forward," he said. He was holding a plastic cup of red wine and staring into the room with her. She wondered what he saw when he looked at the women. "But if you had any interest in being photographed again, I'm putting together a new book."

"I would love to," Elena said.

In the kitchen Caleb was leaning on a counter, holding a bottle of beer and laughing, talking to an older man whose face she couldn't see. Elena stood for a moment in the kitchen doorway, watching him—he didn't seem to notice her—but she couldn't bring herself to go in. There was a door in the hallway with a sign that read *W.C.* in wooden-block letters. She slipped inside and closed and locked the door behind her, splashed cold water on her face until her skin was cold to the touch and stood leaning over the sink with water dripping from her hair. Her face in the mirror was utterly white. Coming to the party seemed to have been a colossal error; she wanted nothing in that moment but to stay alone with her thoughts. She spent some time fixing her water-smudged mascara with a scrap of toilet paper, then sat down on the edge of the bathtub.

There was a stack of books beside the toilet, and the second book from the top had a familiar blue spine. She pulled it out of the pile. *Naked: New Photographs by Leigh Anderson.* The girl on the cover lay facedown on the bed in Leigh's apartment, naked but for a pair of very high heels. Elena flipped to page thirty-four and stared at her own face for a moment. She caught herself wondering if any of her old classmates had seen this book, and if any of them would recognize her if they did. "Do you think you're invisible?" Broden had asked. *I do, actually. Yes. Thanks for asking.* She walked back out to the kitchen; Caleb waved when she came in and put his arm around her waist.

"Dell," he said, "you've met Elena."

The professor smiled, and Elena saw that he didn't remember her. Some years earlier, in a different lifetime, he had written the initials *LUCA* on a blackboard and let the chalk fall to the floor.

"Elena," he said carefully. "And what are you up to these days?"

"I'm a spy."

"What?" Caleb's beer was halfway to his mouth; he put the bottle back on the counter and looked at her, still smiling. "What's that, honey?"

"Actually, I just quit my job today."

"Oh," Caleb said. "Wow. Congratulations, El, I know how much you hated it. Is everything all right? You seem a little . . . ?"

"I'm fine. Actually, I'm better than I've been in a while."

"Oh," he said. "Well, that's good, then. How much notice did you give them?"

"None. I just walked out."

"If you'll excuse me," the professor said.

"You just walked out," Caleb repeated. "So you, um, you have a new job lined up?"

"I'm posing for the photographer again."

"Posing for the . . . wow. The same one as before?"

She nodded and took the beer bottle from his hand, drank for a moment and gave it back to him.

"El, are you sure you want to do that again?"

"Why wouldn't I?"

"Well," he said, "it's just, I don't know, it just seems a little sordid, doesn't it?"

She was suddenly very tired. Her joints ached from miles of walking and she wanted to lie down. "Work is always a little sordid," she said.

6.

Anton received his diploma from Harvard and had it framed in a neighborhood far from where he lived. He was half-afraid he'd be laughed out of the frame shop, but the man behind the counter only nodded and told him to come back the next day to pick it up. Anton took his résumé to an employment agency with the full expectation of being thrown out of the office, but they placed him immediately in a low-level clerical position at Water Incorporated and he was promoted twice within the first six months. The transferability of his skills was truly startling; the confidence required to sell illegal documents was the same confidence required to sit in an office beneath a framed Harvard diploma and pretend he knew what he was doing until he learned the job.

"Con*sul*ting," Anton's father said, with what struck Anton as an entirely unnecessary emphasis on the part of the word that rhymed with *insult*. "What do you consult?"

"Well, we're water system design specialists," Anton said. He was having dinner at his parents' apartment.

"Are *you* a water system design specialist?"

"No, I'm in a support division. I do research, produce reports for the sales teams, help prepare presentations, that kind of thing."

"What qualifies you to do that?"

"Well, the same thing that qualified me to sell Social Security cards to illegal aliens, actually. A certain veneer of confidence combined with sheer recklessness."

His father smiled. "Also, let's not forget, I graduated Harvard," Anton said, and his father laughed and raised his wineglass.

Anton met a cellist at a party that year, a spectacularly talented girl who didn't know he'd never been to Harvard, and he proposed to her eight months later. Sophie and the job together formed the foundation of his new life; between the straight clean lines of a Midtown tower he rose up through the ranks, from junior researcher to senior researcher to VP of a research division. His dedication to the company was mentioned in his performance reviews. He directed his team and came home every night to a woman he loved in an apartment filled with music in his favorite neighborhood, until it all came apart at once and he found himself in Dead File Storage Four lying naked on the floor next to his former secretary in the summer heat.

"Do you know what's strange?" Elena asked. Anton had turned the lights off in the room, and her skin was pale in the dim light through the windows.

"What's that?"

"The building thinks I still work here."

Anton propped himself up on one elbow to look at her face. "*I* thought you still worked here."

"I quit a week ago," Elena said. She was gazing up at the ceiling. "That night I didn't come to you."

"Ah," he said. "I wondered what'd become of you." *Wondered* wasn't exactly the right word. He had lain on his back on the floor till seven P.M. watching the door that didn't open and thinking about the complete dissolution of the life he'd been building, and when he'd gone home that night he hadn't even the energy to lie. "I just stayed late in the office," he'd said when Sophie asked if he'd had another staff meeting.

"And my swipe card still works," Elena said. "It's been seven or eight days, but I can still get into the building at five o'clock to see you. I thought it would be deactivated, but the turnstile gates still open for me in the lobby."

He was quiet.

"I thought I'd be locked out of the system," she said, "but no one's told the building I don't work here anymore."

"You haven't worked here in a week, but you still come to see me at five?"

"Of course," Elena said.

Anton lay down beside her again and held her close. She let

her head fall against his chest. The breeze through the broken window was warm on his skin.

"That first time you came to me," he said after a while. "That first afternoon."

"What about it?"

"Why were you crying?"

She sat up and began reaching for her clothes. "Anton, has Aria spoken to you?"

"About . . . ?"

"Nothing," she said. "What time is it?" She was standing up and getting dressed again, smoothing her hair. She turned on the floor lamp and its yellow light filled the room. He stood up, blinking.

"Ellie?" He touched her shoulder, but she still didn't look at him. "About what? Has Aria spoken to me about what?" But she shook her head again and made a small but final motion with her hand, leaned over awkwardly to put on her shoes.

"Ellie, please."

"I ran into her on the street a few days back. She asked how you were and said she needed to tell you something. That's all. It's none of my business." She didn't meet his eyes. "That's all," she repeated.

"Well." He was watching her closely. She retrieved a tube of lipstick from her handbag and applied it quickly, pressed her lips together once. "I'll see her tonight," he said. "There's a dinner thing uptown."

"A dinner thing?"

"It's my parents' thirtieth wedding anniversary."

"Thirty years of marriage." There were tears in her eyes. "Did they ever cheat on each other?"

"Elena . . ."

"I'm sorry," she said. "I'll see you on Monday, if my swipe card still works."

"Please call me if it doesn't work. I'll be here."

"Goodnight," she said, and left very quickly without kissing him goodbye.

His parents' thirtieth anniversary dinner was at Malvolio's Ristorante on the Upper East Side. He'd been there once some years ago for an event gone hazy in memory—Gary's birthday?—and had forgotten exactly where it was but nonetheless arrived early. Anton didn't feel like sitting at the table alone. He was waiting on the sidewalk out front when Aria pulled up in a silver Jaguar and gave her keys to the valet. He whistled softly.

"Beautiful," he said.

"Isn't it?" She was dressed expensively, wearing a silk neck scarf that made him think of flight attendants.

"Is it new?"

"This year's model." They watched the Jaguar recede.

"Whoever said crime doesn't pay doesn't know you very well."

Aria laughed as she led him into the cool of the restaurant. "I want to talk to you about something," she said when they'd been seated. Their table was in a back corner of the room, far from other customers.

"I thought you might."

She glanced at him strangely, but continued. "I know this is forward of me," she said, "but are you certain . . . is the wedding going through this time?"

"It is," he said.

"And you're definitely going to Italy afterward?"

"That's the plan."

"In that case, I have a proposition," she said. "I think you'll find the terms attractive."

"What kind of proposition?"

"I've been working on a major deal. It involves multiple clients, and they're willing to pay me a lot of money. The catch is," she said, "the deal has to be done in Europe. They're unwilling to risk coming to the United States in the present political climate without the benefit of my product, if you know what I mean."

"So they have the wrong passports."

"Are you trying to get me arrested? Speak a little louder, I don't think they heard you in the kitchen. Anton," she said, "I could really use your help with this. You're going to Europe on your honeymoon."

"True, but I'm also out of the business. I'm a respected junior manager at a major consulting firm." Anton couldn't help but think about Dead File Storage Four as he said this, and tried to focus on the old eleventh-floor office instead. The details of his old office were already slipping away from him. He was no longer absolutely sure, for example, what color the carpet had been. In his memories it shifted unsteadily between gray and blue.

"There would be a substantial commission," Aria murmured. "Ten thousand dollars."

He whistled softly. "What are you doing for them?"

"Plausible deniability, Anton. You don't really want to know."

"You're right, I really don't. Why can't you go to Europe yourself?"

"I've got some things I need to do here," she said. "I can't leave just now."

"I appreciate the offer," he said, "but—"

"There's practically no exposure, Anton. We can set it up so that you're plausibly innocent throughout the whole transaction. You go to a hotel in Europe, you receive a package from me addressed to a third party care of your name and room number, that third party approaches you that evening and introduces himself as a friend of mine, you hand it over to him without opening it, and a short time later a wedding gift gets wired to your bank account. It's that easy. You couldn't possibly be having your wedding at a better time, incidentally."

"Glad it's convenient for you. But seriously, Ari, you call that no exposure?"

"It's ten grand," she said. "For accepting a FedEx package and then handing it to someone. You're a respectable corporate drone on his honeymoon. You have no criminal record whatsoever. You've been out of the business for long enough that no one's paying any attention to you, and you never even have to know what's in the package."

"Aria," he said after a moment, "I don't want to do it. I'm sorry. I'm out of the business."

"I'm *family*," she said.

"And I'm not judging you. It's a hell of a business you've built for yourself, I mean, I sure as hell don't drive a Jaguar." She didn't smile. "I just don't want to be a part of it anymore. That's all."

She was quiet; she sipped her water; she rested her chin on her hand for a moment and stared into space.

"This is the deal of my career, Anton," she said softly. "It would launch me into a whole new sector."

"What's wrong with your old sector?"

"I think it's almost time to get out of it," she said. "These people are in the import-export business. It's an area I'm interested in."

"Well, I'm sorry."

"So am I." Aria smiled, seemingly at nothing and no one in particular, and toyed with a corner of the tablecloth as she spoke. "I can't imagine how uncomfortable it would be for you," she said, "if Sophie were to find out that you didn't actually go to Harvard."

"What?"

"Do this one last thing for me," she said. "Do this one last thing, and then you're finished. I'll consider you retired. You'll never have anything to do with my business again."

"You're blackmailing me."

"I'm helping you to avoid a supremely awkward explanation. Didn't Sophie work nights as a waitress to put herself through Juilliard? And here you just cheated your way into your career. Do you think she'll be very understanding?"

He was staring at her, wordless.

"Because I'm not at all sure that she will," said Aria. "Poor motherless Sophie, playing the cello at nine in her trailer park in California while her father worked two jobs to support his kids. Sophie, who's had a job since she was what, eleven? Twelve? I have enormous respect for her for that reason alone, Anton, but don't you sense a certain, well, a certain lack of open-mindedness when it comes to, shall we say, alternative means of securing an income? She's—"

"Shut up," he murmured, "just shut the fuck up. Sam and Miriam are here."

His parents had entered the restaurant. His mother was wearing the vintage yellow dress she wore only on special occasions in the summertime, an enormous amber brooch resplendent on the front. His father beamed under his summer fedora. They were laughing as they crossed the room. "It's so lovely to see you both," his mother said. They were kissing Anton and Aria and sitting down at the table; his mother was rummaging in her beaded purse for a tissue and blotting sweat from her forehead; they were talking about a restored garden fountain they'd just sold that morning, the white marble one they'd had for so long. They'd had a good week.

"I can picture it," Anton said. "I remember it exactly. Stone birds all around the edges. Beautiful piece." He felt like throwing up but kept his voice as bright as possible. I'd just like to thank the Academy. "How long have you had it?"

"Ten years," said Aria. "I remember when we got it in. You remember how much Sophie liked it when she first came into the store?"

Anton smiled painfully. His father had intercepted a passing waiter and was ordering wine.

"How *is* Sophie?" his mother asked.

"Excellent," Anton said. "She's doing well these days. She sends her regards, by the way, and her regrets and her congratulations."

"Quite a combination," his mother said. "Regrets, congratulations, regards."

"She couldn't get out of rehearsal tonight, otherwise she'd be here."

"Ah, is that it. Sir, may we have some menus? Thank you," his mother said. "She feeling a little calmer these days?"

"*Miriam,*" his father said. The two canceled wedding dates had been difficult to explain to Anton's mother, who had some trouble understanding why anyone would hesitate even momentarily to marry her only child. The wine was being poured, and a basket of bread had appeared on the table. His father raised his glass of wine, so everyone else raised their glasses too. "To marriage," he said. He reached across the table to hold Miriam's hand.

"Thirty years," said Aria. "Congratulations."

"Congratulations," Anton repeated. "Happy anniversary."

"Thank you," his mother whispered. She was smiling, radiant. There were tears in her eyes.

"And to Anton and Sophie," his father said.

"To Anton and Sophie." Aria looked Anton in the eye and smiled as she spoke. "August 28th?"

"The 29th," Anton said. "The wedding's August 29th." His throat was dry. He put down the wine and drank half a glass of water without stopping for breath. It was already August 3rd.

The appetizers were arriving. Aria, utterly at ease beside him, speared a white circle of mozzarella and ate it in pieces from the fork, talking about something—he was having trouble hearing, and also he wanted to kill her and his head was light—and his father said, "And then the next thing I know—" and Aria was laughing but he'd missed the joke. Anton couldn't concentrate. Things were difficult to grasp.

"You seem a little out of it," his mother said finally. "Everything okay?"

"Prewedding jitters?" his father asked.

"No, actually, I'm being blackmailed by my cousin," Anton said.

Aria shot him a look, which he ignored, but he felt it graze his cheek.

"Blackmailed," Sam repeated. "Really?"

Aria shrugged.

"Really," said his mother. "Aria, please explain."

"Well," said Aria, "I'm conducting a transaction." She leaned forward across the table and dropped her voice to a murmur. She repeated the details about the ten-thousand-dollar wedding gift and the FedEx package at the Italian hotel, but added that her plans depended on Anton's involvement in the initial transaction—the successful completion of this deal would open up a particularly profitable segment of the import-export business, which was where she'd been wanting to focus her attention for some time. Aria wasn't entirely sure, she had to admit, why anyone would consider her request for assistance even faintly unreasonable under the circumstances.

"Under *what* circumstances?"

"You left me hanging," she said. "I've been through three business partners since you left the business, and none of them worked out."

"How is that my fault? And she'll tell Sophie about Harvard if I don't do it," Anton said.

His parents were silent. Miriam looked at her wineglass, twisting the stem between two fingers and her thumb. Sam nodded and stared into space, considering the situation.

"Well," his mother said, after some time had passed, "she is *family*, Anton."

"What? Mom. She's *blackmailing* me."

"Listen," his father said quietly, "I can't say I'm down with the coercion aspect, but it does seem fairly low-risk if you think about it." He speared a tomato slice, and looked contemplatively at the wall behind Anton and Aria as he talked. Anton glanced over his shoulder. There was a mural on the wall, painted long ago and cleaned rarely since, a greasy waterscape of gondolas and dim canals. "You sign for a package, you give the package to someone without opening it, in the worst-case scenario you deny all knowledge of its contents, and in any event you get ten thousand dollars wired to your bank account. Do you know what she's sending you?"

"No."

"There you go," his father said, as if that resolved everything. "You keep it that way and come home with a nice little nest egg for your life with Sophie, you don't even know what you did, you help out your cousin at great personal gain and virtually no personal risk. Why not?"

All three were looking at him. Aria was smiling slightly.

"You're only going along with this," Anton said to his mother, "because you don't want me to marry Sophie."

"Oh, don't be silly," his mother said. "Why *wouldn't* I want my only son to marry a girl who's canceled the wedding twice?"

Anton's father raised his hand for silence; the waiter was approaching.

"Who ordered the chicken parmesan?" the waiter asked.

"Me," Anton said, without taking his eyes off his mother's face. She was looking at the waiter.

"I'm the veal," she said helpfully.

"Linguine?" asked the waiter.

"Over here," said Anton's father.

"And you must be the steak."

"I am," said Aria. *"Grazie."*

"Listen," his father said when the waiter was out of earshot, "it

119

seems like a fairly smooth transaction." He was winding pasta around his fork. "I'm not going to lie to you, I think you'd be a fool not to do it."

"Well, that's exactly it, Dad, actually. I don't have a *choice* but to do it."

"But why wouldn't you *want* to?" his mother asked. "I know you lead a different kind of life these days, but ten thousand *dollars*, love."

"You don't understand, I don't have a—"

The waiter was approaching again; Anton fell silent and clenched the tablecloth with both hands under the table.

"Fresh pepper, sir?"

"Thank you," Anton's father said. He leaned back in his chair to allow the pepper mill unrestricted access to his plate.

"Because that was the whole point of Harvard," Anton said when the waiter was gone. "So I wouldn't have to do this kind of thing anymore."

"But you didn't *go* to Harvard," Aria said reasonably.

"But she doesn't know that."

"A marriage has to be based on honesty, sweetie," his mother said. She put down her fork and held her husband's hand for a moment on the tabletop.

"Thirty years," Aria said. She raised her wineglass. "To Sam and Miriam."

"Thank you," his mother whispered. They raised their glasses again. Anton raised his glass too, but he couldn't make himself speak. He set the glass down next to his plate and tried to concentrate on dinner. Look at this holy chicken parmiggiano, this holy salt shaker, the starched purity of this tablecloth. Behold the holiness of my family, serene and utterly at ease in their corruption, toasting thirty years of love and theft in a restaurant on an island in a city by the sea.

Anton paid for dinner. Outside Malvolio's Aria said goodbye and he stared at her flatly until she shrugged and climbed into her silver Jaguar and disappeared into the river of red taillights that flowed south down the canyon of Park Avenue. When Aria was gone his parents kissed him and thanked him for a wonderful evening, said goodnight and walked east holding hands. Anton stood on the corner of Park Avenue and 53rd Street, dazed, a little lost. He glanced at his watch, nine thirty but the summer light was endless—it was twilight still, not night, and the city was hazy. He began to walk south, in the opposite direction of home. After a few blocks he took his cell phone out of his pocket and dialed a cell number from memory as he crossed 49th Street.

"Where are you at this moment?" he asked when Elena answered.

"The Starbucks downstairs from the office."

"Alone?"

"Caleb's working."

"You didn't want to go home?"

"Something like that."

She was waiting in his office when he arrived, cross-legged on the sofa with her shoes on the floor, reading a copy of the *Times* that he hadn't thrown out the window yet.

"You look awful," she said, when he came in and closed the door behind him.

"Thanks. It's hot out there. I might drop dead of heatstroke."

"I meant shaken," she said. "You look shaken."

"Yes, well, I talked to Aria. Why didn't you want to go home?" He sat on the opposite end of the sofa, some distance away from her, leaned his head back on the cushions and closed his eyes.

"Caleb's working late at the lab. It's lonely in the apartment."

"Tell me about Caleb."

"He's a scientist," Elena said after a moment. "We met in my first year at Columbia . . . well, my only year, actually. He's involved in the plant genome project. Would you believe he's the only person I'm close to in this city? It's so hard to make friends here. He's known me since the week I arrived from the north."

"What does that mean, the plant genome thing?"

"It means he's mapping the genes of the *Lotus japonicus*. When that's done, he's moving on to geraniums. Other teams are working on cucumbers and tomatoes. I used to know what the point was, but I'm not actually sure I understand anymore. Anton, are you all right?"

"Not really," he said. "Do you love him?"

"Kind of. I don't know. Yes."

"Will you ever marry him?"

"I don't think so," Elena said. "I think it's almost over. He doesn't want to sleep with me anymore."

"Clear evidence of insanity."

"It's not him," she said. "It's the antidepressants he's on. He can't help it."

"I'm sorry. That's an awful side effect. I didn't mean to call him insane."

"It's okay."

"What's it like," he asked, "living three thousand miles away from your family?"

"Four thousand. I miss them."

"Why don't you live closer to them?"

"Because I never wanted to live anywhere but here."

He nodded, but didn't speak.

"Do you want me to leave?" she asked.

"No, please stay."

They sat together in the quiet, listening to the city, until Anton stood up and went to the broken window. "Have you ever played basketball, Ellie?"

"A little in high school. I was never that good."

"Me either. I realize this sounds a little crazy, but could I interest you in a game of basketball on the roof of the Hyatt Hotel?"

"Absolutely," she said.

He was looking down at the lower roof of the Hyatt. It was connected to their office tower, no more than a four- or five-foot drop below his windows, but the windows of Dead File Storage Four were painted shut. Anton stood back for a moment, considering the problem, and then went to his desk. He picked up his tape dispenser and his telephone before settling on the computer keyboard. He disconnected the keyboard from the machine, acutely aware that Elena was watching him, went back to the window, held it in both hands and swung. Anton turned his face away at the instant of the impact but he felt a sting on the side of his face and he knew he'd been cut. Glass rained down the outside of the building. It wasn't hard to break the rest of the glass away around the edges, and after a while all that remained were a few small shards wedged deep in the window frame. These he pulled out gingerly with his bare fingers and dropped out the window. The air-conditioning system was useless against the breach; the room was flooded suddenly with August, like a southern current moving through an undersea cave. He took off his shirt, folded it, put it over the window frame to guard against any stray shards, and then swung his legs over and dropped down to the rooftop in his undershirt.

He was unprepared for the sound. The city was all around him, and he was lost in the noise. There were trucks, horns, sirens from Lexington Avenue and from the cross streets, but behind these individual noises was the sound he stopped to listen to sometimes when he was jogging alone in Central Park at night. A sound formed of traffic and helicopters and distant airplanes, voices, car horns, conversations and music, sirens and shouting and the underground passage of trains, all combined into a susurration as constant and as endless as the sound the ocean makes. He'd looked down at this rooftop from the eleventh-floor window a thousand times and from that distance it had seemed like the smallest gap between towers, a tiny plateau between the dark glass of the Hyatt and the pale bricks of the Greybar Building, but out here in the sound and the darkness he was overtaken by the empty space around him. An expanse of gravel, lit only dimly from windows high above and from the sky that never darkens over the city of New York, passing clouds reflecting light back down from above. Some distance away on the rooftop, a row of colossal air vents rattled in the shadows. Crumpled-up paper lay all around his feet, every wadded ball of newsprint he'd ever thrown through the window. Two or three pieces of his stapler glinted in the half-light. He heard a sound behind him, and when he turned back Elena had dropped down from the window.

"I'll get the basketball," he said.

But when he found the ball it had lost most of its air, and anyway, the surface here was gravel. He held it in both hands as he came back to her, the rubber warm and too soft.

"It's lost air," he said. "Want to break into a hotel room?" He gestured at the Hyatt across the rooftop, the line of blank windows so close. Elena hesitated.

"I can't," she said.

"We'll say it was my idea," he said. "We'll plead insanity. No wait, we'll plead heatstroke."

"I'm afraid of being deported."

"Why would you be deported? You have a Social Security number and an American passport."

"I don't want to take the risk," she said.

"Funny," he said, "you never struck me as the risk-averse type."

She was silent. Her hair was illuminated by the light from the office windows above and behind her, a frizzy halo, but he couldn't quite see her face. He looked up at the sheer tower walls rising all around them, towers of windows reflecting each other and the night.

"Let's go back inside," he said. He gave her a leg up. She disappeared over the window frame. Anton stood outside for a moment longer in the heat before he followed her. Glass cracked softly under his shoes. The room was dark and so still that for a moment he thought she'd left.

Elena was lying on the sofa with her eyes closed. Her breathing seemed shallow when he came to her, and her skin was clammy to the touch.

"Are you all right?" he asked.

"I'm okay," she said. "I just don't deal with heat very well."

"The heat's deadly." He sat on the floor beside the sofa, near her head, and kissed her hand. Her sweat was salty on his lips. He heard himself asking, "Do you think he knows?" and felt clichéd and a little tragic. All the dangerous joys of the five o'clock hour had dissipated; the room had depressurized and gone dim.

"I don't think so." She didn't open her eyes. "I usually get home before he does anyway. If I don't, I tell him I'm out with friends."

"And he never suspects anything?"

"Caleb isn't *stupid*, he just, I don't know, we've known each other for so long and he's so distracted by his work, he doesn't—"

"Suspect things."

"Right." She opened her eyes, sat on the edge of the sofa for a moment, stood up slowly and took a deep breath. "He doesn't suspect things. Goodnight, Anton."

He stood up and kissed her. She closed the office door behind her, and her footsteps were lost instantly in the white noise of the mezzanine. He glanced at his watch—ten thirty P.M.—and went to the broken window to retrieve his shirt. It was still damp with sweat. A jagged edge of glass had ripped a hole in the sleeve, and when he put it on there was a crumpled black streak across the front where the fabric had been pressed against the outside of the window frame. He looked to the back of the door where his spare shirt usually hung, but he'd worn it home the night before. On his way down in the elevator in the ruined shirt he decided that from now on it would be a good idea to have two shirts hanging on the back of the door at all times, and he felt suddenly exhausted by the command of detail that successful infidelity required.

Outside the city had fallen into a subtropical nightmare. It was even hotter on Lexington Avenue than it had been on the rooftop, and he moved like a sleepwalker through the heat-locked air. It was impossible to move quickly; it took Anton a half-hour to get to the open-till-midnight GAP in Times Square, another few minutes under the fluorescent lights with bored night-shift sales associates and dazed tourists before he left with a new clean shirt in a bag. Outside on the sidewalk he took his old shirt off in front of gawping tourists and buttoned up the new one, overexposed in the lights of Times Square. It was after eleven P.M. but he could see his shadow on the sidewalk.

"Indecent," a passing woman said to him, indignant under a cloud of bleached hair.

"You don't know the half of it," he said, struggling to remove the price tag from the new shirt. He threw the old shirt in a trash can before he buttoned up the new one and stepped out into the street to hail a cab, but there were no empty taxis traveling northward that night, and the new shirt was soaked to his back almost instantly. After a few minutes of waving at full taxis he gave up and descended into the 110-degree hell of the subway system, where he waited a long time for a train to arrive.

When he got home it was well past midnight. All of the lights were on in the apartment, and the door to Sophie's study was closed. She was working. He stood for a moment with his ear to the door. She didn't come out to greet him, and he fell asleep an hour later to the sounds of Bach's First Cello Suite.

In the morning Anton woke and saw blood on the pillow, and remembered the sting on the side of his face as he swung the keyboard into the window. In the bathroom mirror he saw the cut, very small and swollen pink. He removed a tiny piece of glass. It came out clear and shining, a translucent bloody absence between the prongs of the tweezers. He held it up to the light for a moment and then flushed it down the toilet, and only then did he notice Sophie in the bathroom doorway.

"What happened to your face?"

"I cut myself shaving."

"You were shaving with glass?"

"I—"

But she'd stepped away from the door, she was making coffee in the kitchen, and when he tried to bring it up later her mouth tensed and she shook her head and turned away from him. This was the morning of August 4th. "That wasn't *glass*," he told her twice. "That isn't what you saw." But she didn't want to talk about it, that day or on any of the days that followed. The wedding was a silently approaching thing, like a hurricane spiraling closer over the surface of a weather map.

"Are you nervous about getting married?" Elena asked softly. It was almost six o'clock and time had been passing very quickly. In a moment she would stand up and put her clothes back on. In a week he would leave her and fly to Italy on his honeymoon.

"Yes," Anton said.

He tried to imagine coming home to Elena instead of Sophie, tried to imagine light hair instead of dark on the pillow beside him in the mornings, his apartment with the study door flung open and no cello inside, the room converted into a second bedroom, an office, another place for reading books. Sophie living somewhere else, Sophie losing significance with time and fading eventually into the ranks of former girlfriends. He looked at Elena, but she was looking at the ceiling. She reached absently for her handbag, as she always did when they were finished, fumbled around for a moment and came out empty-handed, then reached in again and extracted a tube of Chapstick. She was biting her lower lip.

"Does your fiancée get along with your family?"

But what would life be, with the two of us alone for longer than an hour? Do we depend on the ghosts of the others, Caleb and Sophie, is it the thrill of stealing you from him that makes me want to take you on the floor of the office every afternoon at five ten? Elena was tense and still beside him. He was never sure what made her so ill at ease at these moments, but he assumed it was guilt. A few miles to the north in a basement laboratory, her boyfriend mapped the genome of the *Lotus japonicus*.

"Why are you always so curious about my family?"

"I don't know. I just am. I feel like I don't know you that well."

"Why don't you tell me about your family, for a change?"

"There's not much to tell. My dad's a social worker. My mother's a nurse at the hospital."

"Were you born in the north?"

"I was born in Toronto," she said. "We went to the north when I was three."

"Why?"

"There was a shortage of nurses and social workers up there. They wanted to be helpful. But I've been plotting my escape from the north for as long as I can remember. Let's not talk about the north."

"Okay. Do you have siblings?"

"I have a brother and a younger sister. We used to be close, but she lives at home with her baby and we have absolutely nothing in common anymore. Our brother's a few years older. He works in a diamond mine in the Northwest Territories." She was quiet for a while, looking away. "Weren't you nervous? Selling Social Security cards like that?"

"Why do you ask?"

"I don't know, I was just thinking about it. I think I'd be afraid of getting caught."

"I was afraid in the beginning," Anton said.

"Do you remember the very first one ever?"

"Of course I do," Anton said.

7.

The first one ever was a red-haired girl with still gray eyes at an Irish bar near Grand Central, four weeks out of Ireland when Aria approached her. She was tired and pale, not sleeping well in a crowded apartment share in the Bronx. She wanted to be a pilot. She moved through the evenings efficiently, was as charming as possible and played up the accent a little and wore a tight shirt in order to obtain maximum tips, read aviation magazines at the library, took long walks through the city and wrote postcards full of half-truths to her friends in Belfast on her days off.

"It's difficult to imagine going anywhere," she said. "I can't go home, or they won't let me back into the country. I want to stay here, but I already miss them."

"Miss who?" The fake Social Security card was in Anton's wallet. His hands were steady but his legs were shaking, which always happened when he was desperately nervous.

"Everyone," she said. "Even the people I didn't talk to much, I miss them. My downstairs neighbor Blythe." She took a slow sip of coffee. Anton glanced discreetly at his watch. He had envisioned this as a fast shadowy transaction, take the money and run, but he hadn't factored her loneliness into the equation. They'd been in the coffee shop for nearly an hour and she seemed to be in no rush.

"Your downstairs neighbor."

"Blythe. She must've been in her fifties. Lived alone, dunno if she was ever married or had kids. I never heard anyone come by to see her. She never went out except to go to work, this insurance office down the street. She listened to talk radio all day on the weekends, so there was always voices coming from her place, and I'd hear them all day long. When I first moved into the place it drove me crazy, I mean, this woman's radio was never off, but then after a while I didn't mind anymore. It was nice, I mean, I lived alone too, and always hearing someone talking, it makes you less alone." She blinked and sipped at her coffee again. "What about you? Were you born here?" He realized that she must have very few friends in this city.

"Albany," he lied. His hands were sweating. The lunch-hour crowd was thinning out. He wished she'd stop talking and ask for the card. He was wearing reflective dark glasses that made her look like a ghost across the banquette.

"Is Gabriel your real name, then?"

"Of course," Anton said. He had thought up the alias with great difficulty.

"How old *are* you, anyway?"

"Twenty."

"Twenty," she repeated. *"Twenty."*

"Yeah. Um, think of flight school." He could see the doubt in her eyes. He tried to look as serious as possible, in an effort to appear somewhat older than eighteen. "I mean seriously, whatever my name is or how old I actually am, think how much easier it will be with a Social Security number."

"I could get in without one," she said. "I did the research."

"Still," he said, "I can't help but think it might be easier if the question didn't come up, don't you?"

She looked at him flatly for a moment and then sighed. "Christ," she said. "Okay. How do we do this?"

He leaned toward her over the table; she leaned close, and he was pleasantly surprised to discover that her breath smelled of licorice. "Give me the envelope," he said very softly. "There's only one bathroom here, and I'm going to go in there and count the money while you go up to the counter to pay for your coffee, and then I'm going to leave. If the count was correct, then when you go in there after me your card will be taped to the back of the toilet tank."

"Like in that *Godfather* movie with the gun," she said. "I like that."

In the bathroom he counted the money and put it in his wallet. From his wallet he took out the Social Security card, double-checked the name on it and put it in the envelope. There was condensation on the toilet tank, a cold porcelain sweat. He tried four times, but the tape he'd brought with him wouldn't stick; the envelope kept falling, the tape kept coming away wet and glueless. He was at a loss for a moment until he remembered the gum. He found the last stick in his pocket and chewed rapidly, contemplating the toilet, then stuck the gum to the back of the tank, stuck the envelope to the gum, and opened the bathroom door half-expecting a SWAT team. The girl was paying at the counter. He walked out behind her back and away down the street in the opposite direction of home, his heart pounding. It was a mile before he doubled back toward the Williamsburg Bridge and his parents' store. He took a circuitous route home amid the warehouses.

"It's messy," Aria said. "I don't like it." They were sitting together on the loading dock at the end of the day. The metal loading dock was still warm from the sunlight but a cool breeze was blowing in off the river.

"What's messy about it?" Anton was feeling a little defensive about the *Godfather* technique.

"Anyone could walk into the bathroom and grab the card before she does. Just come up with a better idea."

"What if I can't?"

"You got straight A's in high school," she said, and muttered something in Spanish under her breath.

The solution came to him when he was out with Aria and his parents for someone's birthday, his mother's perhaps, at a restaurant in Chelsea. Anton observed the mechanism of paying: the bill arrives, tucked discreetly into the check folder. Cash is placed in the folder, and even from the next table those bills could be ones, tens, twenties, fifties, hundreds—God bless America and her monochromatic green bills!—and the check folder is taken away and returned with change. If the count is correct, there must be a signal: perhaps the waitress, your co-conspirator, brings a glass of red wine to the table and that's how you know to discreetly hand off the envelope with the Social Security card. Later, as the business expanded, perhaps also a passport. Using a waitress made the moment of transaction difficult to observe, and if the customer were stopped later by the police, the quality of the product was high enough that unless the transaction itself had been witnessed, the most a police officer would reasonably be able to accuse them of would be carrying their Social Security card and passport around with them, which was not recommended but not illegal. "We'll stop doing business in this country," Aria said, "when it's no longer legal to carry our product."

"It's never legal to carry our product," Anton pointed out. "And what other country would we do business in?"

He flew to Italy the morning after his wedding.

Sophie posed for pictures in front of the Colosseum, next to a gladiator with a digital wristwatch. She stood in front of the Trevi fountain while he took picture after picture after picture of her, trying to use up the whole roll.

"Excuse me," she said to a passing tourist, "would you mind taking a shot of the two of us?" Anton was putting the lens cap on the camera as she spoke, and neither Sophie nor the photographer noticed it as the shot was taken. He wanted no photographic evidence that he had ever been in this country.

On the island of Capri she noticed the lens cap.

No, he said, of course it hadn't been on the whole trip. Yes, he was positive. No, seriously, he said, he'd just put it back on after the last set of pictures. It's all right, she needn't be sorry for doubting him. No, hey, it was a fair question. He loved her too. No, he really did. Shh, shh, don't cry. The Norwegian tourist who'd been taking their picture gave the camera back in the emotion of the moment, inexplicably apologetic, and the picture wasn't taken after all.

On Capri Sophie wanted to see the Blue Grotto. It cost thirty-five euros to board a vessel that carried them out along the formidable shoreline. Anton held Sophie's hand and looked up at the fishermen's saints, small figurines wedged into dark rocks above them at impossible heights. Look at this holy island, these saints bestowing blessings from high up on the rocks. Patron saints of luck and strong netting, of tides and fish. Sophie held his hand and looked down at the water.

When they reached the grotto two other boatloads of tourists were already there, the boats idling in the choppy waters a few yards from the shore, and it seemed that it was another twenty-five euros to climb out into a little rowboat that transported two tourists at a time into a small space between the rocks and the sea. The men rowing the tourists into the underworld were friendly and animated, but the whole operation reminded Anton of a conveyer belt—extract money from tourist, insert tourist into cave, return tourist to boat—and he was put off by the unexpectedness of the extra fee. But Sophie wanted to do it; she paid the extra money and waited her turn patiently on the lower deck while Anton watched the progression of tourists in and out of the cave. Most of the tourists who came back were smiling but to his eyes they all looked faintly disappointed, like the crowds he'd seen trickling out of the Sistine Chapel a few days before. "I've heard about the Blue

Grotto all my life," he heard one of them say to another, but he didn't hear the reply. When Anton looked down at the lower deck again Sophie had vanished and there was a flash of near panic when he thought she might have somehow slipped overboard, but then he looked over in time to see her duck her head as the rowboat carried her under the rocks. It seemed she was gone for a very long time.

Anton held on to the railing while he waited for her, the boat tossing in the wakes of the other vessels around them. He closed his eyes and felt in that moment that he could disappear here in this brilliant light so far from Brooklyn, his parents and Aria four thousand miles away.

"Wake up, sleepy. Are you really that bored?" Sophie had appeared beside him.

"No, just enjoying the sun. How was it?" She looked different from most of the others, more alive; he realized that she wasn't disappointed.

"You should've gone," she said. "It was beautiful and blue."

"Beautiful and blue," he repeated. He kissed her and tried not to think about Ischia.

In the morning they woke early in their hotel room on Capri. Anton opened the curtains and sunlight glanced over the tiled floor. Sophie hadn't slept well. She was tired and moody and she didn't want to talk to him. They ate breakfast in incompatible silence and took a taxi to the ferry. Back in Salerno there were a few dead hours. They wandered the streets amid groups of tourists, walked in and out of stores, sat for a while in a café where the waiters greeted them in English. Sophie bought an unattractive skirt. Anton lied and told her he liked it, but she accused him of insincerity and then he had to lie about lying. The train was an hour late leaving Salerno. They sat in a compartment across from a middle-aged woman who spoke even less English than Anton spoke Italian, which he wouldn't have thought possible. When the train was forty-five minutes late the woman tapped her watch and made an exasperated face. *"Italia,"* she said. She shook her head and rolled her eyes. Anton nodded. Sophie was reading a biography of Jim Morrison, frowning slightly, ignoring them both.

They arrived after dark in the city of Naples.

A memory: nine years old on a cold morning in Brooklyn, waiting for the school bus with his mother in the rain. Usually Anton waited with Gary, but Gary was home sick that day and his mother didn't like him waiting alone. The neighborhood was rougher back then. She stood over him with an enormous purple umbrella that a customer had left behind in the store.

"Why would anyone want to be a school bus driver?" Anton asked. His parents encouraged the assumption that he might grow up to be anything, and at nine things were possible that became less possible later on. It was still plausible that he might grow up to be an astronaut, for example, or the king of an as-yet-undiscovered country.

"You just make decisions as you go along, my magnificent child," his mother said. "A or B, two options present themselves, and you choose the one that seems best at the time."

Years later on an island in the Bay of Naples he walked a discreet distance away from the outdoor café where his new wife sat drinking coffee, waved reassuringly at her, and called Aria on his cell phone.

"I'm here," he said. "I'm on Ischia."

"I'll call you back. Are you calling from your cell phone?"

"There's no phone in my hotel room. It's a very small hotel."

"Well, then find a pay phone and call me back at home," she said. "You know I don't discuss business on cell phones. I'm at the Santa Monica apartment."

"I don't have the number there," he said. She gave it to him and hung up.

He went back to the newsstand and bought a phone card. There was a pay phone on the edge of the piazza, by a low stone wall.

"Anton," Aria said, "there's been a slight delay."

"How slight?"

"Three weeks."

"Are you out of your mind? You want me to stay on this island for three weeks?" Sophie was watching him, holding a glass of coffee. She waved when he looked at her. He forced his face into a weak facsimile of a smile, raised his hand and turned his back on her.

"Four at the most," she said. "I'm sorry, Anton. It's out of my hands."

"*Four?* Aria, I'm sorry, listen, I can't . . . Aria, I can't do this. We go back to Rome tomorrow. We fly home Thursday night."

"Well, you don't *have* to do it," Aria said. "It's of course your decision."

"But if I don't, you'll tell Sophie . . . you'll tell Sophie . . ." He was beside himself. He looked over his shoulder again, watching Sophie pretending not to be watching him. She sipped her coffee, gazed out at the harbor, glanced fleetingly at him where he stood with the red pay-phone receiver against his face. Aria was silent.

"Aria," he said, "we're family. My parents took you in."

"And then we entered into business together," Aria said, "and stayed in business, until you abandoned me, and now I'm asking you to do this one last thing."

"I don't want to do this. I'm sick of—"

"I know you don't want to do this," Aria said. "I'm perfectly aware of that. It's a question of what you want to do least: perform this one last transaction, or explain to Sophie that you're a fraud. Which is it going to be?"

He looked over his shoulder. On the other side of the piazza, Sophie sipped at her coffee and looked up at the clouds.

"My commission will be what?"

"Twelve thousand dollars for the extra trouble, secrecy, and an exit."

"I want fifteen."

Aria was silent for a moment and then said, "Fine. Fifteen."

"I also want payment in advance."

"Half now, half when the transaction's complete."

"Okay. I do this one last thing for you, and Sophie will never hear anything about Harvard, and I'm out of the business. Swear on something you believe in. Do you believe in anything?"

"No," she said, "but I swear anyway. No, wait. I swear on my financial independence."

"That's the highest thing you believe in? Financial independence?"

"'Fraid so."

"Jesus Christ. Three weeks?"

"Yes," she said. "Well, possibly four."

He hung up the receiver, closed his eyes for a moment and took several deep breaths, and then took the phone card out of his pocket and redialed.

"Four weeks," he said, when Aria picked up. "What am I supposed to do here for four weeks?"

"You sound tense," she said mildly. "Don't you like Ischia?"

"I'm about to leave my wife on our honeymoon. Wouldn't you be a little edgy?"

"As I was saying, it'll be the easiest deal you ever played in your life. In three weeks a man will come to the hotel and introduce himself to you. You give him the package, you fly home, buy some roses for your wife, and you're done."

"I think this will take a little more than roses, Ari."

"Spend some of the commission on her, then. One of those ten-thousand-dollar I'm-sorry-I-left-you-on-our-honeymoon rings from Tiffany's."

"Oh God, let's not talk about rings. Who's the client?"

"Do you want back in the business?"

"No," he said.

"Then don't ask me who my clients are."

"Fine." Anton hung up the phone and stood for a moment in the sunlight, watching the movement of boats in bright water. The boats in the Sant'Angelo harbor were painted every conceivable color, two colors per boat; yellow with blue trim, red with green, white with red. The light was too bright, the colors a kaleidoscope, sunlight piercingly brilliant off the surface of the sea. He wanted to be sick. He felt Sophie's eyes on him from across the piazza and the thought that he'd considered leaving her anyway made the moment no easier. Three weeks. He walked to the newsstand with its supply of German newspapers, its British tabloids, its daily allotment of two *International Herald Tribunes*, paid for one and brought it back to Sophie. She took the front section.

"Who were you calling?" she asked. She was skimming the headlines.

"The office," he said. "I told them I'd check in." Check in to what, exactly? He imagined his telephone ringing endlessly on his desk in Dead File Storage Four, the empty room, the drift of paper beneath the window, dust gathering on the telephone and pigeons flying in to investigate from the world outside. Elena flashed through him, eyes the color of storm clouds, and he opened the paper but couldn't read. His eyes skipped twice over the same paragraph. Two options present themselves, and you choose the one that seems best at the time.

"You know," he said, as casually as possible, "I was thinking about maybe staying on a while."

Sophie looked up from her café latte.

"Our plane tickets are for Thursday," she said.

The morning after Sophie left Ischia he woke up lonely from a dream he couldn't remember and lay staring at the blue ceiling for some time before he got up. He opened the shutters and the sea was awash in light, Capri a far-off shadow on the edge of the cloudless sky. Down on the piazza were too many tourists, calling out to their children in languages he didn't understand or reading newspapers at the café tables, so he went back to the restaurant at the hotel and ate pasta and grilled squid at a table by the window, looking out at the ocean. In Sophie's absence he felt an enormous amount of space around him.

She would be in Rome today, unless she'd changed her flight. He glanced at his watch and imagined her eating breakfast somewhere, alone at an outdoor café with a clear glass of coffee, reading the *International Herald Tribune*. The thought was almost unbearable even though he was enjoying his solitude, so he went back down to the piazza to call his best friend from the pay phone that stood beside the low wall by the harbor.

"Gary," he said, "I think I'm alone again."

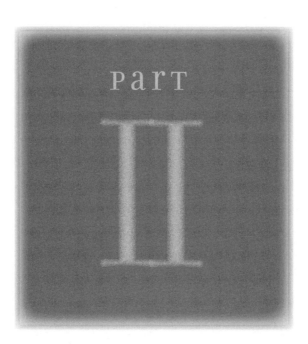

part

II

8.

In a quiet office on the twelfth floor of the new World Trade Center 7, Broden played Elena a tape.

"It can't have been an easy business."

"It was an easy business. I was good at it. It was the easiest thing I ever did in my life."

"Then why did you get out?"

"I don't know, I just gradually didn't want to do it anymore."

"Why not? What changed you?"

"I don't know. It was gradual."

"If you could name one thing." Listening to her own voice all these weeks later, Elena closed her eyes and thought, Why did you keep talking to me? Wasn't it obvious that you were being interrogated? She was strangely angry with him.

"Well, there was a girl. Catina. I'd been thinking about getting out, but it was meeting her, it was talking to her . . . I didn't know before her that I was really going to do it. Get out, I mean."

"A girlfriend?"

"No, not a girlfriend. I sold her a passport."

Broden stopped the tape.

"The tape runs out two minutes later. Did he say anything more about his other clients?"

"No," Elena said. "Just what's on the tape. The woman from Lisbon. And that stuff later on about the falling man."

"Oh, I know all about the woman from Lisbon." Broden was smiling, more animated than Elena had ever seen her. "I spoke with her at great length. Nonetheless, Elena, it's the best tape you've given me. Good work."

"Can I ask you a question?" Elena asked.

"Of course."

"Why was Anton put in a file storage room?"

"I thought it was an elegant solution," Broden said. "We need him close at hand, but the company wasn't willing to keep him once the results of his background check came up."

"What did the background check say?"

"What do you think it said? No one's invisible," Broden said. "There's no such thing as operating under the radar. The background check said he'd never been to Harvard and that he and his cousin were the subjects of an ongoing criminal investigation. Water Incorporated didn't want him, but he was judged a significant flight risk if he lost his job, so a compromise was reached: the company's keeping him in storage while we conduct our investigation."

"Why not just arrest him?"

"Because I don't want to tip off Aria just yet," Broden said. "But at any rate, I called you in to ask you something. Did he say anything to you about staying on in Italy? I expected him back some time ago."

"He didn't tell me anything," Elena said. She was slumped in her chair. She hadn't been sleeping well. She'd gone to Anton's office with a sunflower—a rose seemed too ordinary—at five o'clock on the afternoon when he'd said he'd be back, but the room was empty with papers blowing over the floor. There was a fine layer of dust on Anton's desk. She sat in his swivel chair and spun around once or twice, then went to lie down on the sofa. She lay there for a long time, drowsy and a little sad, watching the movement of loose-leaf paper over the floor. She left the sunflower lying on his desk, but when she came back the next day at five o'clock it remained undisturbed. She visited the empty room every afternoon for the rest of that week, lying on the sofa in the quiet, resting in her memories. She was startled by her longing. By Friday Anton hadn't returned and the sunflower was wilted, so she dropped it out the window onto the roof of the hotel and didn't go back again.

9.

Anton sometimes stood on the balcony of his hotel room on Ischia and thought about the span of oceans that divided him from Brooklyn, and the thought of being four thousand miles away from his family was exhilarating but the days on Ischia were endless. There were contentious phone calls to New York. The sea changed from blue to gray and back again. Anton wandered the narrow streets of Sant'Angelo (he had a hard time thinking of them as streets, these narrow corridors between villas and walled gardens that turned into staircases every now and again), talked to himself by the harbor, read the English-language newspapers and stared out at the sea. He called Aria every third or fourth day and listened to her tell him that the package was still delayed and then hung up on her, which was satisfying the first few times and later tedious. He convinced her to pay him seventeen thousand dollars in consideration of the delays; she agreed but was furious. He tried to call Sophie sometimes, but her phone rang endlessly. She never picked up.

There were a number of brief storms during which Capri vanished from the horizon and wind moaned around the edges of the hotel and came in through the shutters. When the weather was nice he drank endless cups of coffee in the piazza and read the *International Herald Tribune* and worried about the transaction.

"Why are you paying me so much?" he asked her once, when he'd been on Ischia for four weeks.

"Because you've forced me up to seventeen thousand dollars," she said.

"But why did you agree to pay me that much?"

"Because it's important that I move into a new business," she said. "It's worth it to me. You don't need to know why."

Sometimes Sant'Angelo started closing in on him, so he took the bus to Ischia Porto and drank cappuccinos at an outdoor café and watched the ferries come in from Napoli for a while. Once he took the bus all the way around the island, but he remained unmoved by the unchanging paradise of his surroundings and didn't get off until the bus came full circle and reached Sant'Angelo again. By the middle of October the tourists were thinning out; the only other regulars on the piazza were a grim-faced German couple who drank beer and stared at the water without speaking to one other and a man staying in Anton's hotel who always had paint on his clothes and always seemed to be either sketching something or doing a crossword puzzle.

Anton couldn't find any English-language books in Sant'Angelo, which was at first an annoyance and then a genuine problem. He'd been reading two or three books at a time for his entire life, and he was unsure what to do with himself in the vacuum. He made inquiries here and there—a waiter at his favorite café in the piazza, the woman who ran the newsstand, a girl who spoke English in a clothing store by the harbor—and they all told him the same thing: the closest English-language books were in Napoli. At the end of the sixth week of waiting he took the bus back to Ischia Porto and boarded a ferry to Naples, blue Tyrrhenian, drinking a cappuccino on deck as he watched the city approach. It's a civilized country that sells cappuccinos on the commuter ferries, Anton thought, and an affection for the place swelled inside him like music.

For almost the first time he began thinking of later, of after the transaction, of a job somewhere and an apartment in Sant'Angelo, or perhaps just a rented room. Napoli sprawled bright on the hills over the harbor. He made his way inland in stages, basking in the exuberance of being off Ischia—an hour in a café reading a newspaper, time spent browsing in innumerable little shops, a long interval on a bench in an ancient piazza with dreadlocked university students playing drums nearby, seagulls sidling up to the café tables. There were two blissful hours in a bookstore near the university; Anton emerged near sunset with a hundred euros' worth of fiction in a heavy paper bag. No reason to go back to Ischia just yet. The ferry ran late.

He stopped for pizza at a brightly painted little place near the water. Sometime past nightfall he climbed a flight of stairs up to the elegant sweep of Corso Vittorio Emanuele, the lights of boats in the Bay of Naples glimmering far below and Mount Vesuvius a blunt shadow against the southern sky. He looked up at the Hotel Britannique, at the balcony six floors up where in a previous lifetime he'd turned away from the lights of boats and islands and watched Sophie emerge from the shower. He was thinking about the night they'd arrived in Naples, the way the city had seemed an undifferentiated chaos of gray buildings and broken plaster and lights spreading up over the hillside, Sophie's blue linen dress, the singer in the restaurant. He glanced at his watch and decided he had more than enough time for a drink before the last ferry to Ischia.

It took Anton some time to reach the restaurant where he'd dined with Sophie. When he stepped through the door the girl who had been singing that night was onstage again, midsong, and the déjà vu was startling. She wore the same dress as before, tight silver, and she was singing in the same languorous style but something was wrong with the microphone; her voice had a wavery, underwater quality, and it was difficult to make out the words. The restaurant was nearly empty.

Anton took a stool at the bar. The bartender brought the wrong drink. A brief argument ensued. His scotch was set down on the countertop with somewhat more force than was strictly necessary and it didn't taste quite right, but he sipped it anyway and turned in his stool to look at the stage. The girl was singing a song he'd never heard before.

"What's her name?" he asked the bartender. "Uh, the girl, the singer, sua nome? Parla inglese?" The bartender ignored him. The girl was leaving the stage. It wasn't her night, or perhaps the sound quality was to blame. The applause was merely polite. Anton paid quickly and left the restaurant. The night air was cool. The stars were blacked out over the sea, a bank of clouds moving in from the distance. He found the side entrance and waited there, pacing, until the door opened and the girl came out.

"Excuse me," he said.

She drew her breath in sharply and reached into her handbag.

"Wait," he said, "I'm sorry, please don't pepper-spray me, I didn't mean to scare you. I just enjoyed your performance, I don't know anyone here and I wondered if I could buy you a drink. That's all."

She considered him for a moment. Up close she was wearing too much makeup.

"I wasn't going to pepper-spray you," she said. She removed her hand from her bag. He would have guessed her to be somewhere in her early to midtwenties, but she had a voice like a twelve-year-old with an indefinable accent. "Just a drink?"

"Just a drink," he said. "No strings. I just want to talk with someone who speaks English for a while. We'll talk about the weather if you'd like."

"That's sweet of you. I know a place near here."

"I'm Gabriel," he said. "Gabriel Jones."

She smiled, and the hand she extended was so warm that he wondered if she had a fever. "Arabelle," she said.

"Arabelle? That's a beautiful name."

"Isn't it?" She sounded pleased. "I made it up just now. Here, it's further up the street." She was leading him away from the sea, farther around the endless curve of Corso Vittorio Emanuele. They walked for a few minutes in silence, an arm's length away from the street's murderous traffic.

"What's your real name, if you don't mind me asking?"

"Kara," she said.

"Where are you from?"

"Saskatchewan."

"Saskatchewan?"

"Here we are," she said. And he followed her into a low-lit room, a new-looking place with a red-tiled floor and candles flickering. The tables were unoccupied. A lone bartender was polishing glasses behind the empty bar, and there were faint notes of paint and varnish in the air.

"This is a nice place," he said. She didn't answer. She was leaning over the counter to greet the bartender, who kissed her on the cheek and said, "Ciao, Kyla." Anton pulled back a barstool for her. Her skirt rode up above her thighs as she climbed onto the barstool. Anton looked away and caught the bartender's eye. There was something in the man's amused expression that he didn't entirely like.

"Kyla," Anton said, "not Kara?"

"It's Kyra, actually," she said, and ordered a drink in Italian. "No one can pronounce it here."

"Due, per favore," he said to the bartender, who nodded and turned away. "What did I just order?"

"You'll like it. It's grapey."

"Excellent," he said. But the drinks were the color of ultraviolet light and they tasted like sugar and lighter fluid; he swallowed his first sip with difficulty and set the glass down on the bar.

"It's a grape martini," she said. "I think they invented it here. Isn't it something?"

"It's certainly something, but I'm not sure it's a martini. Listen," Anton said, "don't be offended, but I'm going to ask you your name one more time. Just for fun."

"My name's Carrie," she said.

"Short for Kara?"

She shook her head. She was wide-eyed, biting her lip like a little girl trying not to laugh before the punch line.

"So your name's changed. Are you still from Saskatchewan?"

"I'm from Albuquerque." She stared at him for a moment longer and then burst into laughter. Her laugh was high-pitched, silvery, with a hysterical edge that made him shiver.

"Who are you?"

"Oh, come on," she said, "don't go all serious on me."

"Why won't you tell me your name?"

"Because everyone *wants* something. Your name, or a kiss, or your body, or whatever. Haven't you ever just wanted to disappear?"

"I have," Anton said. "I'm sorry. I understand now."

"Can I have another grape martini?"

"Can you at least tell me what country you're from?"

She hesitated.

"Just the name of your country. Your country for a drink."

"Mexico." He held up the girl's glass and gestured to the bartender. The bartender nodded, and began mixing vodka and something that looked like grape Kool-Aid. Anton tried not to watch.

"You mind if I ask again?"

"It's Mexico. Really."

"You don't look like any of the Mexicans I know."

"I'm a gringo," she said. "My parents moved there from the States."

"Can I ask the name of the city?"

"San Miguel de Allende. The kingdom of fake artists and retired Texans." She was already halfway through the second martini and her eyes were bright. "How about you? Where are you from?"

"Brooklyn. How did you end up here?"

"I shot someone," she said between sips. He laughed, hoping she was kidding, but she didn't smile. "Then I took a bus to Mexico City," she continued, "and then I got on a plane. I've been here for years now."

"Why Naples, though? I've heard it can be dangerous here."

"Not for me," she said.

"Really."

"No, see, look . . ." She was fumbling in her purse for something, but then she caught sight of her drink and seemed to lose track of what she was looking for. She removed her hand from the bag and finished her drink and winked at the bartender, who smiled warily back.

"It isn't dangerous here because you have pepper spray?"

"Oh, I don't have *pepper* spray," she said. She opened her purse and held it open for him. He peered in and saw the dull shine of the Beretta between a Hello Kitty wallet and a pack of spearmint gum. Anton leaned on the bar, shaken, while she finished her drink and then held the glass up to the light in case there might be a few hitherto unnoticed drops remaining.

"I hate guns," he said. "I don't believe in them."

"Well, you don't have to *believe* in them," she said. "They'll still work regardless. Can I have another drink?"

"Have you ever fired it?"

She laughed that silvery laugh again and put her glass down. Anton shivered.

"Is it loaded?"

"We're in Napoli," she said. "Be reasonable. Can I have another martini?" He was thinking of Ischia, of the boats in the harbor, of Elena, of his cat, of putting money on the counter and wishing her a pleasant evening and walking away down Corso Vit-torio Emmanuele and never coming back to Naples again as long as he lived, but like a man in a dream he gestured at the bartender, who stepped forward and began mixing another poison-violet drink.

"Last one," he said quietly. "Why do you have a gun?"

"I live alone by the train station. It isn't really safe."

"Tell me your name?"

She smiled.

"Your name for a drink. Doesn't seem that unfair, does it?" Of course it seemed that unfair. He felt horrifically cheap and the evening was spiraling.

"Jane," she said. The bartender set the third drink down on the countertop and she lifted the glass unsteadily to her lips.

"Jane? Really?"

"Jane," she said. "I'm serious this time." She leaned closer to him and beckoned. He leaned in and smelled the alcohol and sweet purple and acetone on her breath. "I'm going to go find the bathroom," she whispered, "and then we're going to do something fun."

"What kind of fun?" he asked, a little desperate.

She inclined her head sideways to indicate the bartender, who was leaning against the counter and staring out the open door at the ceaseless traffic. There were still no other customers. She smiled and cocked her finger at Anton and whispered, *"Bang. Bang."* She blew on the tip of her finger like a gunslinger blowing smoke from the tip of a gun and then fell against the bar in a fit of giggles. "We'll be outlaws," she said. "We'll be like Bonnie and Clyde."

"Are you crazy?"

"No no no, this way ..." She was laughing and could hardly get the words out, "this way we don't have to pay for our drinks.

Relax, there's no one else in here. This place just opened. Do you see a security camera? I don't."

"Come on," he said. "It isn't funny."

She winked at him. "Wait here while I go to the bathroom," she said. She turned away from him and slid unsteadily from the barstool while Anton slipped the gun from her purse into his jacket pocket. Her dress clung to her body like broken glass. She reached for her bag and wavered away from him, sequins glittering down the dim corridor at the end of the room, until her dress flickered out behind a wooden door.

Anton stood up, opened his wallet, and left three twenty-euro bills on the bar—the bartender called after him, he had drastically overpaid, but he was on his way out the door and could not stop—and he began to walk rapidly downhill toward the Hotel Britannique. After a moment he broke into a run. The sidewalk was narrow in places; he had to dodge around people and heard himself gasping with every breath, *I'm sorry, I'm sorry, I'm sorry, I'm sorry,* the words turning into a meaningless sobbing for air, and the traffic was a blur of steel and death and lights at his fingertips. When he looked up he saw that the sky had gone starless. Past the warm soft lights of the Grand Hotel Parker's, past the Hotel Britannique with its faded lobby full of tourist brochures, and then he darted across the street—horns blared, a Vespa swerved to avoid him—and jogged down the stairs toward the water. At the bottom of the steps he stopped running and settled into a loose staggering walk.

On the last ferry to Ischia he slumped over a railing on the outside deck, staring down at dark water and trying not to think about anything. The gun was a solid weight in his pocket. He couldn't stop thinking about the things that might happen to a girl like that, drunk and alone in the seething city of Napoli, making her way home to an apartment near the train station unarmed. He had left the precious English-language books in the bar.

In the morning Anton woke with a pounding headache. He'd only sipped at the violet drink in the bar, but he felt poisoned. He took a cold shower and lay on top of his bed for a while before he went down to breakfast, thinking about what it would mean to never return to New York again.

10.

Just before Aria's fifteenth birthday she returned home to her father's apartment after a weeklong absence, but the locks had been
changed and there was a note on the door next to the eviction
notice *(Went to Ecuador, go stay at your uncle's place)* and from the
street she saw that the curtains were gone from the windows. She
came back to Anton's neighborhood quickly, with enormous bra-
vado and shaking hands. She sat at the table while Anton's mother
fluttered around her, bringing her a plate, a fork, some food, some
coffee, *you poor thing.* When Anton's father heard that his brother

had taken off for Ecuador he almost punched a hole in the wall, and for the rest of that week everyone stayed out of his way. He talked to his vanished brother while he worked, while he did the dishes, in any situation where he was more or less alone and no customers were present: a furious muttered monologue about family and responsibility, punctuated by curses.

But Aria didn't talk about her father at all. She didn't talk about much of anything. She disappeared for long hours, she went to school and worked in the store, she listened to music in her room. She was a polite and quiet presence in their lives that year, always on the margins or just out of sight. Anton's mother did what she could, but Aria was unreachable. After a few weeks there was a phone call from Ecuador. Her father apologized. He just couldn't bear to be away from Aria's mother any longer, he said, so he'd sold everything they had to pay for the plane ticket. The furniture. The dishes. Aria's clothes. All temporary stuff, he assured his daughter. Nothing they couldn't eventually replace. Aria's mother had never felt like marrying Aria's father while they were all in Brooklyn together, but now they were going to be married in Ecuador. They were happy. Sylvia had stopped drinking. It was unbelievable, miraculous, a whole new life. He said Aria was welcome to move to Ecuador and join them, but Aria laughed and hung up the phone.

That was the year Gary introduced Anton to cigarettes, which they felt conveyed a certain hard glamor. The technique was to squint into the distance and smoke as if you'd been smoking for so long that you hardly noticed the cigarette anymore and in fact had no idea how it had ended up in your hand. They practiced smoking under the bridge, separated from Anton's parents' store by several hundred yards and an array of enormous concrete pilings.

"You know your cousin steals?" Gary asked once, when the cigarettes were lit. He passed one to Anton, who took it gingerly—the thing he didn't like about cigarettes was that one end was hot—and used it to stall for time.

"She's fucked up," he said, after he'd exhaled, when it became apparent that Gary was waiting for an answer. "I'm sorry. I can't stop her."

But he realized as he spoke that he didn't really want to. Every time he thought of her he was shot through with strange envy. She was six months older but miles ahead.

Aria had a way of staring at the river while she smoked her cigarettes. Standing in front of the store, under the awning when it was raining. One hand in her pocket, the other holding her cigarette, and she lit one cigarette after another and looked out at nothing, or at Ecuador.

Anton's and Aria's sole chore around the apartment was to do the dishes, because his parents liked to read after dinner. When the dishes were done Aria usually disappeared into the demands of her private life, going out with friends who exchanged inscrutable jokes in rapid-fire Spanish or closing herself in her room and listening to music with the volume turned down low. She saved and saved and bought her own CD player. Anton's father was willing to put down his book to have a conversation if he saw Anton hovering around, but there were two or three hours after dinner when his mother was lost to them; she read with all of herself, immersed, breathing language, and couldn't be reached until she was ready to emerge.

When he didn't have plans with anyone he closed himself into his bedroom to read after dinner, or stayed with his parents in the living room. Anton resented the absence of a television, but there were things he read in books that took his breath away. His mother's collection of travel guides never moved him, but Kirkegaard's last words were *Sweep me up.* He read those three words when he was fifteen years old and his eyes filled unexpectedly with tears.

It was his mother's absence in the evenings that made Sundays important. When it was warm enough she sat with him on the loading dock in front of the store, watching the boats on the river and Manhattan on the other side. Anton would go out by himself around ten and after a few minutes she came to join him with two mugs of coffee, and they sat there together for an hour or so. They didn't talk much; the point was contemplation and silence. In winter they drank coffee in the store, where there were two old chairs behind the counter that were too comfortable to sell, but it wasn't the same as watching the river.

"Does it bother you ever?" he asked her once. "The way we do things?"

"I'm not sure what you mean." It was a Sunday morning, almost noon. He was fifteen years old and they were watching a Brooklyn-bound J train passing over the Williamsburg Bridge. The warehouse was so close to being under the bridge that at a certain point any approaching subway train disappeared overhead.

"I know a lot of it's stolen," Anton said. "The stuff we sell."

"True," said his mother. She had finished her coffee and she held the empty mug clasped loosely in her hands. She was looking at Manhattan, or looking through Manhattan at something else. There were moments when Anton's parents seemed very far away from him.

"Doesn't it bother you?"

"No," she said. "Does that disappoint you?"

"I don't know. Maybe."

She was quiet for a while. "Your grandfather was an official in the Church of Latter-Day Saints. He was a well-respected man, one of those pillar-of-the-community types, but he was terrifically cruel in his personal life. I ran away at sixteen. Was he moral? He thought so. He operated a soup kitchen and a shelter for the homeless during the winter and probably saved lives. There are probably people alive today who were homeless in Salt Lake City in the '60s, and they didn't freeze to death in the winter because of him. Or my sister," she said. "We've had a few misunderstandings, so you haven't seen her since you were tiny, but she's a wonderful woman. She was on welfare because she had three little kids to take care of, and her ex-husband never did pay child support. Once there was a bureaucratic error and she received two welfare checks for the same month. She spent the extra money on new winter coats and boots for the kids and a radio, and her ex-husband found out and threatened to report her for welfare fraud unless she stopped pestering him for child support. Was she immoral? Was what she did wrong? I frankly don't believe so, my beloved child. My point is that it isn't black-and-white, what we do or what anyone else does in this world."

"We deal in stolen goods."

"We deal in goods that would in all likelihood be destroyed anyway. We're a salvage operation."

"But *stolen*. We don't know they'll be destroyed. Someone else might be planning to save them, and we don't own them. They're not *ours*." He blinked and was humiliated to realize that he was ready to cry. He clenched his coffee cup with both hands to steady himself. Adolescence had made him embarrassingly emotional.

"Anton," she said, "sweetheart, I know it's questionable. But we work hard. I'm at peace. Your father's at peace. We sleep well at night. What are our options?"

"Normal jobs?"

"Normal jobs," she repeated. Her voice held an edge. "You've never worked a normal job, Anton. What do you imagine it might be like?"

"I don't know. Less questionable."

"Well, most things you have to do in life are at least a little questionable," she said. She stood abruptly, took his coffee cup from his hands and left him alone on the loading dock.

11.

The day after he stole the singer's gun Anton went down to the piazza and called Gary.

"You want me to kidnap your cat," Gary repeated.

"Not *kidnap*, exactly." Anton had purchased aspirin with great difficulty at a pharmacy near the hotel—the pharmacist didn't speak English, which necessitated a brief game of charades at the counter—but his headache wasn't entirely gone yet. The sharp light of afternoon made him want to go to bed with the curtains drawn, and the gun was a malignant presence in the top dresser drawer in the hotel room. "I mean, he's *my* cat, it's not like you're stealing him."

"Oh, so I'm not kidnapping him in the *technical* sense of the word, I'm just breaking into your apartment, extracting your cat, and then putting it in a crate and shipping it to Italy. Cool."

"No, I'd send you my house keys. No break and enter involved."

"Oh, okay. That changes *everything*."

"Look, and I'd pay your expenses and all the shipping—we're clear about that, right? I'll throw in another fifty for your time if you want. A hundred. Make it a hundred, okay? A hundred dollars for two hours of your time."

"Thanks, but why don't you keep the money and buy a new cat?"

"Because I already *have* a cat. Jim isn't replaceable."

"Yeah, look, it's just a little crazy for me. Isn't there anyone else you could call?"

"You're my best friend. Who else would I call?"

"Sorry," Gary said.

"Two hundred. Would you do it for two hundred?"

"No, I'm sorry, I wouldn't."

"Why not?"

"Because it's crazy, Anton, I'm sorry. I've known you forever. And I gotta tell you, man, you've just been a little out there lately."

"Why? Because I miss my cat? I've been here for six weeks, Gary. It's lonely as hell."

"No, because you left your wife on your honeymoon and now you want me to take the cat from her too, and all this after you cheated on her with your secretary. You ever stop to think about what kind of a person you are?"

"I do, actually. I think about it all the time."

"And you can still sleep at night? Because it's just not admirable, Anton. It isn't. And look, hey, you know I'm not one to judge, I've always been here for you, I was the guy you called and went for beers with every time she fucking canceled a wedding on you, man, but how could you leave your wife on your honeymoon?"

"You don't understand, there were—"

"Oh Christ, let me guess. There were mitigating circumstances."

"Well, yes, there—"

"How fucking mitigating could a circumstance possibly be?"

"Pretty mitigating," Anton said.

"She cheated on you? She tried to kill you? What?"

"No. Nothing like that. It wasn't anything she did. Look, I can't tell you."

"You can't tell me."

"I'm sorry," Anton said. "I just can't."

The phone call ended badly and afterward Anton went to the café closest to the water. It was the only café on the piazza that still kept regular hours, the only one frequented by the fishermen; the other cafés were opening later and closing earlier as the supply of tourists dwindled and colder winds moved over the surface of the sea. He suspected that the nozzle on this particular café's milk frother wasn't cleaned very often—the lattes tasted slightly like yogurt—but the beer was decent and the grilled panini were good. He'd taken to watching the sunset from this place. Anton sat outside in the last light of afternoon, thinking about his cat and about all the things he should have said to Gary.

Later he took a circuitous walk that lasted three hours and returned to the café after dark to get drunk. There were other lonely foreigners in the piazza that night. They came together as the café emptied out and shared three bottles of wine, and when the café had closed they sat together on a pier: Anton, a couple of Germans who spoke English, another American whose name he didn't know. The Germans were catching an early flight back to Munich; after a while they went back to their hotel and then it was just Anton and the other American, some guy from Michigan. Anton sat on his hands and looked down at the water, the slick of lights on the surface. He was cold. The effervescence of the previous few hours was fading. He was starting to think about the singer and her gun and his far-off cat again.

"I can't remember your name," Anton said finally. "Did you tell me?"

"David Grissom."

"Anton Waker. Pleasure." He reached sideways to shake David's hand. "I've seen you around here a few times before tonight. Doing the crossword puzzle. Sketching stuff. I think we're staying in the same hotel."

"Yeah, I've been here a few weeks."

"Long vacation?"

"Staying here a while. Painting," David said.

"You know, that's a skill I always wanted. I could never even draw."

"It's an overrated talent." David seemed uninterested in the subject. "Where do you live?"

"Here. I used to live in New York, but I don't think I'm going back there. You?"

"No fixed address, as they say in the newspapers. I've been drifting around Europe for a while."

"What do you do, aside from traveling and painting?"

"You know, I used to think that was the most banal question," David said. "*What do you do?* I used to think it was synonymous with *How much money do you make?* But lately I've begun to think it's the most important question you can ask someone. *What do you do? What are you doing? What is your method of conducting your life, by what means do you move through the world?* Important information, isn't it? But I'm sorry, I'm rambling. Is that bottle empty? In answer to your question, I travel aimlessly and try not to think too much. I work odd jobs and paint still-life paintings and then throw out the canvases every time I move to a new place, unless I can sell them to tourists, which only happens if I paint landscapes. I'm going to ask what you do in a minute, bear with me, but first, what's the most important question you've ever been asked?"

"The most important . . . ?"

"It's a subject that interests me," David said. "I used to start conversations the regular way—you know, *Hi, how are you, how 'bout this weather we're having*—but then a few years ago, around the time my wife died, I developed an allergy to small talk. So lately I've been starting with that question, and I find it makes all the conversations I'm in more interesting. Also, I'm drunk."

"It's a good question." Anton was quiet for a moment. "A girl in New York asked me something once. She said, *What was it like when you were growing up?*"

"What was it like when you were growing up. That's good. That's very good. I'll remember that one. What do you do?"

"Me?" Anton raised the wine bottle to his lips, drank for a

moment and set it back on the pier. "Nothing good. Nothing at all, actually. I'm not doing anything but waiting. Can't we just ask each other what we *used* to do? Because the present, well, I have to tell you, I don't like the present very much."

"I used to sell cocaine to art school kids in Michigan," David said.

"Really?"

"Not a bad business," David said. "I only left Detroit because my wife died."

"I'm sorry about your wife. I used to work at a consulting firm," Anton said, "but I think it's safe to say that that career's more or less over. Now I'm just waiting to perform a transaction. I've been waiting for a while now."

"What kind of transaction?"

"One I'd rather not do," Anton said. "It's nothing, actually. I just have to give a package to someone, and after that I'll be free. The waiting's killing me, though. I'm not sure there's anything much worse than this."

"Really? You don't think there's anything much worse than sitting on a pier on the southern coast of Italy drinking wine?" David was smiling. "How drunk *are* you, exactly?"

"Drunker than I've been in a while. I meant there's nothing much worse than this *limbo*," Anton said. "This *waiting*. All this waiting, and I have nothing to go back to once the waiting's done. There's nothing left in New York City. It isn't just that my marriage is over, it's that it never should have started in the first place. I don't know what I was thinking. She was a once-in-a-lifetime person, but that doesn't mean I should have married her. There's nothing left there for me there except my cat and a girl I had an affair with once."

"Do you love her?"

"The girl? I don't know. A little. Yes. Okay, the thing is, I miss her, but not as much as I miss my cat."

"Your cat."

"Jim. He's not just any cat, I rescued him when he was a little kitten. I was walking one night with Sophie, my wife, back when we were still just dating. It was raining, and there was this little wet shivering kitten in a doorway. He almost died. Lost an eye to infection. I tried to get my best friend to kidnap him and ship him over just now, but he wouldn't do it."

"That's why I try to avoid having too many friends," David said. "Unreliable species."

"Not as bad as family."

"I wouldn't know."

"You don't have a family?"

"Not really," David said.

"I envy you, man. I wish I didn't have a family."

"No, you don't."

"You're right," Anton said, "I don't. I wish I had a different family."

The evening after the thirtieth anniversary dinner at Malvolio's, Anton took the subway out to Brooklyn. He was tired. His footsteps were heavy on the steel steps up to the loading dock, and his planned speech evaporated when he stepped into his parents' warehouse. There was the stone fountain just inside that had been there for a decade, sold at last, tagged, waiting for transport. He stopped to touch it—Look at this holy work of art, these holy stone birds along the edge of this basin—and ran one finger over the ecstatic curved spine of a finch. He thought he was alone but when he looked up Aria was already watching him. She was behind the counter, leaning on it, the *New York Times* spread out under her elbows.

"How could you do this?" It wasn't at all what Anton had meant to say.

"Anton," she said, not unkindly, "grow up."

"It's not—"

"You're not *really* going to say *It's not fair*, are you?" They were again thirteen, standing under the awning across the street from Gary's father's store; she was explaining how to shoplift but he was a baby and she was disgusted with him, *You just take it from the shelf and then you don't have to pay for it.* The things she was stealing were different now, colossal: entire futures, perhaps lives, and he wondered how he hadn't noticed when her crimes became so enormous. It occurred to him that perhaps he hadn't been paying enough attention.

"Aria," he said, "this is my life. I've done something different. No one else in our family—" he was about to say *has ever gone to college*, but stopped himself just in time. "Aria, listen, I'm getting married, I'm going to have kids someday, and they'll go to good schools because I have an office job and I can support that, and they will never have to do anything even remotely corrupt."

"You're saying they won't have to do what you did."

Anton sensed a trap but nodded anyway.

"Except that you didn't have to do what you did either." He had stepped on the tripwire; the trap snapped shut. "What were your grades like in high school?"

"I hate rhetorical questions." Anton couldn't look at her.

"Straight A's," Aria said. "You could have done anything. You always said you wondered what life would be like with a college degree, well, you could have gone to college. You had the grades. They have scholarships for kids with grades like yours. But you didn't go to college, did you?"

Anton had no answer to this.

"The way I live is my decision," she said. "The way you live is yours. No one ever forced you to be corrupt."

His father was approaching from the back of the warehouse. He was holding a paintbrush in his hand, tipped with paint the color of poppies. "Are we back on the blackmail thing again?" his father asked.

Anton rested his hand on a stone bird to steady himself. "Yeah, Dad, we're back on the blackmail thing again." The curve of stone wings beneath his fingers.

"Well, she's family, Anton. No getting around it."

"She's your niece. I'm your son."

"She's as much my daughter as—"

"Anton," his mother said. "Ari, Sam, what is this?" She had appeared from somewhere in her work clothes, a streak of dust across her shirt. She was twisting a damp rag between her hands. "I heard you all the way in the back."

"This *blackmail* thing again," his father said. "Talk to him, Miriam."

"Oh, Anton, it's an important deal for her, you *know* that. I don't know why you won't help her."

"Well, I don't have a choice but to help her out, Mom, that's the thing. That's actually what blackmail *is*, in case no one ever told you."

"Don't speak that way to your mother."

"Okay. Okay." Strange to realize, looking at the three of them, that he didn't want to see them again. No, that wasn't it; it was more that not seeing them again was suddenly, staggeringly, absolutely necessary. "Tell you what," Anton said, "I'm getting married in three weeks."

"Well," his mother said, "assuming Sophie doesn't—"

"Shut up. Just shut up. I'm getting married in three weeks, and I don't want to see you there. Any of you." He forced himself to meet their eyes. They were staring at him, uncomprehending but starting to understand. "I don't want any of you to come to my wedding. You are not invited. You are not people who I want to see again. Do you understand me? I'm done." His mother was weeping. The look in his father's eyes. "I love you," Anton said. His father made an indecipherable sound. "I love you. All of you. I just can't, I just don't want to, I just don't want to live the way you live anymore. I can't." He was at the threshold, backing out. "I can't. I'm sorry." They stood frozen in place, and something broke in him at the instant he turned away.

But they came to his wedding anyway, of course. They were family. He saw them sitting far back in the last row of the church— not Aria, just his parents, his mother in her favorite yellow dress— and they slipped away before the reception.

Anton sat with David on the pier on Ischia until it was too cold to sit there anymore and the wine was completely finished, then he excused himself and crossed the piazza to the pay phone. He started to dial the Santa Monica number and then remembered that she'd said she'd be back in New York by now. Her phone rang for some time before she picked up.

"*Anton,*" she said. She had taken to pronouncing his name ironically lately, in italics, because he had hung up on her four or five times in a row. "What time is it there?"

"Aria, my darling. Any news?"

"Yeah. We're in production."

"You're kidding me."

"I'm too tired to be kidding you. You woke me up."

"Only, what? Seven weeks late?"

"Six. You know I'm sorry about the delays you've been through. Believe me, it's not that convenient for me either."

"You didn't have to leave your wife on your honeymoon." The moon was setting.

"Yes, well, if I'd known the delay would be this long I would have done it differently, but nine more days and then it's over. The package will arrive on Friday of next week. That evening your contact will come to your hotel. You'll meet him at the restaurant downstairs at ten P.M."

"The restaurant downstairs isn't open at ten P.M."

"He'll be there anyway."

"How will I know it's him?"

"His name's Ali. I'll have more details on Thursday. Just go down and meet him, give him the package, shake hands and you're done."

"Aria, I want twenty thousand dollars."

"Are you drunk?"

"A little, but that's beside the point. What am I supposed to do after the transaction's done? I've lost practically everything. I do this transaction, and then what?"

"What do you mean, *and then what?* You do this transaction, and then you're done. You can come back to New York."

"With no wife and no job? What am I coming back to, exactly?"

"Not my problem," Aria said.

"Do you know what these weeks have cost me? I used to have a job I loved—"

"You wrecked your own life," she said. "You needed no help from me. And now you want me to pay you twenty thousand dollars because you've had to hang out in the Mediterranean for a few extra weeks? Don't push me any further."

"What does that mean?"

"It means that you've already talked me up to seventeen thousand dollars, which is excessive, incidentally, and I'm afraid I've reached the edge of my patience. Just go downstairs to the restaurant on Friday night, hand over the package, and you're done."

"Eighteen thousand five hundred," Anton said.

"You're unbelievable," Aria said, and hung up. The piazza tilted unsteadily in the half-light; Anton made his way carefully back to the pier and sat down beside David again.

"It's finally happening," Anton said. "That transaction I've been waiting for."

"What kind of transaction are we talking about here?"

"I'm not exactly sure, to be honest. It's my cousin's transaction. I'm just the guy who hands the other guy the package. I don't even handle the payment. We've never really been business partners," he said. "She said we were, but I always just did what I was supposed to."

David nodded. "When's the transaction supposed to take place?"

"Soon. It was supposed to be weeks ago. I've just been stuck here waiting. But you know what's crazy? I wish I could stay here, actually, when all this is done. There's nothing for me to go back to in New York. I'm thinking about getting a job in a hotel somewhere during the tourist season, maybe in Napoli, coming back to Sant'Angelo in the evenings after work, reading a book, spending time with my cat if I can get someone to ship him here, walking on the beach, maybe going for a swim. It's the kind of life I think I've always wanted, crazy as it sounds. Just working all day and coming home at night, nothing shady. Seems uncomplicated, doesn't it?"

"Everything's more complicated than it looks, but what's stopping you from doing it?"

"I'm here now," Anton said, "and no one knows me. I could be anyone. But today or tomorrow or the day after that a nice man in a FedEx uniform will park his truck at the gates of Sant'Angelo and walk down to the hotel with an envelope for me, and shortly afterward a man will show up and I'll give a package to him, and then that man will know who I am. Do you see? My anonymity will be completely ruined. And say this man has a good memory and decides someday that he needs to tell someone else about me. Now that he's seen me, now that I've handed him an envelope, he'd be able to pick me out of a lineup or recognize me on the street, and voilà! Any chance of a new life vanishes at that instant. I could stay here in peaceful anonymity, but once I give the guy the envelope, I'll always be looking over my shoulder."

"What if you paid me to do it?"

"To do what?"

"You give this guy a package," David said, "and you never see him again."

"Yes. Right."

"So why can't it be me? I'm broke, I'll do anything. Well, not anything, but I'm a retired coke dealer. Whatever's in this envelope of yours, how much more illegal can it possibly be? *I'm Anton Waker, I have a package for you, here you go, pleasure doing business.*"

"You'd do that?"

David grinned. "For the right price," he said.

The effects of the wine were leaving Anton. He was slightly disappointed to realize that he was no longer quite drunk. "I have to make another phone call," he said. "Let me think about it. We'll talk soon?"

"Soon," David said. He gave Anton a loose salute and lay on his back on the pier to stare up at the sky. Anton went back to the pay phone, searched the scraps of paper in his wallet until he found the number he was looking for.

"Elena," he said.

12.

At four o'clock in the haze of the third Tuesday in October, Elena stood on the corner of Columbus and West 81st Street waiting for the light to change. In her right hand she held a set of keys that had arrived from Italy by mail a day earlier, and she wore a hat pulled down low over her forehead. Her hair was damp with sweat. She was unaccountably nauseated, but she wasn't sure if it was the heat or her nerves. What she was thinking of at that moment, before Sophie appeared on the other side of the avenue, was the note from Anton hidden in the bottom of her jewelry box in Brooklyn.

She almost wished she had it with her, for reference or for companionship, but the girl approaching Columbus Avenue was unmistakably Sophie. She carried a blue handbag and her hair was pinned up away from her face with dark strands escaping; she was the girl met once in passing at a company Christmas party, the girl whose face was a tiny blob in the string section in full-orchestra photographs of the New York Philharmonic, the girl who'd left her husband alone on Ischia over a month and a half ago.

Sophie and Elena stood for a moment on opposite sides of the avenue with cars passing between them, Elena trying to be invisible with her hat pulled down low and Sophie apparently oblivious, gazing at nothing in particular. The light changed and they came within a few feet of one another on the crosswalk. Elena turned back to watch Sophie from the other side of the street. Sophie walked away slowly, seemingly in no rush. She looked up at the trees that lined the lawn of the Museum of Natural History, she looked at the last of the flowers growing under the branches, she seemed lost in a dream. She disappeared down the steps of the subway station, a long block away. Elena counted to ten and then walked quickly west on 81st Street until she found the address. She stood for a moment on the sidewalk, extending this last moment before she entered the building. Nothing is over yet, she told herself. The cat's still inside. I can still turn and walk away. Instead she unlocked the inner door of the building and ascended the stairs.

Anton's apartment smelled faintly of incense. It was a dim book-filled space, with dark wood furniture and soft-looking white carpets, and somewhere a tap was dripping. There were sounds of traffic from the street outside. Elena closed the door behind her and locked it, her heart beating too hard and too quickly. Impossible not to imagine him everywhere.

The cat was emerging from the bedroom in stages, pausing at intervals to stretch one leg at a time; he yawned hugely and padded toward her. One of his eyes was closed and something about the set of his face suggested that it had never opened. She was shaken by his friendliness. Jim dropped to the floor at her feet just as if she weren't an intruder planning on kidnapping him and sending him to a foreign country. She stroked his milk-white stomach and he twisted on his back with his paws in the air. She stood then, opened the door to the closet where Anton had said the pet carrier box would be, and this was the moment when her nerve failed her all at once; in the space of a few heartbeats she was locking the door of the apartment behind her, she was halfway down the stairs, she was out on the street gasping for breath and walking quickly away from there.

"You look a little feverish," the photographer said.

"Oh, I'm fine," Elena said brightly. She had come straight from Anton's apartment and was fifteen minutes early. She sat down on the sofa in Leigh Anderson's apartment, and he gave her a glass of water that she drank all at once.

"Would you like some more?"

"No, I'm fine, I'm fine, thank you. I was just walking a little too fast, and the heat . . . it's as if fall isn't coming this year."

The photographer was nodding absently. "Brutal," he said. "Might as well still be August." He had produced a portfolio from somewhere and was sitting down in the armchair across from her.

"So," he said, "I should warn you, my work has evolved somewhat since I worked with you last. I'd like you to take a look at my current portfolio." He slid the portfolio across the tabletop, and Elena flipped it open. On the first page two girls lay together in a bathtub, half-submerged; the one on top had pierced nipples and a tongue stud.

"It's still very much on the side of art," Leigh said. "Or if it's moved toward pornography, it's in the hinterlands between the two." The next picture was of a woman sitting on a chair, legs spread wide, naked from the waist down with her head thrown back. Elena wanted to ask how this was different from pornography, but the photographer was still talking. "I like to see it as art photography," he said, "but thrown into the deep end, pushed over the edge. The idea is that the viewer is pushed toward the outer edge of—forgive me," he said, "I get a little pedantic on the topic. I've been teaching a photography class." Elena was looking at a photograph of two girls—a different duo—standing in a bathtub kissing, blurred behind a transparent shower curtain.

"Is your rate still twenty an hour?" Elena asked.

"Forty. You're comfortable with the overall aesthetic?"

"Absolutely," Elena said. Not counting the money Anton had sent her to pay for shipping the cat to Italy, she had less than a hundred dollars left in her checking account.

"But what I do need to see at this point," the photographer said, "is what you look like naked."

"But you've seen me naked. I used to pose for you."

"That was nearly five years ago," the photographer said. "People change in five years. I find it puts my models at ease. It may seem paradoxical, but if you think about it . . ." He had stood up from the armchair, and he was closing the blinds. "I need to know what you look like naked—what you look like *now*, because bodies change in five years—and taking your clothes off for the first time is the hardest part." He paused at a window, looking at something on the street, then closed the blinds and turned back to her. "This way, if you're naked in front of me for a few minutes now, it'll be easier to be naked for four hours when we meet next week for the session."

"You said that five years ago."

"It's still true."

Elena took her shirt off. She unfastened her bra and slid down her skirt with no trouble, and found that she could even look up at him once she'd taken off her underwear.

"Please," he said, gesturing expansively.

Elena came out from behind the coffee table, and stood exposed on his living room floor.

"Nice," he said. "You still have a good body."

"Thanks." She watched his face, obscurely anxious. His eyes drifted professionally downward.

"Can you trim?" he asked. "Not a lot, just a bit. Think of making it into a V-shape. Do you mind?"

She didn't, although she was aware that her hands were shaking slightly. She was trying to remember if it had been like this the first time, five years ago, but found that she'd lost the memory.

"Can you turn around for me?"

She turned slowly away from him.

"Stop."

She stood facing his tiny Manhattan kitchen, a closet-sized corner tiled in black with one wall painted the color of an emerald in sunlight. There was a Van Gogh postcard magneted haphazardly to the fridge, explosions of stars in a swirling sky.

"You have nice calves."

"Thanks," she said hollowly. She turned back toward him.

"When are you due?"

"What?"

He winked. "I can always tell," he said.

It took her a moment to understand. "Oh, I'm not *pregnant*."

Leigh didn't look embarrassed, only surprised. "You're positive about that?"

"Positive," she said.

The photographer nodded and began moving back toward the armchair, and she understood this as her cue to get dressed again. She put her clothes back on and they spoke of practical things. Dates, methods of payment, the model release.

Twenty minutes later she found herself standing in the 81st Street Museum of Natural History subway station, looking at the tiled mosaic elephants and bats and sea turtles and frogs, realizing that actually she wasn't positive at all.

"So, what did you do today?" Caleb asked.

He had come to bed earlier than usual but seemed unready to sleep. He lay on his back and she lay beside him with her head in the crook of his arm. Her thoughts were turned toward the Upper West Side, toward the photographer's green kitchen wall and Sophie drifting across the intersection.

"Not much," she said. "I met with the photographer."

"That same one as before, right? Upper West Side?"

"The same one. Yes."

"Have you given any more thought to finding a job?"

"I'm posing for him tomorrow. He pays more now than he used to."

"I meant real work," Caleb said.

"I hate real work." She was trying to keep her voice light.

"Most people have to work, though, sweetie." It was a delicate topic: *he* didn't have to work, and he didn't entirely understand. The closest Caleb could come to imagining what an office job might be like was to compare it to research, which he loved, or to depression, which the pills had eradicated so successfully and for so many years that it was beginning to seem abstract, a half-real memory of six months in the late '90s when he hadn't wanted to get out of bed, something that might have happened to some-body else.

"Aren't you listening? That's not what I'm saying at all," Elena said. "Of course I have to work. I'm not suggesting that any alter-native exists."

"But maybe if you had a different kind of job," Caleb said carefully. "You were happy when you were working as Anton's as-sistant, weren't you?"

"Was I? I don't know, I suppose it's a question of ratio. I was probably less unhappy more of the time."

"Have you thought about going back to school?"

"So I could do what? Work in yet another job? It's work itself, Caleb, it's not the job I happen to be in. I don't mean to go on and on about it, it's just, I'm still . . . I've been working since I was six-teen years old, except for that one semester at Columbia, and the initial shock of work hasn't worn off yet. I still have these mo-ments where I think, *Come on, this can't possibly be it. I cannot pos-sibly be expected to do something this awful day in and day out until the day I die*. It's like a life sentence imposed in the absence of a crime."

"Perhaps you should see someone," Caleb said. He went to a psychiatrist once a month, and came back introspective and a little dazed.

"How could I see someone? I have no health insurance now, and anyway, I don't want to see someone. I don't want to be numbed."

He was quiet.

"I'm sorry," she said.

"It's okay. It must seem like that to you sometimes."

"It does. I'm sorry."

He stroked her face for a moment, withdrew his hand and kissed her on the forehead.

"Well," he said, "we should probably get to sleep. I love you."

"I love you too."

Elena couldn't sleep that night. After a while she got up and went to the kitchen. She turned on the light above the table. The clock above the stove was ticking loudly in the quiet. She was reading a two-day-old newspaper when the telephone rang at midnight.

"It's okay," Anton said when she told him. "Everyone loses their nerve sometimes."

"I'm sorry, Anton. I'll go back again."

"You don't have to," he said, perfectly aware that his former secretary was incapable of leaving a project unfinished.

"Of course I'll go back." She was standing by the kitchen window, which was as far from the bedroom as a person could get and still be inside the apartment.

"Did you get the veterinary records?" he asked. "The vet was supposed to mail them to you."

"I have them," she said.

"What's the weather like there?" He was watching the fisher-men preparing their nets, the first few boats gliding out around the breakwaters. He had taken to going to bed early, for lack of anything else to do in the evenings, and rising at dawn to watch the sunrise and the boats.

"Warm," she said. "Hot, actually. It's as if it's still summer."

"Have you found work?"

"I haven't tried. I've just been posing naked for people."

"People?"

"Art classes. Borderline pornographers."

"Does that kind of thing pay well?" His tone was studiedly neutral.

"Not particularly. No. I think I have to do something else soon, or else commit to it completely." It was impossible to keep her voice from wavering.

"What do you mean, commit to it?"

"I mean actual pornography, not just the borderline stuff." She was looking at her reflection in the kitchen window and thinking that she looked like a ghost; in the window she was transparent against the fire-escape railings outside. "I don't know what to do," she said.

"What kind of job do you want?"

"That's exactly the problem. The thought of finding another job . . ." She was breathing somewhat quickly; she closed her eyes, concentrating on the idea of five-thousand-year-old pine trees, the first cup of tea and the first line of *Gilgamesh*, the first sheet of glass ever held up to the light, and forced the wavering part of herself to be still. She laughed in what was meant to be a carefree manner, but it was a strange clenched sound that escaped her throat.

"Elena," he said, "it's all going to be all right. I'll call you tomorrow or the next day, and we'll figure out what to do. Listen, Sophie has therapy on Thursdays. She's always gone between five and seven."

"I'll go back again."

"Thank you," he said. "I can't tell you how I appreciate it."

Caleb was awake when she came back to bed.

"I'm sorry," he said gently, when she reached out to him. It had been months now, a growing distance, like the gradual tectonic division of continents.

"Yes, I'm sorry too." She hadn't meant to speak so sharply.

"What's upsetting you really?"

"This," she said.

Caleb was silent. It was too dark to see his face, but she knew he was staring up at the ceiling unblinking.

"It's late," he said. "We should go to sleep."

Beyond the fact that Caleb couldn't quite bring himself to touch her anymore, there seemed to be an underlying question of compatibility. He talked about specimens, types of leaves. She found herself grieving for the absolute tragedy of the lost tree in Utah. He talked about cross-sections of bark, the genetic structure of the *Lotus japonicus*, work that was being done on the plant genome project. Elena listened to him and found her mind wandering, wondering if that Utah geology student who felled the four-thousand-nine-hundred-year-old tree felt remorseful, what kind of person could do that, if a person capable of felling a tree to retrieve a broken tool is even capable of understanding the sheer magnitude of his crime; someone must have pointed out to him that the organism he'd killed had been alive three thousand years before Christ, but can a man who thinks so small perceive anything so enormous?

In the morning after Caleb had left for the university Elena stood in the hallway for a while, watching the movement of the goldfish, trying to think ordered thoughts. Phylum Chordata, with us and the otters and the monkeys and the sea squirts; the phylum for all of us in possession of a nerve cord. Class Actinopterygii, the domain of bright fishes. Order Cypriniformes, of carps and minnows; family Cyprinidae, genus *Carassius*, species *auratus*. Fins like orange silk in the water. Memories of childhood cartoons with orange fishes and black cats.

Two days later she stood in the photographer's apartment on the Upper West Side, blinking in a flood of sunlight with dust motes drifting bright around her. She hadn't been sleeping well. Her eyes were heavy. She remembered posing here five years ago, but the memory was so distant that it was almost third-person: the five-years-ago girl had insisted that the blinds be closed even though the sunlight in the room was perfect when they were open, the five-years-ago girl had taken off her clothes but lain on her stomach on the sofa and had to be gently persuaded to turn over. Elena shied away from nothing now, but the difference was more frightening than liberating; she could feel the five-years-ago shadow staring at her from the sofa while she stood in the window in full view of the neighbors across the street, naked from the waist down except for her most perilous pair of high-heeled shoes, alarmed by how little the thought of strangers seeing her in the window concerned her.

"That's beautiful," Leigh said. He was moving around her, taking picture after picture, the faint digital *beep* of the shutter sounding over and over again. "Now take off your shirt."

She did this, and stood naked except for the shoes. She turned her face toward the camera, but she was looking at dust motes drifting through the light.

"Close your eyes," he said, and when she closed her eyes it was harder to balance; she touched the window frame and felt the warmth of sunlight on her hand. "Can you touch yourself a little?"

She found that she could, but that was more or less when the nausea started, and an hour later she threw up in a Starbucks bathroom near the subway.

13.

"You can dispose of my luggage as you see fit," Sophie had actually said, a half-hour before boarding the ferry to Naples.

How does one dispose of luggage? For the first few weeks Anton kept Sophie's suitcase in the wardrobe beside the bed, but its presence was oppressive. On a bright clear afternoon in late October he came up from the piazza and was bothered yet again by the way the wardrobe wouldn't quite close. He lifted the suitcase onto the bed and unzipped it. He was overcome for a moment;

sweet, faint, her hair, her skin. She was the kind of preternaturally organized girl who remained packed for entire vacations, extracting a set of clothes every morning and leaving everything else folded neatly, hand-washing the previous day's clothing in the sink and hanging it up to dry on the hotel balcony overnight, refolding it the following morning. Everything was clean. There were three pairs of pants, several shirts, a skirt, the blue linen dress she'd worn in Naples. He laid it all out on the bed like evidence. There were t-shirts, a wrinkled blouse, underwear, socks. A bra the color of daffodils, a biography of Jim Morrison; he read the first few pages and then returned his attention to the suitcase. It was empty now but for a wadded-up pair of socks, so he began methodically checking the outside pockets. In the first pocket was an Oxford Italian-English dictionary, two blank postcards from Rome, an article about nuclear ethics torn out of a newspaper, and a packet of sugar with a picture of Capri on the back. In the other pocket were two folded maps (Rome and Naples), a partially consumed bottle of water with condensation clinging to the inside, and an envelope addressed to Sophie c/o the New York Philharmonic.

The envelope been opened. Inside was a typed note on San Francisco Symphony Orchestra letterhead, dated August 15th:

Dear Ms. Berenhardt,

As per our telephone conversation of August 4th, it is with great pleasure that I acknowledge your acceptance of our invitation to join the San Francisco Symphony Orchestra for our upcoming season. As discussed, Jacob Neerman from our personnel department will contact you within the next two weeks to work out the details. We are happy to provide a stipend to offset your expenses in relocating to San Francisco this fall. Jacob will discuss the details when you speak with him.

Sincerely,

Arthur Gonzalez

Administrative Director, San Francisco Symphony Orchestra

"San Francisco," Anton said. The room was silent. He carried the letter out to the balcony, where he read it again and then stood for a while looking out at the sea. After a few minutes of this he went back inside. His cell phone was flashing a low-battery warning on the desk, so he picked up the keys and his wallet and ran down the hotel stairs and around the corner to the piazza, where a tourist was using the pay phone. He stood nearby, impatiently shifting his weight, and realized that the page was still in his hand. He read it over a few times and then lost himself for a few minutes watching a passionate soccer game being played by boys on the beach. They were the children of fishermen, of restaurant workers, of the woman who ran the newsstand, and they played on the beach all day while their parents worked, an emotional society of small tanned boys in swim shorts who formed and broke alliances, went swimming individually and came back together again, organized themselves into soccer teams and then disbanded to pester their parents for ice cream.

"Ich vermiss dich so sehr," said the tourist, on the phone.

He wanted to call Sophie and ask when exactly she had planned on telling him that she was moving to San Francisco. *As per our telephone conversation of August 4th.* He remembered August 4th. He had stood in front of his bathroom mirror that morning, extracted a piece of glass from his face with a pair of tweezers and held the shining transparent thing up to the light. Sophie had stood in the doorway and asked if he'd been shaving with glass and then hadn't wanted to talk about it later. Had she really decided to leave him that day? But married him anyway? He'd gone off to work, she'd stayed home and placed a call to San Francisco and then behaved as if nothing was wrong that night? He was incredulous. The whole thing seemed pathetic. He was disgusted with both Sophie and himself. A yellow-and-blue boat was coming into the harbor.

"Ich werde niemals zu dir zurückkommen," said the tourist. She was silent a moment, listening, and then hung up the phone without saying anything else and walked away toward the water. Anton moved in immediately and made the call, but their home phone number in New York had been disconnected. He called Sophie's cell phone, but it went to voice mail and he didn't want to leave a message. Anton hung up and dialed a different number but then remembered that he and Gary weren't necessarily on speaking terms and hung up before Gary answered. He went to the fishermen's café and read a newspaper until David appeared. It was a bleached-white day, cloudless, the sky so bright he couldn't look at it.

"Mind if I join you?" David sat down across the table from him without waiting for an answer. He had green paint under his fingernails. He was carrying his own newspaper. He opened it, folded it carefully to expose the crossword puzzle, and ordered a beer from the waiter before he looked up at Anton again.

"What's the matter?" David asked.

"Something I read." The letter was still in Anton's pocket. He unfolded it and gave it to David. "My wife," he said. "I didn't know she was going to leave me."

David took the letter from him and read it through quickly. "She said nothing about it? No hint?"

"Nothing. I found the letter in her suitcase. I mean, to be fair, I guess I left her first."

"Why didn't she take her suitcase?"

"I don't know. Maybe she wanted me to find it."

"Are you all right?"

"More startled than anything."

"I would be."

"I mean, I was cheating on *her*," Anton said. "I didn't think she'd . . ." He trailed off and there was a silence, during which a fisherman climbed into his red-and-white boat and started slowly out of the harbor. "It's all so pathetic," he said. "I don't know why we got married. It just seemed like the right thing to do, but why would either of us . . ." The *putt-putt* of the motor played counterpoint to the calls of the soccer boys on the beach.

"Hey," David said, "I think Gennaro wants you." Anton followed the direction of his gaze. The owner of the hotel was coming around the corner into the piazza. The white FedEx envelope in his hand shone almost painfully in the sunlight.

Anton felt as if the envelope were floating toward him, a glaring white rectangle that he found hard to look at dead-on. The wait was agonizing, so he stood up from the table and went to meet it.

"Good afternoon," Gennaro said. "This envelope arrived for you. I signed for it, thought I'd give it to you in person."

"Thank you. I appreciate it." It was addressed to an Ali Merino, care of Anton Waker. He recognized Aria's handwriting. She'd used Gary's father's store for the return address. "It's for a friend of mine," he said. "He forgot some papers."

"Ah," said Gennaro. "A beautiful day, yes?"

"It is." Anton raised the envelope to shield his eyes against the sun and tried to smile.

"Well," Gennaro said awkwardly, "goodbye."

"Goodbye." He watched Gennaro recede for a moment before he returned to the table where David was sitting.

"Your package?" David asked.

"After all these weeks."

"You going to open it?"

"No," Anton said. Strange to have it before him after all this time, shining innocuously in the sunlight.

14.

On the third Thursday of October in the city of New York, Elena stood on the corner of 81st Street and Columbus watching the slow progress of a moving truck parked halfway up the block. It had arrived an hour earlier and three men were carrying furniture and boxes between the front door and the truck. Five minutes earlier she had seen Sophie come out and speak to them. Sophie had left soon afterward, walking away down West 81st Street in the opposite direction. Elena counted to ten before she ventured up the hill. It was October 20th, but the forecast called for 85 degrees

Fahrenheit, here in one of the last countries on earth that still used the Fahrenheit system. Her shirt was wet on her back. She made her way up the sidewalk in the deadening heat, and one of the movers winked as she approached.

"Hey," she said, "you know where Sophie is?"

"She went out," the man said. "Running an errand of some sort."

"Oh, okay. I'm Ellie, I'm here about the cat. She told you I'd be coming?"

"No."

"That's strange. I'm Ellie——" She realized that she was repeating herself, but too late——"and I'm taking care of the cat for a couple days. He's upstairs?"

"Who's upstairs?"

"The cat?"

"Yeah, yeah, locked in the bedroom. Go on up."

She ascended the stairs quickly. Inside the apartment a mover was taking apart a table in the middle of the room. He looked up and grunted when she said hello. It seemed to be possible to walk into apartments that people were moving out of without anyone saying much. Her heart was beating very quickly, and there was a disjointedness about the scene—she was crossing the room with the cat-carrying box, although she couldn't remember reaching up into the closet to retrieve it, she was opening the door to the bedroom and closing herself in.

The bedroom was empty. The closet doors wide open, the bed and dresser gone, pale rectangles on the wall where pictures had hung. Jim was lying on the carpet by the window, absorbing sunlight. He raised his head and watched her with his one bright eye. She set the box down in the middle of the floor and opened the cage door, but it turned out that the cat wasn't interested in being inserted into it. He began twisting away from her almost immediately when she grasped him, and he braced his legs on the edges of the opening. By the time she had forced him in headfirst and slammed the cage door shut her arms were stinging with scratches. Jim yowled once. When she looked in through the door he was crouched low, glaring with his single eye.

"I'm sorry," Elena whispered, to everyone. She lifted the box (the cat was surprisingly heavy), and opened the bedroom door just as Sophie opened the door to the apartment. Two movers were indoors now, disassembling the bookcases.

"Elena," Sophie said, "what are you doing with the cat?"

"I'm sorry," Elena said, again.

There was a soft thud. "Jesus, that was my thumb," one of the movers said.

"What are you doing with the cat?" Sophie asked again. She didn't move away from the doorway or look away from Elena's eyes.

"Anton asked me to send him to Italy."

Sophie stared at her, silent.

"He said he misses him," Elena said.

Sophie still didn't speak.

"I'm sorry. I'm just really—I'm sorry," Elena said.

The movers, disassembling the bookcase, worked on in awkward silence. Elena felt that she was becoming transparent under Sophie's gaze. Her knees were weak. She wanted to fall. "I'm sorry," she repeated, and to her utter mortification she realized that she was beginning to weep. She stood frozen in the bedroom doorway with sunlight pouring through her, a shadow, a ghost, gripping the cat box as tightly as possible and wishing to be anywhere, anywhere else, her shoulder aching from the cat's weight and tears on her face, her breath catching, and still Sophie only watched her.

The movers had entirely dismantled the bookshelves now— they lay in a stack of flat boards gleaming dark in the sunlight— and they were wrapping the boards in a packing quilt and bundling the packing quilt with tape. The sounds they made were distant, like actions occurring in another room. Elena began walking forward across the room, trying to come to some internal understanding of what she would do if Sophie didn't step aside from the doorway. But Sophie did step aside, almost at the last moment, and she said nothing as Elena passed by. Elena kept walking, away down the stairs with Sophie looking down from above, until she was out on the street with the cat. She hailed a taxi, asked for Kennedy Airport and closed her eyes in the backseat.

"You okay?" the driver asked.

"Yeah," she said, "fine—" and realized that there were still tears streaming down her face, unabated. Her hands were shaking.

"Where you traveling today?"

"Italy," she said.

"Italy," said the driver. "Without luggage?"

"Without luggage."

"Who flies without luggage? I didn't take you for a terrorist." His tone was jokey; he was trying to make her laugh. She smiled wanly and didn't answer him.

"Wait," she said after a moment, "can we make a stop? I forgot my passport."

"Of course. Wherever you want." In East Williamsburg she carried the cat into the apartment and the cab idled out front while she threw a few things into a small suitcase: some clothes, a manila envelope containing old postcards, a piece of paper hidden in a blue sock at the back of her sock drawer, both the Canadian and American passports, a few things from the bathroom. Halfway to the door she remembered the cat, and went to the kitchen for a can of tuna and a can opener. A phone message in Caleb's handwriting was attached to the fridge: ALEXANDRA BRODEN CALLED PLS CALL BACK. She stood for a moment holding the piece of paper, went to the kitchen phone and dialed the number.

"Please don't ever call me at home again," Elena said when Broden picked up.

"I tried your work first. You didn't tell me you'd left and I need to ask you a question." There was an urgency in Broden's voice that Elena hadn't heard before. "Did Anton ever say anything to you about shipping?"

"Shipping?"

"Shipping containers, or boats, or ports, or travel over oceans, or the import-export business. Anything of that nature. Any mention at all."

"No," Elena said, after a moment. "He never did."

"When did you last speak with him?"

"Just before he left."

"He was supposed to be back weeks ago," Broden said.

"I know."

"Well," Broden said, "we can discuss this tomorrow."

"I have to see you tomorrow?"

"Yes, at four o'clock. We scheduled this three weeks ago."

"I'll be there," Elena said.

She paused for a moment by the goldfish tank and then locked the apartment door behind her and ran back down the stairs with the cat and the suitcase. The interior of the cab was too warm.

"One more stop before the airport," she said. She was opening the window. "Can you take me up to Columbia University?"

"Pretty big detour. What time's your flight?"

"I don't have a flight."

He looked at her in the rearview mirror. "You said you were flying to Italy."

"I am."

"Okay," the driver said.

"Are you from Italy?" she asked after a few miles of silence. They had crossed to the Manhattan side of the bridge and they were racing north up the island, streets passing fast. Flashes of mannequins in store windows, people walking on the sidewalks, whole lives played out between avenues, a bright faux-summer day. All the trees she saw were still green.

"Italy? No."

"Your accent, I thought it sounded . . ."

"I'm from a place you've never heard of," he said, and he winked at her in the rearview mirror.

"So am I," said Elena. She thought for a second about obscure countries and then said, "Kyrgyzstan?"

"Tajikistan," the cab driver said. He looked at her in the rearview mirror, startled. "But I've been to Kyrgyzstan many times. Many times."

"What's it like there?"

"Kyrgyzstan? I don't know. Different from here."

"Everywhere's different from here." The gates of Columbia were on their right. "You'll wait for me?"

"I'll wait," the driver said.

She took her suitcase and the cat with her anyway and made her way through the gates and over the sunlit expanse of the grounds, through a doorway and down several flights of stairs to the underground laboratory where Caleb was working. He looked up from his computer when Elena said his name. On the screen before him line upon line of gibberish ran down the screen. He hit a key and the letters and numbers stopped moving and flickered silently in place.

"Ellie? What's going on?"

Elena set down her suitcase and Jim, who meowed furiously and then sank into a prowling orange fury that moved him back and forth across the carrier.

"Whose cat is that?"

"It's Anton's," she said. "Caleb, listen—"

"Anton your old boss?"

"Yes. Caleb—"

"Why would you have your boss's cat? Your *ex*-boss's cat." He spoke without malice.

"Caleb."

"Are you leaving me?"

Elena found all at once that she had nothing to say. She had planned a speech on the way down the corridor but all the words were fading out in the cool air of the room. She looked down at the floor and nodded.

"You're leaving me," Caleb said. He smiled briefly, ran his hands through his hair and looked at her. "Where are you going?"

"Italy," she said.

"Italy," he repeated. "With no money, and Anton's cat."

"I have a little cash. And I still have a credit card."

"Italy," he said again, very quietly, and laughed.

"Caleb, I'm sorry, I just . . ."

He raised his hand to stop the sentence, and smiled, and shook his head. She smiled back at him, and for an instant there was peace. Then Jim meowed again, more urgently, and she remembered the time and the cab idling out front with the meter running. She picked up the cat's carrying box and the suitcase.

"It's okay," he said. "I'm sorry too, I just couldn't . . ."

"It's all right."

"A lot of it was just the pills, you know. The side effects."

"I know."

"You don't have to go so far away," he said.

"I can't stay in the United States anymore."

"It's a big place, Ellie."

"It's not that. I'm not trying to get away from you. The thing is, look, I don't have time to get into it, there's a flight I want to catch, but the thing is, I'm not an American. My American passport's a fake. I shouldn't have lied to you. Caleb, listen, I have to go."

"What? What do you mean your passport's a—"

"Goodbye, Caleb."

"Ellie, wait," he said, but he didn't make a move to follow her when she turned away. In the cab to the airport she turned to look out the back window at the last possible minute, just in time to see the Manhattan skyline disappear.

At JFK she bought a one-way ticket to Rome and gave the cat over to a red-suited airline representative who promised not to lose him. She used her Canadian passport, half-expecting to be arrested on the spot, and was mildly surprised when she met no resistance. Her suitcase was small, so she carried it with her through security and was grateful that she had something to hold on to as she paced the grayish corridors of the terminal. There was a considerable amount of time to kill before the next flight to Italy.

Elena ate a grease-and-salt meal at a bar beyond the security gates, ordered a glass of cheap wine that she didn't touch, and sat for a while in the airport restaurant thinking about calling home to talk to her family; calling Caleb and apologizing, saying she'd made a terrible mistake, asking him to come get her; calling Anton to tell him that the cat was arriving in Rome tomorrow morning; calling Anton to tell him that in twenty-four hours she would be on Ischia; calling Broden to announce that she would give her Anton Waker if only she could stay forever in New York. Not all of these options canceled each other out, and contemplating all the possible configurations was exhausting.

She spent some time standing at a wall of glass, watching airplanes rise and descend in the gathering twilight. There was still something breathtaking about the ascent.

15.

Elena, buying a Social Security card at the Russian Café:

She arrives a half-hour early and chooses a table by the window, facing out. The Russian Café on 1st Street is a few feet below street level and when Elena sits down she can only see legs passing above the bank of snow, flickering shadows of high boots and dark overcoats. It is late afternoon and the snow is unceasing.

The café is warm, but Elena is shivering. She takes off her coat but keeps her hat and scarf on, she orders a mug of tea and a muffin—four dollars, which is her entire budget for the day because she's been saving all her money for the transaction that's about to occur. The place is nearly empty. An older man in a tweed jacket sits alone at a table on the other side of the door, reading a newspaper and sipping a cappuccino. A couple sits some distance away, laughing at a private joke. They are young, college students perhaps, and the woman's face is flushed in the warmth of the room. Elena holds the tea near her face and closes her eyes for a moment, waiting for the heavy footsteps, the door flung open and the Homeland Security badge flashed in her face and the shouting, the handcuffs, the guns; but when she opens her eyes the room is still tranquil, candlelight on red wallpaper and the shadows of pedestrians still flickering across the top of the window before her and the snow falling outside, the waitress behind the counter still chatting in Russian on her cell phone, the man in the tweed jacket still turning the pages of the newspaper. Of course. Why would her arrest be so dramatic? She isn't armed or dangerous. She's a twenty-two-year-old who goes without dinner too frequently and gets dizzy if she stands up too fast. No need for storm troopers, for the waving of guns. In a moment the man in tweed will take one last sip of his cappuccino, fold his newspaper unhurriedly and stand up from the table, buttoning his jacket as he stands. He will move toward her slowly, he will reach into an inside pocket and remove a police badge and hold it up with a wink as he removes the handcuffs from his belt, speaking confidentially in a friendly voice, *You have the right to remain silent,* and by morning she will be on a northbound plane with an X stamped on her passport. She sips the tea to calm herself and tries to eat the muffin. An hour earlier she had been desperately, light-headedly, agonizingly hungry, but now she can taste nothing and it's difficult to swallow. The man in the tweed jacket turns a page of his newspaper. Elena clenches her hands around the mug of tea, trying to look everywhere at once and bracing herself for the sting; the men exploding through the door with guns drawn or the couple across the room standing up and pulling badges from their hipster jean pockets. Every catastrophe has a last moment just before it; as late as eight forty-four A.M. on the morning of September 11, 2001, it was still only a perfect bright day in New York. But the couple remains in conversation, the man in the tweed jacket sips his cappuccino and reads, the waitress stands by the glass door looking up the steps to the sidewalk and street.

"Still snowing," the waitress says. She's a young woman with straight blond hair and brown eyes, a small scar on her forehead, and she smiles when Elena looks up. "It will be deep tonight, I think."

The door opens a moment later and the man is at her table almost instantly, sliding into the chair across from her and unbuttoning his overcoat, his face red with cold.

"Gabriel." He extends a cold hand. "You must be Elena."

She nods mutely.

"It's freezing," he says. "Jesus." He waves at someone behind her, presumably the waitress, removes a tissue from his coat pocket and blows his nose. "Excuse me," he says to Elena, and the waitress has appeared with a latte. She sets it down in front of him and Gabriel kisses her cheek. "Illy," he says, "you're a saint. Thank you." The waitress smiles and steps back, watching them. Gabriel leans forward across the table and beckons for Elena to lean forward too. His breath is hot against her ear. "I apologize for this," he murmurs, so softly that she has to strain to hear him, "but I need you to go to the back with Ilieva, and do what she says. It's a security precaution that my cousin insists on. Please don't take it personally."

"Here," Ilieva says, "come with me, please." Elena stands and follows her past the brightly lit pastry case, down the red corridor past the bathroom, until Ilieva opens a door marked *Employees Only* and Elena follows her into the storeroom. It is a cramped space filled with boxes and milk crates. An enormous glass-fronted fridge hums in a corner, filled with white cake boxes and ice-cream tubs. Ilieva closes and locks the door behind them.

"Please take off your clothes," she says.

"What?"

"For the wires," Ilieva says. "It is to check for the wires."

"The wires?"

"Wiretapping. The recordings. I'm sorry, my English . . ."

"Oh. I understand." She begins to take off her clothes. It's warm in the storeroom, but she can't stop shivering.

"Your bra also," Ilieva says. She picks up each article of clothing as Elena removes it, patting it down before she returns it to Elena, presumably feeling for recording devices. When Elena is fully dressed again Ilieva makes an unembarrassed search of Elena's coat pockets. She removes and examines the wad of bills, replaces them and continues searching. "No handbag?"

"No handbag," Elena says.

When Elena goes back out into the restaurant Gabriel is where she left him, drinking his latte. He smiles when he sees her but doesn't speak. Ilieva appears a moment later and murmurs something in his ear. He nods.

"I apologize sincerely," he says to Elena. "I know it's intrusive, to say the least. My cousin's a little paranoid about security."

"I understand."

"I hate it," Gabriel says. "The whole procedure. It just seems somewhat necessary these days. The current political climate, et cetera. But anyway, listen, may I buy you a sandwich?"

"Oh, there's no need, I—"

"Seriously," he says gently. "You're looking a little pale."

All at once she is desperately hungry again.

Later on it's difficult to remember the conversation, except that it's effortless and that hours pass before Ilieva brings the check and the snow outside the window sparkles blue and amber in the lights of the street.

"We close early," Ilieva says apologetically. "For the snow." The café is empty but for an older couple eating dessert nearby.

"Bear with me for one last absurd ritual," Gabriel says softly, "and then you're free to work in the United States of America. Will you do exactly as I say for a moment?"

"Yes," Elena whispers.

Gabriel opens his wallet and slides a twenty into the check folder. "That's for the food and drink," he tells her quietly. "Now put in your share." His tone leaves no doubt as to his meaning, and all at once it is the last moment before potential catastrophe again: the whole evening has unwound to this point, *now*, and it's too late again. Elena reaches into her left coat pocket, where the precious stack of bills that she's been accumulating for months resides, but the police don't break down the door. Perhaps it won't happen. Perhaps she'll walk out with a forged passport and a Social Security number, exactly as promised. "Turn the folder so that it opens away from that couple," Gabriel murmurs, "and slide the money in. Don't count it—good—now put the folder on the table and look at me as if nothing out of the ordinary has occurred."

Ilieva takes the check folder and Elena is alone with Gabriel for a moment, and the music playing in the café at that moment sounds like a Russian lullaby. Ilieva reappears with the folder and two glasses of red wine.

"Your change," Ilieva says. "A pleasure, as always."

Gabriel raises his glass. "Red wine means the count was correct," he says softly. "If she'd brought water, I'd be out the door by now. Cheers."

"What are we toasting?"

"My last job," he says, "and your future gainful employment."

"Really? I'm your very last?"

"Well, I have one more tomorrow, actually. But *my second-to-last job* doesn't have quite the same ring to it, does it?" He's reaching into an inside pocket of his jacket, and he passes her the envelope so casually that Elena almost doesn't see it until it's on the table. It's the kind of envelope that film developers use for photos. "Here are some vacation pictures," he says. "You can look at them later."

She takes the envelope and puts it in her bag and the moment of transaction is over so quickly that she's almost unsure it happened. He's still holding up his wineglass, and she smiles.

"Well," Elena says, "congratulations. I assume this isn't the easiest line of work."

"That's just it," he says. "It *is* easy. I could do this forever. But I want something different. What will you do with your new-found legality?"

"I'll stop washing dishes for a living. I'll stop posing naked for photographers. I don't know. Anything."

Gabriel goes quiet for a moment, sipping his wine. "Listen, I shouldn't ask probably," he says suddenly. "This is probably silly of me, but do you have any office skills? Can you type?"

She nods.

"I started a new job last month," he says. "It's nothing that exciting, but I've been told to find a new secretary for my division . . ." She listens for some time to the details of the position, she sips her wine and then the glass of water that follows, and she is stricken by a sense that has come over her before in moments of unreality; it's as if she's stepped outside herself and is observing the scene from afar. At a small table in the Russian Café in a snowstorm she talks to the man she met a few hours earlier and laughs as if she's always known him, just as if they're two old friends out for dinner on a snowy night in New York. Just as if the envelope that Anton slid over the table hadn't contained a Social Security card and an impeccably forged American passport.

"I don't know," Gabriel says in the snow outside the restaurant, walking toward the Williamsburg Bridge, "it's difficult to explain. I just want, I've always wanted a different kind of life than this. This will sound strange, I mean, I know it's crazy, but I always wanted to work in an office."

"You have a corporate soul?"

She's mostly joking, but Gabriel nods as if she isn't and says, "Exactly. Yes."

Late at night on the bridge the cold is deep and absolute. The lights of the Domino Sugar Factory shine over the river, and the snow is still falling. Gabriel tells her he's spending the evening with his parents in Williamsburg. They walk together, talking, and a boat moves silently over the dark water far below.

On the far side of the bridge he calls a car service for her on his cell phone and they stand together waiting for it to arrive, stamping their feet to keep warm until the black car pulls up to the curb. "Let me give you my business card so you can call me about the job. There's just one thing I have to tell you," he says as he gives it to her. "About my name . . ."

The car takes her away from there to the apartment building in East Williamsburg. She leans her head against the window to look up at the snow and it seems at that moment that it's going to get easier now, that the long nightmare of hunger and dishwashing and posing naked is almost over; there's a chance at a job here in her beloved city, something different, health insurance, a new life. The driver, already paid by Gabriel/Anton, grunts something about the neighborhood when she says goodnight. Elena lets herself in through the first door, a steel gate that clangs shut behind her. Her boyfriend is lying on her bed when she opens the door to her bedroom; she can't suppress a gasp. They've been talking about moving in together, and she forgets sometimes that she's given him a key. He grins at her and puts down the book he was reading, *The Botany of Desire*, green-gold apples resplendent on the dust jacket.

"I let myself in," he says. "I hope you don't mind."

"Not at all. I'm glad you're here." She opens the closet door and steps behind it, hidden from his view. She's taking her clothes off; the thought of undressing for Ilieva in the storeroom returns to her, and she blinks and tries to erase Ilieva's face from her mind. "What time is it?"

"Almost eleven," he says. "Where've you been?"

"I went out with a girl from work. Jennifer."

The American passport is cool to the touch. She takes it from her coat pocket and opens it quickly, hidden from Caleb's view by the closet door. The light in the closet is bad but the document seems perfect. The photograph that she mailed to a post-office box two weeks earlier stares back at her.

"A waitress?"

"Yes," Elena says. She's running her fingers over the letters. *Nationality: United States of America.* "She works mornings, usually. You haven't met her. How long have you been here?"

"Oh, a few hours," Caleb says. "Missing you rather urgently, I might add. Are you naked yet?"

Later on in bed she opens her eyes to watch the movements of his shoulders above her, the side of his face, his neck. His eyes are clenched shut. She watches him intently. Trying to concentrate on Caleb only, trying not to pretend that Caleb is anyone else.

16.

It took nearly an hour to clear Customs in Rome. The cat's health records and proof of rabies vaccination were examined at great length, it seemed to her, by customs officials while the cat glared at everyone through the bars of the carrying case. When she was finally allowed to leave the airport Elena took a silver shuttle train to the central station, Termini, and found that there was some time to kill before the next train to Naples.

There were men posted in Termini, a few women too, police

officers with dark uniforms and sharp white leather belts. She tried to walk casually and to carry the cat on the side facing away from the police officers, deeply afraid and simultaneously cursing herself for paranoia. It was morning in Italy, three A.M. in New York. She had another thirteen hours before she failed to show up for her appointment with Broden, and she imagined that still more time would pass after that missed appointment before the machine of inquiry would begin to roll into motion, before agents arrived at her apartment, before her passport was tagged—perhaps hours, perhaps a day—but she was traveling on the Canadian passport, not the American; would that make a difference? She wasn't sure. Nothing made sense anymore. She was exhausted but wired, scattered, alive, her thoughts moving in circles like a flock of dark birds.

Elena carried the cat and the suitcase onto the first train to Napoli, and watched the sun rise over the Bay of Naples from the train. In a small lurching bathroom onboard the train she let the cat out of the carrier, opened the can of tuna she'd brought from Brooklyn and watched while the cat ate frantically and purred. Some hours later she found herself standing in front of the pink hotel on the island of Ischia, unsure what to do next. The restaurant seemed open, a waiter moving about setting the tables, but all at once she needed more time. She didn't know what to say to Anton; they had left it that she would call him once she had the cat.

Elena turned away from the hotel and continued on down the cobbled street, which curved and opened into a large piazza. There were three cafés here, their outdoor areas distinguished by different styles of umbrellas, and a harbor full of painted boats. She stood for a while in the sunlight by the water's edge, looking at the boats—they moved against each other in the harbor ripples, soft sounds of wood on wood—and at the far side of the harbor a sheer face of rock rose up to become a tree-crested hill, connected to Sant'Angelo by only the narrowest strip of beach. The weight of the cat was suddenly too much; she turned back to the piazza and made her way to the closest café area, to a table shaded by an immense white umbrella. Her heart was pounding and her head was light, the sleeplessness of the previous night falling down around her. She was dizzy. The waiter approached and said something. She stared at him blankly and smiled, a little panicked. He repeated himself in what sounded like halting German.

"He's asking if you'd like some water and a menu," a woman at the next table said conspiratorially.

"Oh," Elena said. "Thank you. Um, si. Per favore. And also a café latte. Please."

Two men were sitting together a few tables away. They had been talking intently over coffee but at the sound of her voice one of them looked over his shoulder, did a double-take, glanced at the cat, stood up slowly and came to sit at her table. His hair was longer than she remembered, and he looked like he'd been spending some time in the sun.

"Elena," he said.

Later Anton held her in the room as she lapsed into sleep, looking up at the blue of the ceiling. The cat climbed on top of him and fell asleep on his stomach.

Later still Anton went down to the pay phone in the piazza, found his phone card and dialed a number from memory.

"I wish you'd just let me call you from my cell phone," he said when Aria answered. "I think it'd be cheaper."

"We've talked about this," Aria said. "To what do I owe the pleasure?"

"I have the package. It came yesterday."

"Excellent. You haven't opened it?"

"No."

"Good. Don't. You'll think I'm paranoid, but I'm going to call you back in three minutes from the pay phone on my corner. Tell me the number of the pay phone on Ischia."

"You're not serious," he said, but she apparently was. He stood by the phone for a few minutes until it rang.

"Your contact will be in the restaurant at ten P.M. tonight," she said. There was static on the line.

"I still want twenty thousand dollars," he said.

"I'm paying you eighteen. The money should be in your checking account by now."

"Aria," he said, "what do these people do?"

"You want back in the business now?"

"I need to know," he said. "You said in the restaurant that night that they're import-exporters, but what do they ship?"

"What difference does it make?"

"I was lying awake thinking last night," said Anton. "It's too quiet here, and I've been by myself. I can't sleep sometimes. If they're going to blow up the subway system, Aria, I'll tell Sophie about Harvard myself."

"Really," she said. "If I told you they were smuggling bomb materials, you'd tell Sophie about Harvard?"

"I would tell everyone about everything," he said.

Aria was quiet for a moment.

"If you don't want to be my business partner anymore," she said, "the least you could do is stay out of my way."

"Explosives are a step too far for me, Aria. I take the subway to work."

The silence was so long this time that he thought he might have lost her. After a moment he said her name.

"I'm still here," she said.

"Then tell me what they're shipping."

"I suppose it can't do too much harm to tell you, at this point. You know how hard it is to immigrate to the United States," she said.

"Well, yeah, that was the foundation of our business plan. What does that have to do with . . . ?"

"They help people enter the country. That's all."

"I'm afraid I don't quite—"

"Fine. What they do, Anton, is they help lovely young ladies from ex-Soviet republics start new lives in the United States. Is that clear enough for you?"

"Trafficking," he said. "Aria, please tell me you're joking."

"We've always helped immigrants once they arrived in the country," Aria said. "Is it such a stretch to help them arrive in the first place?"

"How did you get involved with these people?"

"The importers? They're the people who brought in Natalka," she said.

"Who?" The name caught briefly on some outcropping of

memory, but tore off and left only hanging shreds. Anton knew a Natalka. He had met a Natalka. An impression of red lipstick, of cigarette smoke. A memory, or was it just that he'd met so many Russian girls who wore bright lipstick and smoked cigarettes that he heard a Russian-sounding name and his memory offered up a stock photograph? He couldn't quite see her face.

"Natalka," Aria said. "You sold her a passport."

And she snaps into focus. Natalka's in her twenties, but her hair is white. Not platinum blonde white, like the Norwegian girl whom he'd dated briefly in high school. Natalka's hair is white-silver, white-decades-early, cut in a slightly uneven bob. In a recess of memory she sits across from him at a table in the Russian Café, raises a cigarette to her lips and smiles. She inhales with the languid desperation of a girl who will very soon be out of cigarettes and is trying to make the current one last as long as possible. Ilieva comes to the table, and when she asks to take their order Natalka smiles at Ilieva's accent and speaks to her in Russian. Ilieva comes alive at the sound of her own language; they talk for a moment and then Ilieva brings a small black coffee, into which Natalka pours so much sugar that Anton half-expects the coffee to congeal into sludge. He realizes that she's trying to make her coffee as meal-like as possible, and his heart drops a little. He buys her a sandwich and watches her eat.

"How did you come here?" he asks her. It's a question he's been asking almost everyone lately. Their stories are seldom uninteresting. He has half-baked ideas about writing something someday—working title: *A Totally Fictional Guide to Immigrating*

Illegally to New York—and to this end he's been taking some notes in the evenings.

"In a box," Natalka says. "I came here in a box." She lights a new cigarette with shaking hands, and lifts it quickly to her lips. She's gone pale; her smile has vanished; he presses her no further. And it's only several years later, holding a pay-phone receiver to his face on the island of Ischia, that he understands what she meant.

"Shipping containers. It's shipping containers, isn't it?"

"Bright boy," said Aria.

"Do you know what happened to her?"

"To Natalka? No idea. She put me in touch with the people who imported her in exchange for a discount on her passport, and that was the last time I spoke with the girl."

"I don't think it's right."

"No," she said, "of course you don't."

"Aria, you know what happens to girls like that."

"All of them? Anton, grow up. It's a way of entering the country. What would their lives be like, in these places they come from? These radioactive little Ukrainian towns, Anton, these dark little villages without jobs, these fallen-down countries where everything's corrupt? It isn't that there's no industry in these places, it's that they *are* the industry in these places. They can be strippers and call girls there or strippers and call girls here, and here at least they stand a chance. When you think about it, Anton, do you disagree with me?"

"No," he said after a moment. "I don't disagree with you."

"Besides, you're helping a friend."

"You're many things to me, Aria, but *friend* isn't exactly—"

"No," she said, "I mean you know someone who's arriving on the next boat."

"What? Who?"

"Ilieva went back to Russia two months ago. Her grandmother was dying and she wanted to see her, but then she couldn't get a visa to come back to the United States and she got stuck over there. Think of everything she's done for us over the years."

"She's done a lot."

"So do something for her. Go downstairs to the restaurant tonight, and give the FedEx envelope to the men who are bringing her back to New York. The interaction's over in five minutes, and you're done. Ilieva's boat moves unmolested into the port at Red Hook. The shipping container is driven away and unloaded, and she's back in New York on Monday morning. You can come home tomorrow, make up a story for Sophie about a nervous breakdown or something, and life resumes its former course."

"And life resumes its former course," he said. He was watching Elena. After they'd made love in the hotel room and slept for a while she had wanted to go swimming, and he'd left her to change while he came down to call Aria. Now Elena was crossing the piazza barefoot, wrapped in a towel and headed for the beach. "Why does she have to come back in a shipping container? Couldn't you have just sent her a passport?"

"There wasn't time. She told me she was in some kind of trouble. She wanted to get out of Russia quickly and it was the best I could do on short notice."

"Aria, promise me you'll leave me alone after this."

"This is the last job I'll ever ask you to do."

Elena stepped out of sight along the beach.

"Do you remember that night," he said, "when we were fourteen and I cut your hair in your bedroom?"

She was quiet for a moment. "Why?"

"I don't know. I was just thinking about it today. There was a certain time in our lives when we didn't have to become so . . . well, so adversarial, for lack of a better word."

"I don't consider you an enemy," Aria said.

"What do you consider me, then?"

"Listen," she said, "I'd love to stay on the line and talk, but I have things to do. It's just business, Anton. Remember that."

"Just business," he repeated.

"Goodbye, Anton," Aria said, and she disconnected before he could respond. He hung up the phone and followed after Elena.

She was in the water. He watched from the beach while she swam out to the breakwater, pale and full of grace. She swam beautifully. She climbed up onto the breakwater rocks, turned and waved at him. That was the moment when he knew; he saw the slight swell of her body when she turned toward him, the weight of her breasts when she raised her arm, and he understood why she had come to him.

"Oh my God," he said, aloud. Elena turned her back on him to look out toward Capri, a small hopelessly erotic figure with his shorts clinging wet around her legs (she'd brought no swimsuit from New York), and the feeling of falling in love was literal: a fall, handholds breaking away in the descent. She swam back to him and he wrapped her in a towel. She sat curled up tight against his side, not quite shivering but not quite warm either, and he held her close with his arm around her shoulders. While she was out at sea he had taken off his wedding ring. Now he buried it with his free hand, pushing it as deep as it would go into the sand.

17.

Ilieva moving over the ocean:

It is dark, but dark isn't a strong enough word. It is ink, purest black, purest absence-of-light. The air is dense and still. There are fifteen girls in a small room squared out of the middle of a shipping container. They sit shoulder-to-shoulder with their backs to the walls, as they have since the ship left Lithuania. If you want to lie down you have to move to the center, but they can't all lie down at once, there isn't room, so they often fall asleep sitting upright and wake up disoriented with numb legs and painful backs. Time comes to a standstill. They long for fresh air. The ship is so enormous that they feel no movement of waves; there is only a faint steady vibration of engines that surrounds them in their metal room. Their imagined lives in America are heady and bright but when they drift off to sleep with their backs to the walls they have nightmares. It's sometimes hard to tell the difference between being awake and being asleep.

The captain lets them out at intervals, when it's safe, but the intervals are too rare and the claustrophobia is pure agony. There's a girl from Kiev who will do nothing but sit in the corner and weep. The others try to comfort her, but none of them happen to speak Ukrainian and the girl from Kiev speaks neither Russian nor English. Ilieva closes her eyes in the stifling darkness and thinks the same thought over and over again: I will never go home again. She draws her knees to her chest and tries to vanish into memories. The girl from Kiev sobs once beside her, and Ilieva takes her hand. The hand is hot and fevered, and the girl is shaking. She's sick and has been for days now. She won't eat or drink. She whispers something through her tears.

"I'm sorry," Ilieva murmurs, in Russian and then in English. "I don't speak Ukrainian. I don't understand."

But the girl keeps whispering, and after a while Ilieva does understand her, even though the girl's delirious, even though they have no language in common. *I miss my family. I am so afraid. It takes so much to come here, and I've left so much behind.*

18.

"Where did you come from?" David asked in the evening.

Elena had been on Ischia for less than six hours, and she'd slept for a while and gone swimming. Now she sat with Anton and David on the piazza, eating pizza, and Anton had his arm over her shoulders. Over the past few days the breeze from the sea had grown cooler. One or two other stragglers from the tourist season were inside the restaurant, but no one else sat outside. A waiter had come around and placed a candle on the table, and David seemed ill at ease and restless in the flickering light.

"New York," Elena said.

"I meant originally."

"A place you've never heard of," Elena said lightly. "A town up in northern Canada."

"I've been to Canada. I've been traveling since my wife died."

"Not this far north, trust me."

"I took the ice road to Tuktoyaktuk," David said.

"You've been to *Tuktoyaktuk*? You're serious?"

"I was trying to get as far north as I could," he said. "Which town are you from?"

"Inuvik."

"I spent a few days there."

"In Inuvik? Why?"

"I liked it there," David said. "I was there in the winter and the northern lights were beautiful. The sun never came up, but I liked living by moonlight."

"It's small," she said. "Everything's always either muddy or frozen. There's nothing up there."

"You're talking about a lack of employment?"

"No, I'm talking about a lack of everything. A loss of potential. It's hard to explain. There's just . . . it's a narrowing of possibilities," she said. "Even the smartest people end up doing nothing much with their lives, because there's nothing to do. It's not just Inuvik, it's everywhere in the world that's small and remote. Fewer things are possible in places like that."

"I think I understand. Do you believe in ghosts?" David asked her.

"David," Anton said, "the poor girl just got here." He couldn't seem to lift his hand from her thigh under the table.

"You know how much I hate small talk."

"I hate it too," Elena said. "It's small."

"Well said."

"I don't think I believe in ghosts," she said.

"Have you ever seen one?"

"No. If I had I'd believe in them." She was tired, and a short time later she excused herself and went to bed. David sipped at a glass of coffee and stared out at the harbor.

"I like her," David said, when his coffee was done.

"So do I." Anton was perfectly content for the first time in memory.

"What's she doing here?"

"I have no idea." Anton knew exactly what she was doing there, but he didn't want to talk about it. The night was too good; the stars were bright, the coffee was perfect, in a few hours the transaction would be over and he would be perfectly free. There was Elena and soon there would be a child, and he was already thinking about names. *Esme. Michael. Zooey. Lucille.*

"I have no idea what I'm doing here either." There was an edge to David's voice. "I'm thinking about leaving tomorrow."

"Why are you leaving?" Anton was surprised by the loneliness that overcame him at the thought of this.

"Look, you'll think I'm crazy." David was leaning back in his chair, looking up at the stars.

"I promise I won't."

"I felt this, well . . . this *prickling* at the back of my neck today. I know it sounds absurd, but I don't know how else to say it. I was sitting on that wall over there this morning, my back to the harbor, just reading the newspaper, and that feeling comes over me. I turn around, and no one's watching me. But the last time I felt like that, the last *two* times, I saw her a little while later."

"Saw who?"

"My wife," David said. "If I stay here now I'm just marking time on this little island, waiting for her to appear again. How long can you flee from a ghost? She's been dead for five years now. I don't know why I'm afraid of her. I mean Christ, it's *Evie*. It's just my wife. I love her. But I'm afraid of the dead."

"Who wouldn't be?" Anton was uneasy. He didn't know what to say.

"Ideally, no one. Ideally, we'd, I don't know, we'd *embrace* them, man, we'd just fucking *accept* the fact that they walk among us and get on with our lives. It shouldn't be that big a deal, you know? Things overlap sometimes."

"You think they walk . . ." Anton didn't want to hear the answer to the question, so he stopped midsentence and let it hang in the air.

"Aren't you listening? I *saw* her. Twice."

"After," Anton said carefully.

"Yes, fucking *after*. I went up north after she died, like I was telling Elena. There's nothing up there, but that was the point—I wanted to get away from everything, from the whole nightmare of the last few months. I think I was just trying to get as far away from the cancer ward as humanly possible, actually. I sold all my stuff, I broke the lease on my apartment and headed north. The landscape up there was so beautiful, I can't even describe it. There was almost no daylight, just darkness and then twilight, and the moon was brighter than I'd ever seen. I could see the northern lights out the window of my hotel room. I stayed in Inuvik for a while, then I took the ice road up to Tuktoyaktuk and rented a snowmobile one day. I rode a bit out of town. It's silent up there, but the snowmobile was loud, and I just wanted to be there in the silence for a minute. So I stopped the snowmobile, and I felt like someone was watching me, so I turned around and there she was—" David gestured, and in the movement of his hand Anton almost saw her. "She was standing on top of the snow in her wedding dress. She was only there for an instant, just a flash, but she smiled at me and I could smell the vanilla perfume she used to wear."

"And then again?"

"Yes, again. I got out of the arctic as fast as I could, headed down to Sault Ste. Marie for a while, and then I went to Europe and I saw her in the crowd in Athens. And you're thinking, *Right, you saw her in the crowd in Athens, whatever.* You can see *anyone* in a crowd in Athens. There's too many fucking people there, that's the problem with the place, and everyone on earth sort of looks like someone else from the back. But I was walking, and I saw a black woman wearing a long blue dress far up ahead. My wife was from Kenya, and her wedding dress was blue. This woman in the crowd was moving in and out of view. I started following her, but I couldn't get close. And just when I'm thinking, *Come on, get a grip, she's been dead for years now,* Evie turned around and *smiled* at me. It was just like we'd been temporarily separated and she was waiting for me to catch up."

The implications of this caught Anton with a sudden chill.

"Ghost stories," he said weakly, and made an attempt at a lighthearted laugh.

"The thing is," David said, "I'm not unafraid, I keep hoping I'll stop seeing her and then, I don't know, get some kind of peace in the world—but if she left, I mean really left, if I didn't think she was still somewhere close by, I think I'd miss her even more. So there's no way out of this one, is there."

"You ever see her when you were with someone else?"

"No. I only see her when I'm alone."

"Then we'll sit out here for a while. The other night," Anton said, "on the dock, you said that for a certain sum of money you might be willing to do something for me."

"Make me an offer," David said. "God knows I could use some traveling money."

"Would you do it for five hundred euros?"

"You'd pay me five hundred euros to give an envelope to someone?"

"I don't know these people. It might be dangerous, they might—"

"It's a deal," David said. "I'll be fine."

When the restaurant had closed they sat on a low stone wall by the harbor, looking at the boats. The sense of impending freedom was exhilarating. Earlier in the day Anton had called his old bank in New York and had the eighteen thousand dollars from Aria wired into a local checking account where he'd already moved the bulk of his savings. Now he sat by the harbor with David in the half-light, thinking of a bright new life that would start tomorrow, thinking of getting a job somewhere and living with Elena and the child in Sant'Angelo.

"What time is it?" David asked. Anton felt his tension in the air.

"A little after nine. She won't appear if I'm with you, will she?"

"No," David said, "she won't."

"Then I'll wait with you," Anton said. "I'll wait with you till it's time."

They walked out past the harbor and along the narrow strip of beach that tethered Ischia proper to its satellite, the islet that rose out of the water on the other side of the harbor. It was very nearly its own island and no one lived there. A few hotels lined the edge of the islet that faced the harbor, but sheer rock rose up behind them. A path curved around the hill to the right. They started up the hillside, but the path was hard and steep. After a little while they turned and leaned on a bank of sand and soapstone, looking back at the village. On the other side of the harbor Sant'Angelo was a wall of lights, houses terraced up the hillside. Anton could see the hotel from here, on the edge of the lights near the piazza.

"What was she like?" Anton asked.

"Evie? It's a funny thing, you know. People die, you remember them as angels. It gets harder and harder to remember what was real. She wasn't an angel . . . I mean, look, I was dealing coke and she was handling the money. So she wasn't necessarily *good*, you know, in any kind of an absolute law-abiding non-drug-dealing sense of the word, but she was good to me. We were good to each other."

"All that matters, I guess."

"I think so, personally. What about your wife?"

"My wife? I don't know. My wife canceled our wedding twice. My wife was already planning to leave me and move to San Francisco when we left New York on our honeymoon. We disappointed each other."

"You don't love her?"

"I do. I did. But not enough. I don't know why either of us went through with it. Look—"

A single light had blinked on in the restaurant of their hotel, a weak shine over the water. It was hard to tell at this distance, but through the far-off windows he thought he saw figures moving. Four people, setting up chairs at a table.

"We have to go back," Anton said. "Listen, you go first. Try not to let them hear you. If they hear you, tell them your name's Anton Waker and that you'll bring the package down in a few minutes. I'll be four minutes behind you. We meet in your room."

David nodded silently and moved away from him down the path, and Anton felt a sudden guilt. He was sending David off alone, the man's ghost wife could be smiling in the air around any given corner, and then he remembered that he didn't believe in ghosts and felt like an idiot. He spent a few minutes after that staring at his watch while David crossed the length of beach and disappeared into the shadows at the edge of the piazza. It wasn't quite four minutes, but Anton couldn't take it anymore and followed him.

There was no one on the beach. The boats bobbed quietly against the piers, soft sounds of waves calmed by the breakwaters. The piazza was deserted. The front door of the hotel was unlocked, as always. Anton slipped in almost silently, heard the soft murmur of voices from the restaurant. A faint impression of light down the corridor. He looked up the stairs and saw David crouched low at the top of the staircase. David smiled and gave him a silent thumbs-up: he had crept in undetected. Anton let go of the door, too soon—it slipped out of his hand and closed loudly, and the murmur of voices stopped. He was silent. The men in the restaurant were silent. David was silent; he had clenched his hands together white-knuckled and he was glaring at Anton. Anton closed his eyes and thought of praying, but he'd never been to church and had nothing to pray to and the world felt less than holy at that moment.

"Hello?" someone called out, in English. Anton signaled to

David—*stay*—and walked down the darkened corridor that separated the foyer from the restaurant.

A single light was on over one of the tables by the window. Otherwise the restaurant was dark, upside-down chairs on the tables casting shadows on the walls. Four men sat watching him. They were in their thirties, of indeterminate national origin, well dressed. They gazed blandly at him, except for the man sitting to Anton's right, who smiled and gestured at an empty chair.

"Please," he said, "join us."

A bottle of wine stood half-consumed on the table. One of the men was casually folding a map and putting it away as Anton sat down. Another was shuffling papers into a neat little pile and turning them over blank side up.

"What brings you to the island of Ischia, my friend?" The man's accent was British with Eastern European undertones.

"I'm writing a guidebook," Anton said. He cursed himself for stupidity as he said this, but it occurred to him that Aria didn't know about the guidebook so perhaps all wasn't lost after all, maybe the slip wasn't ruinous, maybe they'd still believe he was David Grissom and that David Grissom was he.

"A guide to Ischia in the off-season?"

"To the world in the off-season."

They were quiet for a moment, then one of them laughed and raised his wineglass. "To the world in the off-season," he repeated. "Cheers." The others raised their glasses too. "Some wine?"

"Thank you."

One of the men poured him a glass of wine. A reaction seemed to be expected, so Anton sipped at it and nodded appreciatively. He was aware that he appeared perfectly calm—an old gift, extraordinarily useful in his first career—but his nerves were spun glass. The wine tasted like nothing. It was a dull shock that this moment had actually come; all these strained lost weeks of waiting for the transaction, and the transaction was at last about to occur.

"The wine's excellent," he said. "Thank you."

"Anton Waker, I presume," the man with the British accent said.

"Who? Oh, no, actually, I'm David Grissom. I'm afraid you've mistaken me—" It seemed like the perfect time to make his escape; he smiled apologetically and stood up to leave, but someone grasped his arm.

"Sit, sit, you think we'd renege on our hospitality so quickly? Come now, a small misunderstanding, sit with us a moment anyway. It's a beautiful evening, and as you say, the wine is excellent. Alberto," said the man with the British accent. "Ali for short. This is Claro, Mario, Paul."

Claro said something in another language and the others smiled. Anton smiled too, trying to look as politely clueless as possible and wondering what their real names were. He was acutely aware of his heartbeat. "And you might be wondering," Ali said, "why Ischia on a Friday night in October?"

"Why Ischia," Mario repeated. His accent was, if not exactly British, clipped in a manner suggestive of an expensive British education.

"Because I like peace and quiet," Ali said.

"Hard to find anywhere quieter than a tourist destination in the off-season," Anton said.

"A man after my own heart. Every tourist destination goes quiet in the winter, but not many places go as quiet as this. There are no cars. There are no tourists. The shops are boarded up; the market hardly opens. And my new favorite restaurateur is kind enough to extend his hospitality." He raised his glass again. "To Gennaro," he said. The others repeated him, except for Paul, who only smiled. "You're staying here at the hotel, Mr. Grissom?"

"I am."

"You wouldn't know a man by the name of Anton Waker, would you? A fellow guest?"

"Anton Waker," Anton repeated. His fear had faded. He felt exactly as he had when he was selling Social Security cards in New York—that perfect serenity, the steadiness that overcame him. He was like a fish slipping back into water, like a bird rising back into the air. He sipped his wine and swirled it in the glass, considering. "The name's familiar. Yes, actually—" He stilled the glass but the wine continued moving for a moment—"I do know the man you mean. Brown hair, medium build? He's in the room next to mine upstairs."

"You know him well?"

"Waker? No, I barely know him at all. We've said hello once or twice."

"Did he mention when he was checking out?"

And the fear crashed down upon him again. "I only know him to say hello in the hallway," he said. "We've never really talked." His legs trembled a little under the table, but his hands were still.

Ali nodded. The others looked at him steadily. Anton feigned a yawn.

"Forgive me," he said, "it's been a long day. If you'll excuse me, I believe I'll retire for the evening. Thank you again for the wine."

"Don't mention it," Claro said. "Would you ask Waker to come downstairs?"

"I will. Goodnight." Anton heard them speaking in some other language as he moved away along the corridor and neared the foot of the stairs. He knew it wasn't Italian, but he couldn't otherwise identify it. It wasn't quite Russian. David was standing at the top of the stairs; Anton motioned him to be still. He walked up the stairs and moved past David, knocked loudly on the door of David's empty room, opened and closed the door, and then took off his shoes and tiptoed in his socks back to where David stood.

"Listen," Anton whispered, "I think this is different from what I thought it was."

"What do you mean?"

"I think it's more dangerous than I thought."

David shrugged. "I'll be fine," he whispered. "Although I wish I had a gun."

"What?"

"I always carried one when I was dealing coke. Never fired it, I just liked to have it in my pocket. Go get the package."

Anton opened the door to his room and closed it behind him. Elena had dozed off with the bedside lamp on, and she was improbably lovely in the yellow light. Jim was curled up close against her side. She awoke with a start and sat up blinking.

"What time is it?"

"Ten fifteen. Shh. Go back to sleep."

But she was wide-awake now, watching him. He was on his hands and knees, fumbling under the wardrobe. His fingers touched the edge of the FedEx envelope.

"What are you doing?" she asked in a stage whisper. "What's going on?"

"It's happening," Anton murmured. He pressed a finger to his lips.

"That transaction you were telling me about?"

"I don't want them to hear your voice. Will you lock the door behind me and turn out the light?"

She nodded and he slipped back out into the hall. The door locked behind him with a sharp *click*; Anton winced at the sound and the light under the door blinked out. David stood motionless at the top of the stairs.

"Just go down there and say you're Anton Waker. When they ask, you have a package for them."

"Anton Waker." David's eyes were alight. Almost any adventure is better than limbo. "You're seriously paying me five hundred euros for this?"

"When this is over," Anton said, "I just want a different life. It's worth five hundred euros to me."

"Fair enough."

"They might bring up my cousin," Anton said softly. "Her name's Aria. Aria Waker. She's the one who's orchestrating this thing."

"Aria Waker," David whispered. "I'll remember."

Anton opened his wallet, counted out five one-hundred-euro bills and gave them to David, who fanned them out to examine them and smiled before he stuffed them in his pocket. Anton gave David the FedEx envelope with the passports and David started down the stairs.

"Wait," Anton whispered. He whispered into the keyhole, "Elena, open up," and she unlocked the door instantly. He slipped back into the room and removed the singer's gun from the top dresser drawer. Elena drew in her breath when she saw it glint in the moonlight—he ignored her—and back out in the hallway he pressed the gun into David's hand. "Here," he said. "Just don't fire it, okay?"

"Don't worry, I won't," David whispered. "Thank you." He was putting the gun in the pocket of his sweatshirt. "Are these guys that dangerous?"

"I assume so, frankly."

"Hey," David said, "at least you're honest."

"Thank you. I'm trying."

David Grissom descended the stairs.

At the top of the staircase there was nothing to do but wait. In the locked room behind him Elena was silent. He heard Jim's movements—a jump from the bed to the dresser and then from the dresser to the floor, soft thudding landings—and willed the cat to be still. He heard the voices down in the restaurant, indistinct from here, the murmured greetings—he heard his own name—and then a period of conversation that he couldn't quite make out. He crouched low in the shadows, straining to hear. Time was passing very slowly. There was time to take in every detail around him: the shadows of the banisters, the gritty texture of the hallway linoleum under his hand. It began to seem that it was taking too long. He glanced at his watch and fifteen minutes had passed. And then chairs scraping back, and a sound—something small and hard had fallen to the floor. And then, quite clearly, "You came armed, Mr. Waker?"—but as hard as he tried, he could understand nothing else, until finally, ". . . a walk on the beach?" and he heard David's voice, nervous now— "At night?"

The voices were becoming clearer; the group was moving toward the foot of the stairs, toward the door. There were footsteps, a muted "No please—after you," the door of the hotel opened and closed. The building was silent. Anton knocked softly on the door to his own room, where Elena was waiting.

"What's happening?" she whispered.

"They took him outside." Anton closed the door behind him. The moonlight through the sliding glass doors was brilliant. He could see Elena clearly but he couldn't meet her eyes. She sat cross-legged on the bed, watching him. Anton went to the balcony door and waited with his forehead almost against the glass, until the men came into view on the strip of beach that connected Ischia to the islet. As silently as possible Anton slid open the glass door a few inches, and the room was filled with the sounds of ocean and wind. The men were walking in a tight group, dark receding figures on the sand, and he couldn't tell which one was David. On the other end of the beach they stopped. There seemed to be some discussion; after a moment they started up the path that curved around the edge of the hill, dim shadows in the moonlight until they disappeared from sight. Anton waited.

Inside the room they were perfectly still. Jim was sitting on the bedside table now, regarding him seriously with one shining eye. Elena sat on the bed and Anton stood by the sliding glass door straining to catch some glimpse of movement in the darkness of the islet. He kept glancing at the bedside clock. Five minutes passed, then ten. Long silence and then a sharp bright sound, a ripple over the surface of the night gone so fast that he thought at first he might have imagined it—If I turn and Elena's face registers nothing, then I *did* imagine it and the gun didn't really go off— but when he looked over his shoulder Elena had pressed the palm of her hand to her mouth and there were tears on her face. The sound was repeated once, twice. Three bullets; she was shaking; she was going to scream.

"Don't make a sound," he said.

Elena stared at him for a moment and then went into the

bathroom. The light flicked on under the door and he heard water running. He closed the sliding glass door but left the wooden shutters open a few inches, watching through the crack.

Some time passed before he saw them again. A group of figures, four now instead of five, making their way over the hillside. They came back over the strip of beach toward the pink hotel and he stopped breathing when they came close to the building, but no one entered. There were soft voices and footsteps on the cobblestones outside the hotel door. Someone laughed. He stood frozen by the door of the room, but he could hear almost nothing—an impression of voices, of departing footsteps—and a long time later a car started up on the road beyond the edge of Sant'Angelo and receded.

19.

In an apartment on the bright sharp edge of New York, glass tower, Aria sat alone on a white leather sofa. She'd paid extra for noise-blocking windowpanes, and the silence in the apartment was all but absolute. A telephone lay on a marble table near her knees. She had been sitting there for an hour when it began to ring; the sound made her jump; she glanced at her watch and picked up the phone to look at the call display, which said ITALY and nothing else.

"It's done," Ali said.

"Thank you. We'll speak again soon."

The line went dead. Aria set the receiver down on the glass coffee table and sank back into the sofa. The room was large and bleached of color; white walls, white carpet, white leather, white phone. All of this was by her own design and usually the absence of color soothed her, but at this moment it was making her feel like a ghost. She closed her eyes again and realized that her hands were shaking. She was dizzy. After a long time she stood up and walked unsteadily to the bedroom, took her suitcase down from the closet shelf. She packed quickly, in a daze. She put on her coat and left the apartment.

20.

Outside in the street Aria hailed a taxi. From a pay phone at La-Guardia Airport she called Anton's parents' apartment.

Anton's father answered.

"Sam," she said.

"Aria?"

"I'm going away," Aria said. "I'm leaving tonight, and I'll be gone for a while. You haven't heard from me, okay?"

"Well, okay. Is something the matter?"

"Sam, I'm sorry. I'm just—I'm really sorry."

"Has something happened?"

"Perhaps you'd better sit down."

"Wait." He was on a cordless phone. His wife was lost in a book in the living room. He carried the phone past her and closed the apartment door behind him, walked out through the vast dim warehouse to the loading dock and closed that door behind him too. Summer had finally broken; it was cold outside and he wasn't wearing a jacket. He stood on the loading dock with his back to the wall. "Okay," he said quietly. "Tell me what you know."

"Listen," and her voice was choked, she didn't sound like herself. It occurred to him as she began to talk, in a small part of his mind that remained rational and detached against the unspeakable thing she was explaining to him, that he had never known her to cry before. Even when she was eleven, when her mother was deported on a clear March afternoon. Strange child.

"I don't understand," he said after a moment. Her building was visible somewhere across the river in the mass of bright towers around the lost World Trade Center. She had pointed it out to him once, but he wasn't sure now which one it was. Manhattan was as distant as another galaxy tonight, an indifferent constellation of tower lights.

"Sam, there was an accident." And she began to explain it all over again, a complicated story about a deal gone wrong, a misunderstanding, a body that couldn't be recovered without bringing both the FBI and the mob down upon them, but he was having a hard time listening or a hard time understanding, he wasn't sure which. He held the phone to his face and stared at the river.

When the phone call was over he went back into the store and locked the loading-dock doors behind him. The door to the apartment was a shadow at the back of the vast room, and he couldn't bring himself to pass through it again. On the other side of the door his wife sat reading. She would look up when he came in; he would kneel down beside her and begin to speak. He couldn't do it yet. He turned on the lights over the back corner of the warehouse, where two figureheads he'd recently started restoring stood waiting for paint. Sam stood looking at them for a while. They were beautiful to him, and in a distant way he understood that it was important to stay busy for a little while, to keep his hands occupied even though they were shaking. From a supply cupboard in the back he fetched his paint and his chisels. He thought there might be a way of surviving Aria's news.

One was saved from the sea near Gibraltor. She depicted a strong-faced woman arcing forward, her arms disappearing into the folds of her gown and her gown disappearing into the folds of carved waves. One was rescued from a shipwreck off the Cape of Good Hope, barnacles adhering like stars in her hair. In her arms she cradled a fish. Both figureheads were women, but this was by no means a given. His mind wandered over other figureheads he'd read about as he worked. Some took the form of dragons, of lions, of princes and kings. The clipper-ship *Styx* had a figure of the devil. All the Corsair's ships set out with a pegasus, and the nineteenth-century ship *Flying Cloud* bore an angel with a trumpet. During the reign of Henry VIII, the preferred British figurehead was the lion. The British privateer *The Terrible* had a skeleton at the helm. The French ship *Revenant* set sail with a corpse.

After a long time he caught himself staring blankly at the figurehead, unmoving, and he realized that his hands were shaking again. He glanced at his watch; it was eleven P.M. and the light under the apartment door had gone out. His wife was in bed. He had survived the first few hours. He blinked and leaned in close to his work. He had been removing the hard pale rings of ancient barnacles from the carved hair of the figurehead from the Cape of Good Hope. Delicate work with a blade-thin chisel. She had drifted to the bottom of the ocean in a cloud of silk and oranges, while a storm tore the surface of the sea far above. Pieces of the merchant ship had descended around her, ribbons of silk unfurling from the broken holds. Some men had drifted downward with the broken ship, he'd been told, but others rose up toward air with the oranges, climbing up onto the rocks and clinging there until the storm had passed, plucking floating oranges from the sea around them and setting off waterlogged for the nearest town. After a while he set down his chisel and began repainting the fish the figurehead held. He gave its scales a shimmering blue-green cast, and painted the inside of its gasping mouth a pink the shade of guavas.

At midnight Samuel Waker stopped painting and went outside to look at the river, at Manhattan shining on the other side. The East River moved over the bedrock riddled with the tunnels of deep underground trains and connected with the Hudson, flowing southeast past the Statue of Liberty, out of New York Harbor and out into the Atlantic. These night seas that circle countries: the Atlantic becomes the Mediterranean at the Strait of Gibraltar, and beyond the island of Sardinia the Mediterreanean becomes the Tyrrhenian Sea. On a Tyrrhenian island Anton sat on his hotel balcony, unblinking. In the room behind him Elena lay motionless, far from sleep. David Grissom had been dead for less than six hours. The moon was a crescent in a clear dark sky.

Anton closed his eyes. Far out over the surface of the Atlantic Ocean, a container ship was moving away from him.

part

III

21.

When Broden left Waker Architectural Salvage she drove deeper into Brooklyn, east down Graham Avenue into a neighborhood that was bleaker, less expensive, where even now in this era of glass-tower condominiums all the windows still had bars. On the block where Elena had lived an organic grocery store had sprung up and also a hipster clothing boutique, asymmetrical dresses hanging bright between a run-down bodega and a hardware store. Broden parked by the boutique and walked down the block to Elena's building, rang twice, but no one was home. She got back in the car and took an aspirin—she felt the beginnings of a headache—and turned left on Montrose Avenue. There was the subway, and a small bakery beside it. She parked and bought a couple of croissants before she drove back toward Manhattan. She couldn't stop thinking about the dead girl in the shipping container, about the girl's parents waiting for news of their child in some distant land. She called her daughter from the car, but it was getting late and Tova was already in the bath.

"You haven't seen her yet today," her husband said.

"I know," Broden said. "I'm trying to get home before bedtime."

She took a detour in order to pass in front of Anton's parents' store again. Anton's mother was still on the loading dock, staring out at the river with no expression on her face. Anton's father was outside now, kneeling beside her with his hand on her back, speaking to her intently. Broden slowed down, but neither of them looked at the car as she passed. At the end of the block she sped up again and passed over the bridge to the spired city.

Broden was tired. There was no case to speak of at this point and no one involved was talking and the whole mess was going nowhere, but back at the office she called Anton's wife in San Francisco. She had tried before and left unreturned messages. This time Sophie answered the phone and said that she'd left Anton in Europe and as far as she knew he was still there, and could Broden please pass on the message that it would be nice if Anton would come back and sign the annulment papers one of these days. Broden asked if she could tell her anything about Elena James. Sophie went silent, and then said that Elena James had stolen Anton's cat and that was the last time she'd seen her. Broden asked her what she was talking about and Sophie got angry, said she didn't feel like getting into it and she knew nothing that she hadn't already told her and actually she'd really like to just be left alone if Broden wouldn't mind.

There was a tape that Broden had pulled out earlier in the day. The first tape Elena had ever given her, a few months before she disappeared. After Broden hung up the phone she put on her headphones and pressed play on the machine. The recording begins with a rustling sound—Elena has reached into her bag to activate the machine—and they speak for a moment about points of origin and distant towns.

Anton: *"Yellowknife?"*

"A small northern city. Then you fly from Yellowknife to Inuvik."

"How long does all of this take?"

"A long time."

"How long?"

"Twenty-four hours. Sometimes longer in winter."

"How much longer?"

"Days. The northern airports close sometimes when the weather's bad."

"A distant northern land. How long since you've been back there?"

"I haven't."

"Haven't what?"

"Haven't been back."

There was a light commotion here, a rustling sound on the tape; Elena was reaching into her purse, fumbling around. A click and then the tape went dead. She told Broden at the time that she'd reached into her purse to get a lozenge and turned the device off by accident, and that the lozenge was because her throat was dry and that was why her voice sounded funny.

Broden took off her headphones, stood up and stretched. It was seven thirty. In other offices she heard people working, a soft murmur of activity and computer keyboards, but when she left her office to put the tape away all of the other doors were closed. Back in her office she looked up a map of the Northwest Territories—there was Inuvik, a tiny red dot on the northern edge of the world—and she thought about involving the Canadian police, placing a call to the RCMP detachment at Inuvik, but there was no real reason to believe Elena was there. The distance between Inuvik and New York was almost dazzling in its extremity.

Broden stood by the window for a moment, thinking of Sophie's odd comment about Elena taking a cat, before she returned to her desk to make a phone call. The phone rang four times in Elena's old apartment before Caleb picked up. They'd had a few tense conversations early on and Caleb was no more endearing this evening than he had been previously; the announcement of Broden's name was greeted with an audible sigh.

"I told you," Caleb said, "I don't know anything."

"Tell me about the cat." To Broden's utter amazement there was silence at the end of the line, so she decided that perhaps Sophie wasn't insane after all and pressed further. "Whose cat was it?"

"She said it belonged to her ex-boss."

"Can you describe it?"

"What? The cat? I only saw it for a minute. Okay, it was orange. It only had one eye."

"She was going to Italy to be with him," Broden said, testing him.

"Look," Caleb said, "she had every right."

"Did she?"

"Now you know as much as I do. Anyway, it's none of your business." He hung up the phone and Broden didn't call him back.

The traffic was heavy between Broden's office and her apartment; she crept home slowly with classical music playing on the radio. Broden arrived home a few minutes too late to kiss her daughter goodnight. Tova had gone to sleep with a blue barrette in her hair. She stirred when Broden gently removed it, but didn't wake. Broden put the barrette in her jacket pocket. She stood in the bedroom doorway for a long time watching Tova sleep.

22.

Anton tried to find David's family and got nowhere. Two days after the gunshots he left Elena alone on the balcony in the morning— she was staring at the sea, at the horizon, at the cat, at everything except him—and went out into the hallway. No one else was at the hotel so late in the season and Gennaro's presence was inter- mittent, but he still looked around before he slipped into David's room. The room was unlocked. He closed and locked the door behind him, stood blinking for a moment in the warm dim light. The curtains were drawn, the balcony doors closed.

The lamp on the bedside table was on, shining down on a single yellowing lime. An easel was set up by the dresser. When Anton opened the balcony shutters and the room flooded with sunlight he saw that the easel held a small canvas, about ten by ten inches, with an unfinished painting of a lime. Odd to see the same lime, on the same bedside table before the same robin's-egg wall, as it had existed two or three days earlier; on the canvas it was alive and gleaming, almost photo-real, a brilliant green. Short brushstrokes radiated outward around it; the white of the table, the blue of the walls. Strange, he thought, to rent a room overlooking the Tyrrhenian Sea and then close the shutters and paint a piece of fruit on a table. There were four or five canvases stacked against the wall, paintings of limes in waxy perfect detail.

Anton moved the contents of David's room into his in stages. First the stack of lime paintings and then the clothes, stuffed into a backpack that he found under the bed. The dresser was empty. He threw out the paltry contents of the bathroom—a toothbrush, toothpaste, a razor, a bar of soap—and on his final pass through the room he saw the last painting. It was small and square, perhaps eight inches by eight inches, propped up on top of the dresser. A portrait of a white man and a black woman. The man had dark hair and brown eyes—it was a shock to recognize David—and in the painting he held the woman close. She was startlingly beautiful, with very high cheekbones and enormous brown eyes, and she wore a pale blue dress of some floaty fabric that exposed her collarbones. There was something about the way the air around her was painted; Anton leaned in closer. They were standing together against a brick wall, and there was the faintest disturbance in the bricks, the slightest electrical charge, a haze, and then he understood: Evie had a halo around her. An opening line from a novel he'd once read came back to him unbidden—*We are not alone, this side of death*—and he took the painting and left the room very quickly, leaving the door ajar. He locked the door of his own room behind him.

When he went through the backpack he found almost nothing. Worn clothing, a plastic bag with two new-looking paintbrushes, an unmarked house key on a plain metal ring. An address book. Anton took the address book with him when he left the hotel, sat down on a low wall by the harbor and turned on his cell phone. Then he remembered that he was supposed to be dead, so he turned it off again and dropped it discreetly into the water. It landed with a little splash and flashed silver for a moment like a sinking fish. He turned back to the piazza and went to the pay phone, where he opened the address book and flipped through page after empty page. It wasn't that the book was new; its cover was worn, the edges blunted. It was just that in all the years David had carried it with him he'd only seen fit to write down nine telephone numbers, and six of these were 1-800 numbers for various airlines. The others were Margaret (no last name), the Northern Lights Hotel in Inuvik, and the Gallerie Montaigne in Duluth. He called Margaret first.

"Hello," he said, when a female voice answered. "Are you Margaret?"

"I used to be."

"You used to be?"

"I changed my name to Margot when I left Sault Ste. Marie," she said.

"Okay. Margot, do you know a man named David Grissom?"

She was quiet.

"I have his address book," Anton said. "Yours was the only name in it. I thought—"

"Who are you? Why do you have his address book?"

"Listen," Anton said, "there's something . . . look, I don't—"

"Oh God," she said. "Something's happened to him."

Hard not to look across the harbor at the islet, its sheer side rising up behind a single row of bright-painted shops and hotels; hard not to imagine what might lie on the other side of that hill, shallow-buried or maybe lost to the sea, but Anton forced himself to turn away from the thought.

"There was an accident," Anton said. He looked down at the red pay-phone buttons and felt the islet at his back.

"Is he . . . ?"

"Yes," he said quietly, and on the other end of the line she began to weep. Anton closed his eyes for a moment.

"He has no family," she said.

"None?"

"Well, there's a sister," she said. "Somewhere in India, or maybe it was Bangladesh. She belongs to a cult or travels with a guru or does yoga or something. I don't think they ever spoke."

"His parents?"

"His mother ran off when he was a little kid. He hasn't seen her since he was three or four. His father's dead."

"Are there friends? Cousins? Anyone?"

"We were living in a commune together for a while," she said, "so there were always a lot of people around, but no one—he was never—he wasn't close with anyone."

"No one except you."

"No one except me. He'd just been drifting for years, since his wife died. He came down to Sault Ste. Marie for a few months after he'd been up in the arctic, then he said he was going to Europe and I never saw him again. You said I'm the only name in his address book?"

"The only one."

"I should go," she said. "Thank you for telling me. At least maybe he's with her now, you know?"

"With who?" he asked, but she'd already hung up. He realized what she'd meant a second later. He had that same ground-falling-from-under-him sensation that had overcome him when he'd looked at the painting earlier and had to collect himself. He called the Northern Lights Hotel in Inuvik, but the woman who answered told him that they kept no records. He asked if she remembered a David Grissom, but realized how silly the question was as he spoke. It had been years since David had traveled through the far north. The woman had only been working there for a month, she said. She was kind and Anton half-wanted to stay on the phone longer. He said goodbye and called the Gallerie Montaigne in Duluth, but the number had been disconnected.

Anton put David's address book in his pocket, bought a panino and a latte at the fishermen's café and brought them up to the room. He opened the balcony door and stepped around Jim—the balcony was just large enough to accommodate two deck chairs and a fully extended cat—and kissed Elena on the forehead. She looked up at him and almost managed a smile but her eyes were glassy.

"You should eat something," he said.

"I'm not really hungry."

"Yeah, but that's what you said yesterday." He found a place to sit with his back to the sea, his spine pressed against the railing and Jim close against his leg. He tore off a small piece of sandwich.

"I'm really not—"

"Just this one little piece."

"Okay." She ate slowly, watching the horizon.

"I called a girl he knew. From his address book. She says he has no family."

"None?"

"Almost none. An estranged sister somewhere in Asia. Here. Another piece."

"I'm—"

"One more bite."

"Fine." Her face was pale and she'd been crying. She was all but translucent in the sunlight. "But what are you going to do?"

"I think I should wait here," Anton said.

"For what?"

"Maybe his sister will come looking for him someday. Look, I don't know what to do. But staying here is the only thing I can think of that seems even halfway honorable."

"Maybe the police will come looking for you."

"It's possible," he said. "Have I told you how sorry I am to have gotten you involved in this mess?"

"A dozen times."

"Whatever you decide to do, Elena . . ."

"Is it a kind of penance?" Her voice was flat.

"Is what a kind of penance?"

"Waiting here at the scene of the crime."

"Maybe. Yes."

"You might wait here forever. It's possible that no one will ever come looking for him."

"I know," he said.

She said she wanted to go and he gave her ten thousand dollars. She insisted it was too much but he insisted she take it. He saw her off at the ferry. Afterward he took the bus back to Sant'Angelo. He walked past the hotel and through the piazza, along the narrow sand beach to the islet, past the strip of hotels on the far shore.

The path that David had walked on his last night on earth curved up around the far side of the islet, but at a certain point it faded out into brush and loose rocks. Anton came upon a broad sloping ledge and found that he could go no further. The cliff rose above him, and it was a sheer drop down to the water below. He looked for footprints, but it had rained twice since the last time he'd seen David. He looked down at the sea, but there was nothing on the rocks and the current seemed rapid. A seagull landed on the surface of the water and was carried quickly away from the shore.

He'd half-hoped for a ghost. He wanted to turn and see David somewhere nearby, smiling at him perhaps, telling him that it was all right, but David's absence was absolute. The ledge was empty, the day clear and bright, the sea glittering below. Anton was perfectly alone except for the seagulls. Far off in the distance, the white triangle of a sailboat moved over the water.

The pleasing rhythms of evening: pouring cat food into the porcelain bowl, cold water splashing over Anton's wrists as he filled another bowl with water in the sink. Jim brushed against his leg and then settled down over the water bowl, lapping steadily. Anton crouched down to scratch behind his ears, and the cat purred without looking up.

In the days after Elena left, he settled into a quiet routine. Once or twice a week he took the bus to a larger town to buy groceries and cat food. He went to Naples every so often and bought three or four English-language novels, but they were expensive and he was always running out between trips. Most nights he studied Italian from a Berlitz textbook, alone in his room with the cat asleep on his desk. After a few months he understood the waiters in the fishermen's café (the last café still open in all of the shuttered-for-the-season village), but the language of the fishermen remained inscrutable. It was a while before someone told him they were speaking Neapolitan, which in his understanding wasn't quite Italian but wasn't quite not Italian either. After a while his own Italian was good enough to get a menial job in an enormous hotel two towns over, one of the few places that stayed open year-round. He was a dishwasher in the restaurant and then they made him a porter.

Anton wore a bright uniform and carried suitcases and came home exhausted at the end of the day, made good tips sometimes from the English-speaking tourists. He worked hard and spent time with the cat and studied Italian in his room at night, reread the books in his slowly growing library, tried not to think too much about anyone he loved.

At first he kept Jim indoors, but the cat gazed at the seagulls with such undisguised longing and the improvised litter box on the balcony was becoming a problem, so Anton took Jim out on the beach one evening. Jim moved close to the sand at first, hissing at rocks and trying to look everywhere at once, but then he gradually relaxed enough to begin pouncing on seashells.

He took Jim down to the water early in the morning and then again late at night, when everyone was sleeping and the ocean was his. The cat was orange in daylight, pale in the moonlight. He stalked Anton's shadow and dug for things in the sand. Anton would sit on a rock and watch him or look at the water. When Anton stood up and began to walk along the shore the cat came with him, never very far from his feet, executing complicated maneuvers in his lifelong efforts to catch his own tail.

The cat slept in a far corner of the bed, curled and independent, although he sometimes stepped on Anton's chest to wake him in the morning. Anton always woke unpleasantly, sick with memories of gunshots. Most of his dreams involved people disappearing into thin air: alone on the abandoned dream island he wandered from house to house and then out to the empty piazza, the silent beach. Out onto the pier where the abandoned boats bobbed gently in the dead sea, through abandoned houses, abandoned cafés, the abandoned restaurant with four chairs and a bottle of wine set up at a table, the whole abandoned dream landscape suffused with dread.

23.

Elena was back on Ischia at the beginning of April, standing pale on the threshold when Anton opened the door. It was an ordinary evening after working the day shift at the hotel two towns over, and Anton hadn't changed out of his uniform yet. He'd been drinking an Orangina and reading *La Repubblica* at his desk, stopping to look up the occasional word. There was a soft knock on the door just before midnight and Anton thought everything was over. He stood up, straightened his jacket, and opened the door with tremendous formality, expecting either the Italian police or a

EMILY ST. JOHN MANDEL

thug with a gun or David's sister or some combination of the above. Elena stood for a moment like an apparition before she fell into his arms, or tried to; her body got in the way. Holding her was awkward. She was immensely pregnant. It was night and she had been traveling for hours. She sank down on the bed and closed her eyes for a moment and didn't answer right away when he asked if she was all right. He asked if she was sick and she said no, just tired, but her tiredness had taken on the force of illness. She trembled and her hands were cold.

"I've missed you so much," she said. "I'm so sorry I left."

"Shh. Shh. It's okay. Are you hungry?" She nodded. He brought her spaghetti and calamari from the restaurant downstairs, which had just reopened that week—the tourists were coming back to Ischia, a slow but widening trickle that would become a torrent by June. He gave her the plate and asked where she'd been, but she was too tired for coherence. She'd gone immediately to France because she spoke the language, and then she'd spent the winter moving slowly through the country in the cold and the rain. Working odd jobs here and there, trying to decide whether to come back to Ischia or not.

"I was afraid you might have gone home to the north," he said. "I thought I might never see you again." He held her close and she rested her head on his shoulder. "Don't you miss your family?"

"More than I can say," she said. "But if I go home to the north pregnant I'll never leave again. I'll be like my sister and just get stuck there forever."

She drifted off in the middle of a story about a grand hotel in Marseilles where she'd worked in the laundry room, woke seconds later from a dream about snowmobiles and said, "He knew where I was from."

"What?"

"People from the south, you tell them you're from the far north and they think you grew up in an igloo, but he knew what it was like up there. Can you believe he'd actually been to Inuvik and Tuktoyaktuk? It's so dark up there," she said. "It was cold in Paris in January, but I kept thinking, *I could be up there.* Where it's dark and there's nothing. The sun doesn't even rise in the winter. You live by moonlight for weeks."

"Ellie, you should rest."

He took the plate of spaghetti from her hands, set it on the desk behind him. She was slumped over on the edge of the bed. He knelt before her and began unbuckling her shoes.

"You kept the painting," she said. She was looking up at the small painting of David and Evie, propped up against the wall on top of the desk. Elena's shoes were stylish, red and shiny like lipstick, and the left buckle was somehow stuck. Anton struggled with it while she talked. Her feet were swollen. "You wouldn't think a night could last that long," she said. "My sister won't talk to me anymore, did you know that? I don't even know why. I think it's because I left her there. I used to call her from New York City, and she wouldn't come to the phone . . ."

"You should rest," Anton murmured. "You've been traveling too long."

24.

The case had gone cold, all loose ends and questions. Anton's parents wouldn't admit that Anton was missing, let alone that he was dead, which meant there wasn't even a missing-persons case, and Aria had yet to resurface—in candid moments Broden thought the odds of apprehending Aria were relatively slim, given that the woman made passports for a living—which meant there wasn't actually much of a false-documents case either. Aria's one and only known associate—a man whom she'd met once in front of her apartment building, who'd been overheard mentioning a pickup at the docks at Red Hook on the day Broden had last spoken with Elena and who had said nothing interesting since—was followed for three uneventful months until Broden's supervisor decided that trailing him was a waste of manpower. The girls who had survived the shipping container languished in an immigration facility upstate, awaiting their hearings. They knew very little about the people who had imported them to New York, and they didn't know the name of the girl who had died. Efforts to track the origins of the container had gone nowhere; the company that had paid for shipping turned out to be a shell corporation in Estonia, its corporate address an abandoned post-office box.

Broden's director agreed that the case had stalled, and Broden's days were far too long and too frantic. No one had time for hopeless cases. But she was attending a conference in Geneva that April and it was a small matter to extend the trip by two days, to fly south to Rome and board a silver train at Termini and follow a story about a cat down the coast to Naples, where she paid a taxi driver to take her to the docks.

She bought a ticket for Ischia and boarded the next ferry. At the very least, she told herself, it's a day on a beautiful island. But her next thought was that it was yet another day without her daughter and her throat tightened. When she'd emptied her jacket pockets to pass through airport security she'd found a blue plastic barrette; she'd carefully removed it from her sleeping daughter's hair some months ago and it hadn't left her pocket.

"You're never here for her," her husband had said as she was packing for Europe, and Broden couldn't deny the accusation. Her work required long hours. There were days when she left for work before Tova was awake and came home after Tova had gone to bed. The child had turned seven while Broden was in Geneva.

"Ischia!" a crew member shouted, and Broden stepped out onto the dock. She traveled by taxi to the town of Sant'Angelo, where the driver let her off at the top of a long hill and told her he could go no farther.

She went first to the hotel where Sophie had said they had stayed. It was a warm day; the doors of the restaurant had been thrown open, and one or two waiters moved about in the cool shadows of the interior. An orange cat was sleeping in a beam of sunlight just inside the threshold.

Broden knelt awkwardly on the cobblestones and touched the cat's soft fur. The cat started awake, but only one eye opened. He purred when Broden stroked his head.

"He likes you," a man said in Italian. He stood a few feet inside the restaurant. An immaculate man in his fifties, well dressed. Blue sea glinted through the windows behind him.

"I like him," Broden said. "Who does he belong to?"

"He's the hotel cat," Gennaro said. "He keeps the mice away."

"So he doesn't belong to anyone in particular?" It had been some years since she'd had occasion to speak Italian, and the language felt awkward to her. She was sure she was mispronouncing important words. The cat turned over on his back so Broden could stroke his milk-white stomach.

"Well, he's Anton's cat, I suppose. But we've all adopted him."

Broden was still for a moment, her hand on the cat. She stood up slowly to look at him.

"Anton's cat," she said carefully. "Are you saying . . . is Anton here?"

"He lives here," Gennaro said, "but he works in another town during the day."

Broden smiled. "He lives here?"

"You know him?"

"I'm a friend of the family," she said. "His mother said he might be here and I was hoping to see him. Do you know what time he'll be back?"

Gennaro glanced at his watch. "He usually eats dinner here around seven," he said, "but it's still only the afternoon. Is he expecting you?"

"It's a surprise," Broden said. "Is there somewhere I might wait for him?"

"There's a piazza just around the corner."

"When you see Anton, will you tell him I'm waiting for him?"

"Of course."

She walked away down the hill and the piazza opened up before her. It was only April but summer had started early. The air was hot and tourists already wandered the cobblestones, buying newspapers at the newsstand and linen dresses at the clothing boutique by the still-closed seafood restaurant, and two out of three cafés had outdoor tables and umbrellas set up in the sunlight. Broden chose a table with a pleasant view of the harbor, ordered a cup of coffee and a sandwich and settled down to wait.

An hour passed, and then two. The boats moved in and out of the harbor. She paid and went across the square to another café for a change of view. She drank more coffee, ordered another sandwich, bought a paper and read it cover to cover, then sat for a long time watching the boys play on the beach. She had brought a novel with her—a thick paperback about spies that she'd picked up in an airport—but she didn't care for the opening and put it back in her bag.

There's something unnatural about being alone in paradise, and the loneliness was strange and unexpected. She watched the stream of tourists and realized that she was surrounded by couples and children. She missed her husband and daughter. She was thinking of Anton's parents, remembering his mother sitting slumped on the loading dock, staring out at the water with no light in her eyes. There was no doubt in Broden's mind that they believed Anton to be dead, and she found herself trying to imagine what unfathomable set of circumstances might compel her to turn the police away if she thought her child had been murdered. In her mind's eye she saw Tova lying on the ground like a broken doll, and the thought was so blindingly horrific that she had to close her eyes for a moment and force herself to think of nothing.

In her wallet she was carrying an identification card. *Anton Waker, Water Inc., 420 Lexington Ave.* Broden looked at the photograph in the warm end-of-day light. Anton Waker stared into the camera, just another office worker, smiling slightly. Nothing in his calm gaze suggested that he'd sold a Social Security number and fake passport to his secretary, or that the diploma on the wall above his desk was a fake, or that he came from the kind of family that sold stolen goods and imported girls from Europe in shipping containers.

Broden had been waiting for nearly four hours. The sun was dropping low in the sky but the heat was undiminished and tourists milled about on the beach. She closed her eyes and leaned back in her chair. Listening to the seagulls, the voices, the waves and the movement of boats in the harbor.

"You know," Anton said, "I could never figure out where they hide the magnetic strip."

Broden opened her eyes. The man sitting across the table in a t-shirt and jeans bore little resemblance to the pale young office worker on the surface of the identity card.

"It's the black border around the picture," Broden said. "That's what the scanner reads in the lobby."

"Who are you?"

"I'm Alexandra Broden." She reached into her pocket for her badge and set it down on the table between them. "I work with the State Department, Diplomatic Security Service. We're the division that investigates passport fraud."

"Well, I don't know anything about passport fraud."

"I'm afraid it's a little late for that," Broden said. "I have you on tape."

"I doubt that," Anton said, with considerably more confidence than he felt at that moment. He had stopped by the hotel on the way to the beach and Gennaro had told him that someone wanted to see him, and now he wished there was some way of silently warning Elena not to come to him. She had been back on Ischia for three weeks, and she spent her afternoons reading on the warm sand under an enormous sun hat. He found himself looking for her among the tourists.

"Your first sale was to a waitress," Broden said. "She worked at an Irish bar near Grand Central Station. She wanted to go to flight school."

Anton was looking down the beach but he couldn't see Elena. In a hazy recess of memory she reclined on the floor of his office and reached casually into her handbag. *What was it like when you were growing up?* His heart was beating very fast. "That's a nice story," he said, "but I'm afraid I don't know what you're talking about."

"Who else? Federico. He was from Bolivia, and he scared you a little. He made a joke about shooting you, so the waitress called Aria from behind the bar and she came and took you away from there. Shall I go on?"

Anton was silent. He had spotted Elena among the tourists. She was sitting on the sand near the water's edge under the shade of her sun hat, looking out toward Capri.

"There was Catina," Broden said. "Catina from Lisbon. She was reading a magazine when you came into the Russian Café."

"Do you still talk to Elena?" Anton asked flatly.

"No," she said, "Elena's served her purpose for me. But if *you're* still talking to Elena, you should understand the position she was in. She was facing deportation if she didn't cooperate."

"Back to the arctic," Anton said. He tried to smile, but it was a painful wince. "I probably would've done the same thing."

"But I'm not here to talk about Elena," Broden said, "although I'd be interested to know what became of her. I'd prefer to talk to you about a shipping container."

"I'm afraid I don't know very much about shipping containers."

"Then let me describe one to you." Broden's voice was calm. "A blue shipping container of uncertain origin comes into the dock at Red Hook in Brooklyn. It's unlike most shipping containers, in that it has a makeshift air pipe, and this air pipe leads to a secret room. The room's seven feet eight inches by eight feet, and it holds fifteen girls."

"Sounds crowded."

"Crowded doesn't begin to describe it, actually." Her gaze was steady. "Your friend Ilieva described it as a kind of living death. Imagine being locked into a room moving over the surface of the ocean. The air's coming in through a small pipe, and there's no light. The darkness is complete. Here's the thing: one of the girls died in transit, and no one knows her name. These girls carry no identification."

Ilieva: standing by the pastry case in the Russian Café, talking to the other waitress and laughing, bringing him a latte unasked and kissing him on the cheek, listening to him all those years ago as he explained the way it would work, asking intelligent questions while they were setting up the system. Ginger ale means I'm in danger. If I order it, go behind the counter and call Aria and tell her to come for me. Red wine means the count was correct. Water means it wasn't. Ilieva laughing, Ilieva speaking in Russian to the old Eastern European men who used to come into the café sometimes, Ilieva gliding across the room with a glass of wine and a slice of cheesecake. Ilieva trapped in an airless room with a dead girl moving over the sea. Hard to reconcile this last horror with the serenity of his memories.

"All we know about her is that she was approximately seventeen to twenty years old and spoke only Ukrainian," Broden said. "We tried to identify her, but the investigation went nowhere and none of the other girls knew her name. After a few weeks in the morgue she was buried in Potter's Field along with the rest of the unclaimed and anonymous bodies that New York City had to offer that week, and her family will likely never know what happened to her. And it would be a terrible tragedy even if this were an isolated incident, but it isn't. Shipping containers are an area of particular interest to me."

A response seemed expected of him. "You've dealt with other shipping containers," he said. He didn't want to know the answer.

"One other, years ago, when I was with the NYPD. It came into the docks at Red Hook, the same as this last one did. There were certain similarities in the shipping manifest and the design of the secret room was almost identical. The docks can be chaotic,"

Broden said. "Sometimes containers get misplaced. That particular container was lost in the stacks for nearly eight weeks."

"Eight weeks," Anton said. He felt ill.

"We don't know why the importers didn't make efforts to find their container," she said. "It's possible that our investigation was getting too close to them and they didn't want to take the risk. In any event, the container held eleven young women from Eastern Europe. The coroner's report listed them as being between the ages of eighteen and twenty-two, but I think one of them was much younger. This is the trade you're a party to, Mr. Waker."

"The thought of these shipping containers . . ." Anton couldn't finish the sentence.

"It isn't what you wanted," Broden said.

"It isn't what I wanted. Of course not, of course it isn't. If I'd known . . . who would want something like that?"

"It's more a question of who would accept something like that," she said, "as a cost of doing business."

"You're talking about Aria."

"Yes. And beyond that question—*who would accept something like this?*—the next question is, *who will stop something like this from happening again?* These shipments won't just stop. It's a lucrative trade. I know you tried to turn your back on Aria's business, but Aria's business continues with or without you."

"I'm not sure what you want from me," he said.

"I want you to tell me where Aria is, to start with."

"I don't know where she is. I'm sorry."

Far down the beach, Elena was half-hidden by her sun hat. She had moved closer to the water so that her feet were lapped by waves.

"I visited your parents a few months ago," Broden said.

A waiter had appeared. Anton ordered an Orangina. "You want anything?"

"No."

"How were they?" he asked, when the waiter had left.

"Your parents? A little out of it, frankly."

"What do you mean, 'a little out of it'?"

"I mean shaken," Broden said. "I mean your father's hands were shaking while he was touching up a figurehead, and your mother looked like she hadn't slept in a week. When I came to the store your mother was sitting on the loading dock, just staring at the river. She told me you used to sit there with her."

"Yes. I did."

"Then I asked your mother where you were," Broden said, "and she said, *He's in a far-off country.*"

"Those were her exact words? A far-off country?"

"A far-off country. That's what she said. And I wasn't sure what she meant by that," Broden said, "but it seemed to me that she wasn't just talking about Italy."

"We had a dog when I was little," Anton said. There was strain in his voice. "It was my parents' dog from before I was born, and me and Aria used to play with him. We were really little, maybe five at the most. Anyway, the dog got old and sick and my parents had to have him put to sleep, and then when me and Aria asked where the dog had gone, my mother said, *He's gone away to a far-off country.*"

"I see. Do your parents still think you're dead?"

Anton was silent.

"I don't know," he said finally. "I don't speak to them anymore." The waiter had returned with an Orangina. He lifted the bottle to his lips, grateful for the distraction.

"To tell you the truth, I wasn't entirely surprised by your parents' demeanor. I thought you were dead too." She was looking steadily at him. "I think you were asked to perform a transaction," she said, "but it wasn't like all the other transactions you've performed over the years. Something went wildly wrong for you. Aria told your parents you were dead, and then I think she fled the city."

"She could be anywhere," he said.

"The penalties for dealing in false passports are stiff these days," Broden said. "Now that you've turned up alive, I'm afraid you're in a certain amount of legal peril. I have you on tape describing the way the operation worked. I can produce a witness who bought a passport from you. And Ilieva speaks highly of you, don't get me wrong, but she won't lie under oath. You're looking at a decade in a federal prison. But I'll tell you a secret, Mr. Waker. I'm much more interested in finding the origin of that shipping container than I am in having you prosecuted for selling fake passports. If you were to tell me where Aria is, I might be willing to negotiate."

"I don't know where she is," he said. He had a strange feeling that he might be dreaming. All his thoughts were of Elena, of the unborn child, of how to keep them safe, and his heart was beating very quickly.

"I'd like you to hear something." Broden reached into her bag and placed a small electronic device on the table between them. "This is a phone call that was taped some months ago."

She pressed a button and over the sounds of the ocean Anton heard a voice. A man speaking in a British accent: *It's done.* And then Aria: *Thank you. We'll speak again soon.*

"When was this recorded?" he asked, but he already knew. His voice was unsteady.

"That call was recorded two days before the shipping container arrived in Red Hook," Broden said. "This was the night of Friday October 21st. It was early evening in New York, eleven P.M. in Italy. Aria was gone by the time police arrived at her apartment."

The night of Friday October 21st. Standing by the sliding glass doors in the darkness of his hotel room, waiting in silence as four shadows came down the side of the islet and passed by the hotel. Footsteps on the cobblestones, a laugh, a car starting up the hill beyond the gates of Sant'Angelo. They had called Aria ten or fifteen minutes later.

"But if by *done* they meant me," Anton said, "I wouldn't be sitting here, would I?" He was suddenly very tired. *This is my last job,* he remembered telling Elena, over a glass of wine in the Russian Café on a snowy night some years earlier, and the memory made him want to laugh or weep. The jobs since that night had been all but unsurvivable.

"The point isn't that you're still alive," Broden said, "although that's certainly an interesting twist. The point is that when Aria heard those words she thought you were dead, because that was the outcome she was expecting." Broden was putting the device away. "A detective visited your parents the morning after the call went through. Your father insisted they knew nothing and that they'd heard from neither you nor Aria, but your mother was too distraught to speak. When I went to see them two weeks later, your mother was talking about far-off countries and your father's hands were still shaking."

Anton looked away from her and his eyes filled unexpectedly with tears.

"You've known her all your life," Broden said. "She's family. Even if you don't know for certain exactly where she is, where do you think she *might* have gone?"

"I don't know."

"How close is Aria to your parents?"

"Close," he said. "They talk all the time."

Broden took a cell phone out of her pocket and flipped it open. "I have the number for Waker Architectural Salvage programmed into my phone," she said. She was looking at the cell-phone screen as she spoke to him, scrolling through the contacts in her address book. "I can't imagine how happy your parents will be when I tell them you're alive and well. If I call them now, how long do you think it will be before Aria knows?"

"Please don't," he said.

"Why not?"

"I think it's possible that the only reason I'm still alive," Anton said, "is because my cousin thinks I'm dead."

Broden glanced up from her phone. "Yes," she said dispassionately. "I think that's entirely likely."

Elena was coming up from the beach, making her way slowly toward the piazza. Anton saw her approach and all but panicked, tried to think of a way to silently warn her not to come to him, but some distance from the table she seemed to catch sight of Broden's face and in an instant she had turned away from them. He looked at Broden. She had followed the direction of Anton's gaze, and now she watched Elena recede for a moment.

"It's a boy," he said softly. "We're going to call him David."

They sat in silence for a few minutes, both watching Elena. Elena was walking slowly, trying to lose herself amid the tourists. Broden's voice was quiet when she finally spoke.

"Do you know who Aria's working with?"

"I never did."

"These people aren't delicate," Broden said. "They don't like to leave witnesses. You seem willing to risk your own life, but are you willing to risk Elena's? What about your child's? Suppose one day a friend of Aria's comes to pay you a visit, a quiet professional with a silenced firearm in his jacket. I hope Elena and your child aren't with you in that room."

The beach was emptying gradually, and he couldn't see Elena anymore. The sun had set and the tourists were disappearing into the restaurants and hotels. The breeze off the water was cool, and only a few other people were still sitting in the outdoor cafés. There was no one near them.

"Look, you seem to have a life here," Broden said. She held the phone open in her hand. She put her other hand in her jacket pocket and her fingers brushed the hard edge of a blue plastic barrette. On the other side of the Atlantic Ocean, her daughter was walking with her nanny in the park.

Broden was silent for a moment before she spoke again. "For your child's sake," she said, "I'm willing to pretend I never saw you. I'm willing to leave this new life of yours intact. If you give me what I want, I won't tell your parents or Aria that you're here."

"You'll leave us alone."

"I will," Broden said. "But only if you tell me where Aria is."

The sun had dropped below the surface of the water and the sky was darkening, a cool breeze moving over the water. He was aware of every sound around him. The quiet of the waves against the sand, the wood-on-wood of boats moving against each other and against the piers, the faraway voices and laughter of tourists, an inconsolable small child being carried back to a hotel. He wanted to run from the piazza and dive into the water and keep swimming till he drowned or reached the north coast of Africa.

"Do you have an address?" she asked.

"I have a phone number." Anton had written it down the day he'd arrived on Ischia, and now he found it among the innumerable scraps of paper in his wallet. "That's a landline into an apartment in Santa Monica."

Broden took the scrap of paper from his hand, looked at it for a moment and then folded it into her notebook. "Santa Monica? Do you know for certain that she's there?"

"No, but that's where she goes when she leaves New York. She's been renting it for a few years now. I don't know what she does out there."

"Thank you," Broden said. She was standing, zipping up her jacket and putting her notebook away. "I'll need to be able to contact you if I need any further information."

"You know where I live," Anton said.

Broden turned and walked away from him. Anton left money on the table for the Orangina and followed her at some distance, up the hill past the pink hotel to the gates of Sant'Angelo. She got into a taxi. When her car had disappeared around the curve of the island Anton walked back down the hill into the village of Sant'Angelo, under the archway beyond which no cars were allowed. Down the cobblestone road past the hotel where he'd lived all these strange long months, back into the piazza and then out along the narrow beach with the harbor on his left, the breakwaters long shadows in the water on either side.

The lights of Capri were bright in the distance. A child's plastic bucket lay discarded on the sand. Sant'Angelo seemed deserted now, everyone dining somewhere indoors, the boys from the beach gone home for the evening. It was a clear night and there was movement all around him, seagulls wheeling through the darkening air. He thought, Look at these holy boats in the harbor. Look at the holy darkness of the islet against the first few stars, look at this beautiful island where I will live with my beloved, with our child, with my ghosts and my guilt. Look at this holy woman coming down the holy beach toward me, eight and a half months pregnant with a holy sun hat in her hands.

Acknowledgments

With profound thanks to my editor, Greg Michalson, for his invaluable editorial guidance; to Caitlin Hamilton Summie, Steven Wallace, Fred Ramey, Libby Jordan, Rachel J.K. Grace, Rich Rennicks, and all of their colleagues at Unbridled Books for their hard work, talent, and support; to my wonderful agent, Emilie Jacobson, and her colleagues at Curtis Brown; to Kim McArthur, Devon Pool, and their colleagues at McArthur & Company; to Mandy Keifetz and Douglas Anthony Cooper for graciously reading and commenting on early drafts of the novel; to Louisa Proske for her assistance with German translations; and to Kevin Mandel.

Note: the line "We are not alone, this side of death", quoted in chapter 22, is from an unfinished novel by Douglas Anthony Cooper and appears by generous permission of the author.